American Beauty

American Beauty

Stories

by

Allen M. Steele

Five Star • Waterville, Maine

In memory of Zack,
my companion for fifteen years:
cool water, plenty of squirrels to chase,
and a warm place to sleep

Table of Contents

Introduction: Mishegos

For those who need to ask: *mishegos* (pronounced *me-she-goss*) is the approximate phonetic spelling of a Yiddish word which means "a collection of different things." I'm not Jewish—as Charlie Chaplin once remarked, I don't enjoy that privilege—but my wife is, and I picked it up from associating with her family. It's a great word, and one which adequately describes the contents of this book, my fourth collection of stories.

At first glance, this is an odd assortment. Two are about robots, and one is about a dog; two involve alternative histories (not the same one), one is about time travel, and a couple of others are set in outer space. One is a spy story, and another is about surveillance of a different kind. One is set in a world created by another writer, while two more are parodies of popular culture. So while some may relate to one another, there doesn't seem to be a clear connection between all of them, even though all except one were written within a brief period of time.

Yet there's a common denominator: they're all about America. Indeed, this book may be seen as a companion volume to an earlier collection, *All-American Alien Boy*, which consists of stories set in the United States in the near future. One of my favorite subjects has been this country. Some years ago, a British editor once told my literary agent that he was rejecting a novel that she had submitted to him because he felt that my work was "too American." He meant that as criticism, but I took it as a compliment. Yes,

9

I'm an American writer—says so right here on the label. Get used to it (and by the way, sorry to turn down *The War of the Worlds*, but we feel that H. G. Wells will never have much of an audience here in the States—he's too English).

One of the overlooked charms of science fiction is that, although it's about the future, frequently it's also a surrealistic image of our present. Very often, the writer isn't fully aware of this; that's why so much SF goes out of date very quickly, not so much because historical or technological trends surpass the events of a given story or novel, but because the author didn't realize that his or her work was really a warped reflection of the period in which it was written. That's the downside; the upside is that, while much of mainstream literature is permanently locked into one particular time period, SF is much more flexible, its subject matter more malleable. So SF can serve as a means by which we examine our present condition, although in a sneaky sort of way.

These stories are about the period and place in which they were written: America at the cusp of the 21st century, a time of both wonder and fear, of excitement and uneasiness, of fond remembrance for things past and anticipation of things yet to come. Some day not too many years from now, we'll look back upon this time, and with any luck we'll be able to say that we were fortunate to be here.

Some notes about these stories: how they were written, and why.

Agape Among the Robots—Agape, in this context, is an ancient Greek word; pronounced *aw-gah-pay*, it means a higher form of love. This is one of the few times I ever tried to write a love story; although it's ostensibly about robots, it's really about the people who built them, and how very

10

often our creations reflect our inner selves. It's also something of a tribute to Isaac Asimov's robot stories, and a reconsideration of the Three Laws of Robotics. Deadheads may note that there's a sly reference to the Grateful Dead in this story (hint: check out the names of the robots, and also those of the supporting characters). And, oh yes, it was nominated for a Hugo Award for Best Novelette in 2001.

Her Own Private Sitcom—Andy Warhol once predicted that, in the future, we'd all be famous for fifteen minutes. That future has arrived with a vengeance; we now have people who feel their lives are unfulfilled if they haven't gotten their fifteen minutes. And likewise, there are those who subconsciously take their cues from TV, behaving as if they're performing in front of a live studio audience, with a laugh-track in the background. The media is no longer merely the message, but a way of life.

Every so often, technology catches up with a science fiction story almost as soon as it's published. Miniature cameras now allow users to put themselves on websites in real-time, and "flycams" are already in development. Privacy is rapidly becoming a luxury, not a right. Pray that you haven't had your fifteen minutes yet . . . or that you won't become part of someone else's.

Green Acres—Did you know that marijuana was not only once legal in the United States, but also one of its major cash-crops? That bit of knowledge has become forgotten in the last seventy years, stamped down by generations of anti-drug propaganda. I gave up smoking pot a long time ago, yet I still use cannabis by-products on a daily basis—I wash my hair with hemp shampoo, use hemp lotion for my skin, and have a couple of items of clothing that are made from hemp cloth—and they would be much less expensive if this country got past the federal legislation that was muscled

11

into law in the 1930s in order to aid the cotton industry.

This is an alternative-history story about what might have happened if the Marihuana Stamp Act had been defeated in Congress. A thought experiment, really, yet of all the stories I've written, this one had the most difficulty being published; it was rejected by every SF magazine and anthology before Scott Edelman, the editor of the now-defunct *Science Fiction Age*, reconsidered and invited me to submit it to him again. After it was published, it came within one vote of getting on the final ballot of the Hugo Awards.

Missing Time—When I was a journalist back in the '80s, I worked as a staff writer for *Worcester Magazine*, the weekly alternative newspaper of Worcester, Massachusetts. One of my jobs was covering the City Council meeting every Monday night; I'd sit up in the gallery and take notes on what was going on, and write up the more interesting moments for that week's edition.

Worcester was the second-largest city in New England at that time, yet it was a town that was struggling with many urban problems, not the least of which were low self-esteem and a failure to envision itself as anything more than Boston's poor cousin. Yet while there were those who tried to take progressive steps to turn things, their efforts were often thwarted by a narrow-minded handful who, for one reason or another, didn't want any changes to the status quo. One of the latter was a certain powerful member of the City Council who regularly voted against propositions which could have done the city a lot of good, usually in the name of saving the taxpayers' money. All well and good, but there's such a thing as being penny wise and pound foolish. Taxes went up anyway, while the city remained in the dumps.

12

A few years after I left Worcester, which was simultaneous with my giving up journalism to become a full-time SF writer, this gentleman was elected mayor. Not long after I moved to St. Louis, I was invited to contribute a piece for *Worcester Magazine*'s 20th anniversary issue. This story is the result: a time-travel yarn, but also something of an open letter to Hizzoner. He took it well—I received a postcard from him shortly thereafter, saying that he liked the story—but I don't think he got the point. Or perhaps he did, but just decided to ignore it.

Graceland—One of my all-time favorite SF novels is *To Your Scattered Bodies Go*, by Philip Jose Farmer. Although I usually avoid contributing to shared-universe anthologies, when Phil Farmer invited me to write a story for *Tales of Riverworld*, this was something I couldn't pass up. It's also a homage to some of my favorite rockers, with John Lennon, Keith Moon, and Jim Morrison as the lead characters.

Appropriately enough, this story was written during a rock concert. On the day I received Phil's letter, I was about to drive to Bonner Springs, Kansas, for a two-day outdoor show by the Grateful Dead. Seeing an opportunity to do something interesting, I took along a notebook and pen, and during the afternoons while I waited for the gates to open I sat in the shade of a willow tree and wrote this story, trying to incorporate everything I saw and heard around me into my tale. So this is a story about rock 'n' roll, channeled through the Riverworld.

Jake and the Enemy—Another story about robots, related to the first one . . . but really, it's about dogs. We may eventually get household robots, but no matter how advanced they may be, they'll never be as smart as the average mutt. This is about a duel between canine and machine, and it's also a tribute to my own Jake, who passed

13

away a year before this was written.

Warning, Warning—Okay, I'll fess up: I was a big fan of "Lost in Space" when I was a kid. I saw it when it was originally aired, and thought it was the best space show on television. And for awhile, it was: "Star Trek" didn't come on the air until a year later, and even then I didn't see it, because its first season wasn't aired in Nashville, my home town; instead, we got to see "The Porter Wagonner and Dolly Parton Show."

When the Sci-Fi Channel started carrying re-runs of "Lost in Space" in the '90s, I caught up with my childhood favorite. This time around, though, I saw something that had escaped my young eye: while the first season was still pretty cool, the second and third season episodes became increasingly awful. Or maybe I did notice this when I was young; I recall losing interest in the show midway through the second season. The reasons for this are well-known, of course; when "Batman" became a runaway hit, all the other SF or SF-like TV shows tried to emulate it by "going camp," and this was what ruined not only "Lost in Space" but also "The Man from U.N.C.L.E." and "Voyage to the Bottom of the Sea."

Anyway, this is my take on "Lost in Space," and an explanation for why there's such a dissonance between the first season (the good one) and the second and third seasons (the bad ones). It's also an homage to lost adolescence, and the terrible truths we learn as we become older.

The Fine Art of Watching—This is the end result of an aborted attempt to write a spy novel, sort of an updated Ian Fleming thriller. For various reasons, I decided to give up on what would have been titled *The Glass Sky* midway through Chapter Four; however, there was enough of a SF element to the first two chapters that I was able to rewrite

14

them as a story for *Analog*; it was published under the pseudonym "John Mulherin" just in case I decided to change my mind, which I didn't.

All the technology depicted in this story presently exists, including the means by which the purloined information is encoded and concealed. Likewise, the setting is real; I visited the Getty Center a few months before I wrote this story (and, although it doesn't appear here, I was given a backstage tour of its art conservation lab by one the scientists who works there). And I owe a large debt to my friend Harlan Ellison, who not only told me where the surveillance van should be parked, but also helped me solve a problem I was having with the story; Harlan makes a cameo appearance here, albeit under a different name.

A Walk Across Mars—The fourth installment of a series in which I've tried to reimagine the American space program as it might have happened if the U.S. had gone into space during World War II and then followed the outline laid out during the '50s by Wernher von Braun in *Across the Space Frontier* and *The Conquest of Space*. The first stories of "Alternative Space" were "Goddard's People" and "John Harper Wilson" (included in my collection *Rude Astronauts*) and my novel *The Tranquillity Alternative*; this is the story of what happened during the 1976 American-Russian expedition to Mars. It can be read independently of the others, but there is a certain progression nonetheless; if you're interested in the background, you might want to find the earlier stories.

Tom Swift and His Humongous Mechanical Dude—Another artifact from childhood, revisited as an adult. I loved the Tom Swift, Jr. books when I was a boy, and borrowed them from my next-door neighbors who had a complete set, yet even then I knew that Tom and his buddies were square beyond belief. I mean, Tom had a girlfriend, but he didn't even kiss her? And why didn't his father ever take away the keys to the amphibicar and ground him?

Today, though, I'd give anything to meet a teenager who was just as smart as Tom Swift Jr., but who wasn't a sockhead with baggy pants and an attitude cultivated by hours zoned out in front of MTV. There are a few, granted, and I consider myself fortunate to know some of them. However, the children of the Baby Boomers haven't been well-served by Tom Jr.'s generation, and now we have Tom Swift III and Junior Bud all around us. They'd be funny if they weren't giving each other gang signs. So this is about what happened to Tom's kid after the old man became a billionaire. It's a parody, sure. But tell me it ain't true.

And there you have it. A big, heaping plate of *mishegos*. I hope you enjoy reading these stories as much as I enjoyed writing them.

—Whately, Massachusetts;
October, 2002

Agape Among the Robots

When Samson met Delilah, the first thing he did was crush an apple against her head. Delilah didn't react in any way; she sat calmly on the park bench, her hands folded primly in the lap of her long purple dress, staring straight ahead as wet pulp ran down her face and into the neckline of her lace collar. She didn't even look up as Samson walked around the front of the bench, bowed from the waist, and gallantly offered his hand.

In the Samson Team control van, though, we were either cracking up or gaping at our monitors in dumb surprise. All except Phil Burton; glaring through the one-way glass window, almost apoplectic with rage; his mouth opened and closed several times before he finally managed to give utterance to his thoughts.

"W-w-w-what t-t-t-the . . . what the hell was that?" he demanded. "W-w-who pr-pr-programmed th-th-th-tha-that . . . ?"

"Nobody programmed it, Phil," I said. I had worked with him long enough to intuit what he meant when his speech impediment got in the way. He looked sharply my way, and I hastily coughed into my hand to hide my grin. Phil had a tendency to think people were laughing at him even when something else funny was going on. "Honest. I checked Samson's routine myself. That wasn't supposed to happen."

"I-I-I know th-th-th-th . . ." Phil shut his eyes, took a deep breath, and silently counted to ten. While he was

17

counting, I glanced past him at Keith D'Amico; although he was still chuckling, he had already checked out his own screen. He caught my eye and shook his head. No, he didn't have a clue as to what went wrong either.

"Phil, Jerry . . . I've put Samson in standby mode." This from Donna Raitt, seated at the console on the other side of me. Unlike Keith and me, she hadn't lost it when Samson had assaulted Delilah with a deadly fruit; she was watching her screen, her hand cupped over her headset mike. "It looks like D-team has done the same," she added quietly. "I haven't heard from Dr. Veder's group yet."

"Oh, but you will . . . you will." Keith was doing his Yoda impression again. "Beware the dark side, Luke . . ."

"Knock it off." Phil had managed to get control of his stutter. He glared at Keith, then turned back to me. "Okay, I believe you. It's a glitch, that's all." He glanced out the window, taking a moment to study the two robots frozen in the wooded atrium. "Access his memory buffer from the beginning of the test up to when Donna put him on standby."

"Death Star in range within ten seconds," Keith murmured.

If Phil heard that—and judging from the annoyed expression which briefly crossed his face, he did—he chose to ignore it. He turned to Bob, the kid operating the remote camcorders. "You got everything, didn't you?"

"What . . . oh, yeah, yeah, it's all here." Bob was wiping tears from the corners of his eyes. "Do you want a copy, Dr. Burton?"

"No, I want you to delete the whole thing." Bob stared at him in surprise, and for a moment his hands moved to the editing board. "Goddammit, of course I want a copy!" Phil snapped. "Run it off now! Move!" He returned his attention to me. "C'mon, Jerry, gimme everything you got . . ."

"Coming right now." I had already loaded a fresh 100 MB disk. A few deft commands on the keypad above my lap, and a bar-graph appeared on my screen, indicating that the data Phil wanted was being copied. I looked again at Keith; behind Phil's back, he had his right hand raised, and he was counting off the seconds with each finger he folded into his palm. Five . . . four . . . three . . . two . . . one . . .

"Delilah Team just called in." Once again, Donna had clasped her hand over the wand of her headset. "Dr. Veder wants to meet with you in the test area . . . umm, right now, Phil."

The color vanished from Phil's face. "Uhh . . . t-t-tell her I'll b-b-b-be there as . . . as . . ."

My terminal chirped. I popped out the disk, shoved it into Phil's hand, then snapped my fingers at Bob. He ejected the DVD from the camcorder, slapped it into a jewelbox, then passed it to Keith, who tapped it against Phil's shoulder. That seemed to wake him up; he blinked a few times, then turned to snatch the DVD from Keith's hand.

"He's coming now," Donna said quietly into her headset. "Sorry for the problem. We had a problem here, but . . ."

"Stick to the rules. No contact except between team leaders." Phil took another deep breath, then clapped the two disks together as he turned sideways to squeeze past her and me as he headed for the control van's door. "Wish me luck."

"May the Force be with you," Keith said, and I shot him a look which told him that I'd like to stick a light-saber where a Jedi couldn't find it. "Good luck," he added, albeit reluctantly.

19

"Thanks." Phil grabbed a roll of paper towels from the shelf near the door. Then, almost as an afterthought, he looked back at Keith. "Wipe the memory buffer, will you? I don't want this to affect the next test." Then he stepped out of the van, slamming the door shut behind him.

For a moment no one said anything, then everyone collapsed in their seats. "Man, oh man," Keith muttered, covering his face with his hands. "I thought he was going to have a stroke . . ."

"Thought *he* was going to have a stroke?" Donna shook her head. "You should have heard what was going on in D-team's trailer. Kathy sounded like she was ready to . . ."

"Are you off-line?" I asked quietly, and her eyes went wide as she lunged for the mute button. Keith chuckled as he reached for the two-pound bag of Fritos he kept stashed beneath the console. I glanced at Bob; he said nothing as he hunched over his screen, replaying the test on his monitor. Fresh out of MIT, he had been working for LEC for less than five months now, and only very recently had been assigned to the R3G program. He was wisely keeping office politics at arm's length, nor could I blame him.

Through the window, I watched Phil as he walked toward the bench where Samson stood frozen, his right hand still extended. He glanced nervously toward the opposite side of the atrium, then he tore a wad of paper off the roll and began hastily wiping the apple shards off Delilah's spherical head. I had to wonder why someone on her team had felt compelled to put her in a dress. Perhaps to accentuate her feminine role; although the test was supposed to work out bugs in their handshaking procedures, the scenario Phil and Kathy had mutually devised was supposed to playfully emulate a quaint, old-fashioned courtship. So far, though, the results weren't very promising.

20

"Oh, such a nice man," Keith said, propping his sandals up on his console as he shoved a fistful of chips in his mouth. "Look, he's cleaning . . . uh-oh, here she comes."

From behind him, Dr. Katherine "Darth" Veder came stalking through the trees, her hands shoved in the pockets of her lab coat. Even before he saw her, Phil must have heard her coming, for he fumbled with the roll in his hands as he reluctantly turned to face her.

"Oh, boy, is she pissed or what?" Bob murmured.

"What," I replied, and Donna arched an eyebrow knowingly.

"Dum-dum-dum-dah-de-dum-dah-de-dum," Keith hummed. "Volume, please. I don't want to miss this."

The van was soundproofed, but we had a parabolic mike aimed at the test area. Donna started to reach for her board to activate it. "Don't," I said quietly, shaking my head at her. "Let's let them handle this themselves." Smiling a little, Donna withdrew her hand.

Keith sighed in disgust, then pulled on his headset and tapped a command into his console. I had little doubt that he was patching into Samson's external mike to eavesdrop on their conversation, if it could be called that. Through the window, I could see Kathy yelling at Phil, her small hands gesturing wildly as she pointed at him, at Samson, at Delilah, at our van, and back at Phil again. Although Phil's back was half-turned to us, his hands were almost as busy, first making gestures of supplication and apology, then briefly returning to his sides—he was probably counting to ten again—before rising again to make irate motions of his own.

Donna rested her elbows on the console and cupped her chin in her hands. Bob picked up the month-old issue of *Spin* he had placed on top of one of the mainframes. Keith pawed at his bag of chips, watching with interest while the two team leaders ripped into each other.

"I wish these guys would hurry up and admit they're in love," he muttered.

Meanwhile Samson and Delilah patiently waited nearby, ignored yet omnipresent, as stoical as only robots can be.

Okay. Time to backtrack a bit.

You know about LEC, of course . . . or at least you should, if you pay attention to TV commercials, browse the web, or visit shopping malls. Lang Electronics Corporation is one of the three major U.S. manufacturers of consumer robots; it started out as a maker of IBM-clones in the early '80s, then diversified into robotics shortly after the turn of the century, introducing its first-generation robot vacuum cleaners and home sentries about the same time that its closest competitors, CybeServe and Cranberry, entered the market with their own household 'bots. CybeServe was the leading company, and solidified that position after it was bought out by Mitsubishi; Cranberry, on other hand, was hurt by poor sales and a reputation for making second-rate 'bots that tended to forget instructions, burn actuators, and taser the mailman. By the time CybeServe and Mitsubishi merged, Cranberry had laid off one-third of its employees and was on the verge of declaring bankruptcy.

This left LEC somewhere in the middle. It remained strong enough to fight off hostile takeover attempts by larger electronics companies in both America and Japan, and its Valet and Guardian series of home 'bots held their own in the marketplace, not only selling as many units as CybeServe but even surpassing their sales in Europe. The success of its first-generation robots prompted LEC to invest considerable capital in developing a second-generation series of universal robots. Biocybe Resources in Worcester, Massachusetts, had recently introduced its Oz 100 biochips, pseudo-organic microprocessors capable of handling 100,000 MIPS—Millions of Instructions Per Second, the robotic equivalent of megabytes—and LEC had built them into its Gourmand, Guardian III, and Companion 'bots, successfully bringing them to market nearly two months before CybeServe brought out their rival systems. It also helped that CybeServe's 'bots were more expensive and that their CybeServe Butler had an embarrassing tendency to misunderstand questions or commands given in less than perfect English ("Is the dishwasher running?" No, it's still in the kitchen. "Answer the door, please." But it hasn't asked me anything. And so forth.).

(If all this is beginning to make your eyes glaze over, please be patient. Home 'bots may be rather commonplace these days—if you don't already own one, chances are one of your neighbors does, and your kids may be dropping hints about how nice it would be to find a CybeServe Silver Retriever or a LEC Prince barking and wagging its tail beneath the Christmas tree—but I'm relating events which occurred about ten years ago. It may seem like business talk, but it has quite a bit to do with the story at hand, so bear with me, okay?)

CybeServe wasn't about to let itself get stampeded the way Cranberry was several years earlier, so after it spent a small fortune working out the bugs in its second-generation 'bots and an even larger fortune in consumer advertising, it took the logical step: the development of a third-generation, all-purpose universal robot, one which could serve as butler, housekeeper, sentry, cook, chess-player, dog-walker, babysitter . . . you name it. And just to put the icing on the cake, CybeServe intended its new 'bot to be human-like:

bipedal, about six feet in height, with multijointed arms and legs and five fingers on each hand.

This was probably the most significant factor, for with the exception of a few experimental prototypes like Honda's P2 of the late '90s, virtually every robot on the market looked like a fire hydrant, an oversized turtle, or a vacuum cleaner with arms. A human-like robot, however, would not only be aesthetically familiar, but it would also be able to adapt more readily to a household environment, since it would be able to climb stairs or place objects on tables.

Although CybeServe tried to keep their R3G program secret, the cybernetics industry is small enough—and the Robot Belt along Route 9 in Massachusetts short enough—that it was only a matter of time before word leaked out of its Framingham headquarters. The fact that their R3G project was codenamed Metropolis, an ironic allusion to the robot in the 1927 silent film directed by Fritz Lang, was a clear signal that CybeServe meant to pull an end-run around its rival in Westboro.

When Jim Lang, LEC's founder and CEO, learned that CybeServe was actively engaged in the development of a third-generation 'bot, the lights stayed on all night in the fourth-floor board room. The following morning, Slim Jim summoned his department heads to the executive suite, where he read them the riot act: LEC was now in a race with CybeServe to be the first company to produce a third-generation universal robot.

As luck would have it, though, the company wasn't caught flat-footed; during their spare time, two of its senior engineers had already been working on third-generation robots.

Where Phil Burton or Kathy Veder managed to find any spare time at a company where everyone in the R&D divisions typically puts in a 7-by-14 work week is beyond me, yet nonetheless these two had been using their downtime to tinker in their labs. On their own initiative, both Phil and Kathy had drafted plans for universal 'bots which would utilize the new Oz chips being produced by Biocybe. Since the Oz 3Megs were capable of processing three million MIPS, this meant that a third-generation robot could have the approximate learning ability of a Rhesus monkey, as opposed to a second-generation 'bot with the IQ of a well-trained mouse.

The fact that they had designed their robots independently of each other, without one being aware of what the other was doing, was no great surprise to anyone. Phil Burton was in charge of the division which developed the Companion robot, while Kathy Veder was the senior engineer behind the Guardian III. Their departments were located at opposite ends of the LEC quad, and their staffs shared little more in common than the company cafeteria. Not only that, but the two couldn't be more unalike: Phil Burton, tall and rather skinny, with thinning blond hair and a lifelong stutter which betrayed his shyness; and Kathy Veder, short, plump, with unruly black hair which was seldom combed and an aggressive manner which bordered on outright hostility (hence the nickname). A pair of über-geeks who couldn't have agreed on the proper pronunciation of "banana" if someone threatened to take away their Usenet accounts.

Nonetheless, Lang was delighted that they already had a head-start, and asked them to show him their work. However, Kathy was a little more reluctant than Phil to comply; in fact, rumor had it that Jim had to memo Darth three times before she finally coughed up her notes and blueprints, while Phil delivered his material almost immediately.

The rest of us chalked up her reticence to peer rivalry, never realizing that there was something else going on just under the surface.

Lang carefully studied their plans, talked to some of his other geeks—myself included—and eventually reached the conclusion that, although each robot was designed differently, they were so fundamentally similar that either could serve as LEC's entry in the R3G race. However, since the company didn't have the time, money or resources to manufacture two third-generation 'bots, it was one or the other. To make matters worse, there was no accord among the brain trust upon which robot should be chosen; Kathy's people were solidly behind her Guardian IV design, while Phil's group was equally convinced that Companion II was the superior system.

Jim Lang loved strategy games. He collected antique chess sets and backgammon boards, and was renowned among Go enthusiasts as something of a master. Indeed, when LEC was a small start-up company in the late '70s, its first major product had been a modular pocket game system, the now-forgotten Lang Buddy. So it came as no great surprise that his solution took the form of a competition.

Dr. Burton's group and Dr. Veder's group were divided into two teams, respectively code-named Samson and Delilah, with Dr. Burton and Dr. Veder as their leaders. Each team was given a substantial R&D budget and access to the same material resources, not the least of which were copies of the Oz 3Meg chips. However, the members of each team would not be allowed to talk to one another or share notes; only the team leaders were given that privilege, if they saw fit to do so.

The objective of Slim Jim's game was the fast-track development of a fully-operational, self-learning universal robot within six months. At the end of this period, each team would let their robots be tested—first by themselves, then interacting with each other—in a series of environments approximating real-world conditions. The team which produced the best robot would not only see their system enter mass-production, but they would also be awarded large bonuses, along with royalties from the sale of each unit. Indeed, the members of the winning team could very well walk away with several hundred grand in their pockets.

It was a hell of an approach, to be sure, and over the course of the next six months I didn't get much sleep, let alone very many free weekends or holidays. Yet Samson itself was built within only three months, and we began installing and testing its conditioning modules shortly thereafter. Although we knew that, on the other side of the quad, behind a pair of keycard-access doors, Delilah Team was spending an equal amount of effort on their own 'bot, we had little doubt who would come out ahead. In fact, I was beginning to price Porsches.

But building a new robot is one thing. Dealing with the human factor is quite another.

"Okay, Samson," I said, "fix me a peanut butter and jelly sandwich."

"Yes, Jerry." The voice which came from his mouth grid sounded almost exactly like Robert Redford's. That had to be Donna's choice; she was a movie buff, and *Butch Cassidy and the Sundance Kid* was one of her favorites. So was Keith, but at least he hadn't again sampled Dennis Hopper's vocal patterns from *Blue Velvet*. That had been a little scary.

27

Samson turned and walked toward the small kitchenette in one corner of the training suite. The suite resembled a large, two-room apartment, with everything you'd normally find in a well-furnished bachelor flat; in fact, some members of the team crashed there overnight when they were too tired to drive home. The only difference was the two-way mirror on the wall above the couch; behind the reflective glass, Donna and Keith were quietly watching the session from the observation booth.

Samson had no difficulty finding his way to the kitchen; his three-dimensional grid-map had already memorized the suite, and even when we rearranged the furniture Samson quickly relearned his way around. As he trod past the dinner table, the coffee in my cup sloshed slightly over the rim. "We're going to have to work on the shock-absorption," I murmured as I jotted a note on my clipboard. "Maybe some padding on his treads."

"I'll take it up with the shop," Donna's voice whispered in my earpiece, "but they're not going to be happy about it." I knew what she meant. Although Samson's frame was constructed of lightweight polymers, he still weighed more than two hundred and fifty pounds. Still, we couldn't have a robot who shook the room every time he walked by.

Samson stopped in front of the kitchen counter. In earlier tests of his cooking repertoire, we had laid everything out he needed in plain sight. This time, though, the counter was clean. Two days earlier, we had stocked the kitchen, then spent the better part of the afternoon showing him what everything was and where it was stored. If his conditioning module had properly tutored him, he should figure it out with no problem.

And sure enough, Samson reached up to the cupboard above the counter and, ever so gently, pulled out a jar of peanut butter and a loaf of bread. He carefully placed them on the counter, then turned to the refrigerator, opened it, and accurately selected the grape jelly from the nearly identical jars of mayo and mustard placed next to them. Sometime later we'd put two different flavors of jelly in the fridge, but right now his artificial vision was doing well to recognize and read printed labels.

Samson located a butter knife in the utensil drawer, and laid it on the counter next to the jars of jelly and peanut butter. He had no problem opening the bread loaf—although it had taken him several hours to learn the trick of loosening twist-ties without ripping open the wrapper—but I held my breath as he picked up the peanut butter. Before I led Samson into the room, Keith had deliberately tightened its lid as firmly as possible, then bet me ten bucks that Samson couldn't open it without breaking the jar. But this time Samson clasped the rubberized fingertips of his left hand around the lid and, while holding the jar steady in his right hand, gradually exerted pressure until he unscrewed the lid.

"Very good, Samson," I said. "You're doing well." I glanced at the window and rubbed my thumb and fingers together. Donna chuckled as Keith muttered an obscenity, and now I had beer money for tonight.

"Thank you, Jerry." Although the cyclopean red eye in the center of Samson's forehead didn't turn my way, I knew that he could see me nonetheless. Although the eye contained two parallax lenses, Samson's bullet-shaped head contained a variety of motion and heat detectors which continually updated my location in the room. We had already tested their capability by putting a cat in the room; although the cat, frightened out of her feline wits by this lumbering man-thing, had constantly raced around the

29

apartment, growling and spitting and raising her fur whenever Samson came near, the robot had deftly avoided trampling her underfoot. The SPCA probably would have objected, but it was better to have our 'bot get acquainted with house pets during the teaching phase than receive lawsuits later.

Samson spread peanut butter across one slice of bread, then grape jelly across another—"A little more jelly, please, Samson," I asked, and he complied—then he successfully closed the two halves together without making a mess. He located a small plate in another cupboard and placed the sandwich upon it, then picked up the knife again and cut it cleanly in half.

So far, so good. Then he began to take the sandwich apart, carefully pulling apart the two halves of each section and laying them on the counter, much as if he was . . .

Oh, no. I shut my eyes, shook my head. "Samson, what are you doing?" I asked, even though I already knew the answer.

"Jerry, I'm fixing the peanut butter and jelly sandwich," he replied. "Please tell me what is wrong with it."

From the observation booth, I could hear Keith and Donna whooping it up. I scowled at the window—Keith better not try using this as an excuse to welsh on his bet—then I looked back at Samson. "Samson, there is nothing wrong with the sandwich," I replied, speaking as I would to a small child who had erred. "My previous instruction was a verbal colloquialism. In this context, to 'fix' any form of food means 'to prepare,' not 'to repair.' Please remember that."

"I'll remember, Jerry." Samson stopped what he was doing, began putting the sandwich back together again. "I'm sorry for the misunderstanding. Are we still friends?"

The last might seem odd, but it was part of the approval-disapproval protocol programmed into Samson's conditioning module. Although Samson couldn't know the meaning of friendship—or at least, technically speaking, not as a human emotion—it was part of his repertoire to ask for forgiveness when he made an error. That had been Phil's idea; not only would it give third-generation robots a closer resemblance to humanity, but it would also give their owners a more user-friendly means of checking their onboard systems. Casual queries like "are we still friends?" or "am I bothering you?" sound more benign than "error code 310-A, resetting conditioning module, yes/no?"

"Yes, Samson, we're still friends," I replied. "Please bring me the sandwich now."

I turned back to the dinner table, picked up my lukewarm coffee and took a sip, then clicked my pen and started to make a few notes. Behind me, I heard Samson walking over to the table, bearing my lunch. Through my earpiece, Keith was asking Donna if she wanted to go to Boston for dinner tomorrow night, and Donna was saying—as usual—that she was busy. I'd heard this before. Donna had recently divorced her second husband and Keith had never married; the two were friends and colleagues, but their attraction was anything but mutual. Donna was understandably reluctant to strike up a workplace romance, and particularly not with the likes of Keith, who thought fart jokes were the height of . . .

"Jerry, look out!"

Donna's warning reached me just an instant too late. I looked up just as Samson slammed a peanut butter and extra-jelly sandwich into the side of my face.

Maybe that sounds funny, in a Three Stooges kind of way, but mind you this came from a robot capable of

31

picking up one end of a six-foot couch without perceptible strain. The sandwich was soft, sure, but the plate upon which it rested was hard; even if I had known what was coming, it's still likely that I would have been knocked out of my chair.

I sprawled across the tile floor, more surprised than injured, with grape jelly drooling down into my right eye and peanut butter plastering my hair against my face, the plate rattling against the table. Towering above me was Samson, six feet of cobalt-blue robot, his right hand placidly returning to his side.

"Jerry!" Donna screamed. "Are you . . . ?"

"Samson, shut down!" Keith bellowed. "Samson, code S . . . !"

"No, Samson!" I yelled. "Code B-for-Break!"

"Code B understood." Samson double-beeped and became motionless, yet his chest diodes remained lit.

Good. He had obeyed the orders of the person closest to him. Had he shut down, as Keith's Code S instruction would have made him do, there was a chance that the abrupt loss of electrical current might have erased the last few moments from his memory buffer. Code B, on the other hand, simply returned him to standby mode.

I sat up quickly, glanced toward the window. "It's okay, I'm all right," I said. "I'm unhurt. Just stay where you are."

Even as I spoke, though, I heard the door open behind me. Glancing over my shoulder, I saw Keith just outside the room. The last thing I wanted was for him to barge in and start throwing questions at Samson, so I waved him off. He hesitated, then he reluctantly shut the door, leaving me alone with the robot.

I let out my breath, then I clambered to my feet, walked over to the sink, and wetted some paper towels. There was a small bruise on my cheek, but I didn't find any blood mixed in with the peanut butter and jelly; the shirt, though, would need a trip to the dry cleaner. Cleaning up gave me a chance to calm down a little; when I returned to the table and picked up the chair, I was ready to talk to Samson once more.

"Samson, come back on-line, please," I said as I sat down, and the 'bot gave me a single beep. "Do you remember what you were doing before . . . uh, just before I gave you the Code B?"

"Yes, I do, Jerry. I gave you the sandwich you asked me to fix for you."

So far, so good. His new usage of the word "fix" indicated that his short-term memory wasn't impaired. The rest, though . . . "Samson, you didn't give me the sandwich. You hit me in the face with it. Do you remember doing that?"

"Yes, I do, Jerry."

"Why did you do that? Hit me in the face with the sandwich, I mean?"

"It seemed to be the right thing to do."

I expected to hear something from the booth; when I didn't, I touched my ear with my right hand, found my earpiece missing. Sometime during the last few minutes, it had become dislodged, probably while I was washing my face at the sink. But I didn't want to interrupt the conversation to go searching for it, so I let it pass.

"That was the wrong thing to do, Samson," I said. "You could have hurt me."

"I'm sorry, Jerry. Please forgive me."

Again, it may seem strange for a robot to ask a human for forgiveness, but this was another aspect of Samson's conditioning. For him, begging forgiveness was an acknowledgement that he understood he had made an error and a tacit statement that he would never do it again. And indeed, he never would, not in a thousand reiterations of the same sequence. Unlike humans, robots don't make the same mistake twice.

Yet getting nailed again with a PB&J was the least of my concerns. "I'll forgive you if you tell me why it seemed like the right thing to do."

Silence. I had posed the question the wrong way. "Samson, why did you think hitting me in the face with the sandwich was the right thing to do?"

"Because I want to do the right things for you, Jerry."

Great. Now we were stuck in a logic loop. Yet this was the second time today he had struck someone else—either another robot or a human—with an object he was supposed to give to them. For such an occurrence to happen twice in such rapid succession couldn't be a coincidence. Time to try a different tack . . . "If you want to do the right things for me, Samson, then how do you feel about me?"

"I love you, Jerry."

Wha-a-a-t?

Even if he sounded like Elizabeth Taylor rather than Robert Redford, that response couldn't have shocked me more. Samson was programmed to learn the identities of his human operators and accept them with platonic, selfless affection. Agape, if you want to use the seldom-used term for such a condition (and, no, it's not pronounced *ah-gape,* like the way you may stare at something, but as *ah-gaw-pey*). Since Samson had become operational, I had spent well over a hundred hours with him in this room, patiently instructing him how to make the bed, wash dishes, vacuum the floor, program the TV, fetch me a soda, answer the front door and greet guests, play various board games, and feed the cat. If I were to ask Samson how he felt about me, he should have replied, "I like you, Jerry. You're my friend."

Love was not supposed to be in the algorithms. I was pretty damn sure he didn't know what he was saying. But what was it that he *meant* to say . . . ?

Once more, I heard the door open. Looking over my shoulder, I saw Donna urgently gesturing to me. I wanted to continue this train of thought, yet since I didn't know exactly what to say next, perhaps now was a good time to grab a Coke. "I like you, too, Samson," I said as I stood up. "Let's take a break. Code B."

"Code B understood," Samson said, and there was another double-beep as he went off-line again. If I didn't return in ten minutes to rescind the order, he would automatically come back on-line again, then seek out the nearest wall-socket and plug himself in for a recharge. Until then, he was an inert hunk of machinery.

Right. An inert hunk of machinery who had just proclaimed his love for me.

I found Phil in the observation booth, bent over one of the monitors as he studied the video replay of the session. He didn't look at me as I came in, but moused the slidebar on the bottom of the screen to review my interview with Samson. Keith was seated in his chair on the other side of him; he glanced in my direction, then quickly looked away. I noticed the cordless phone near his left elbow; that explained how Phil had gotten down here so quickly. Keith, you prick; you're always ready to crack jokes behind the boss's back, but whenever you get a chance to suck up to him . . .

35

"Why didn't you let Keith shut down Samson?" Phil asked quietly, still gazing at the screen. At least he wasn't stammering this time.

"I wanted to make sure we didn't lose anything from Samson's memory." I stepped aside to let Donna slide past me, but she remained behind me, standing in the open door of the darkened booth. "This was the second time today Samson has attacked someone, and I wanted to find out why."

Phil shook his head. "Sorry, Jerry, but that's an unacceptable risk. If there's something critically wrong with his conditioning protocols, we can't let him stay activated after an accident." He turned to Keith. "Download everything from his buffer and give them to me, then erase his memory of this test."

"Hey, whoa, wait a minute! I just spent two hours in there with him! You can't just erase everything because . . . !"

That ticked him off. Phil slapped the desk as he rose to face me. "D-d-d-don't t-t-tell me wh-whu-whu-what I ca-ca-ca-ca . . ."

"Damn straight I can!" I snarled back. "That's my conditioning routine you're screwing with here, Phil, and this is the second time today you've told Keith to wipe the memory buffer!" I jabbed a finger at the motionless robot on the other side of the window. "And in case you didn't notice, that stupid friggin' thing just said he *loves* me! Now there's got to be a reason for that!"

Phil stared at me in astonishment, and I can't say I wasn't rather amazed myself. In the four years that we had worked together, we had seldom raised our voices to one another. We weren't great friends, but even after the stress of the last six months, it was hard for the two of us to get really mad at each other. Unlike, of course, his stormy rela-

36

tionship with Darth Veder . . .

And it was then, deep within my brain, that a couple of synapses sparked in a way those two particular synapses had never fired before. Phil and Kathy . . .

Okay, time out for a little soap opera. *True Geek Romance*, or perhaps *Computer Wonks In Love*. Either way, here it is:

A long time ago, in a galaxy far, far away . . . okay, so it was about twelve years ago, just across the Charles River on the MIT campus . . . there were two post-grads working in the Artificial Intelligence Lab, both studying advanced AI as applied to robotics. A nice couple of kids in their late twenties; neither of them much to look at, and hardly the type you'd imagine prancing hand-in-hand through the lily fields, but hey, love isn't only blind, but it's also got a bizarre sense of humor. They found each other, they worked together for a time as colleagues, then close friends, then . . . well, you get the picture.

But it didn't take. That's the problem with romances among highly intelligent people; they *think* too much about what they're doing, instead of just letting their *cojones* go their own merry way. They were a mismatched couple, or at least so they told themselves, prone to argue about every little detail, whether it was about the theories of Norbert Wiener or what kind of pizza to order tonight. Late one evening, after the latest tiff, she stormed out of his Cambridge apartment, and he retaliated by throwing her books into the street, and that was pretty much the end of that. They both received their MIT doctorates only a few months later, and since each of them already had jobs awaiting them on opposite sides of the country, they left Massachusetts with scarcely a final goodbye.

But every great affair has a touch of irony. A decade

went by, during which time LEC decided to diversify into consumer robotics. Jim Lang hired corporate headhunters to recruit the best cybernetics talent available, and as fortuitous circumstances would have it, the two former lovers were lured back to Massachusetts. Imagine their surprise when they discovered that they were now working for the same company. Different divisions, perhaps, but the same company nonetheless.

So now it's twelve years later, and they were still trying to work out their relationship. Only this time, they'd built robots which program themselves by observing human behavior and imitating it.

"Keith, Donna," I asked, "would you mind excusing us for a moment?"

Keith stared at me before he realized that I wanted him to leave, then he shrugged and rose from his chair. Donna gave me a quizzical look, but didn't say anything as Keith closed the door behind them.

Phil waited until we were alone before he spoke. "Whu-whu-whu-what d-d-d-do you w-w-wa-wa-want t-t-t-to . . . ?"

"Phil, sit down and count to ten." He glared at me but took my advice anyway, taking the seat Keith had just vacated. While he was counting, I crept to the door, put my hand on the knob, waited a couple of seconds, then yanked it open. Keith stood just outside, pretending to scratch his nose. He mumbled something about getting a cup of coffee and scurried down the hall. I shut the door again just as Phil had reached ten. "Okay now?" I asked.

"Sure." He let out his breath. "All right, Jerry, what do you want to talk about?"

"Okay, just between you and me . . . are you seeing Kathy again?" Phil's mouth dropped open, and for a moment I thought he was going to start stammering again. I saw the denial coming, though, so I headed it off. "Look, everyone knows you two were once an item. Frankly, I don't care, but if it makes any difference, I'm not going to tell Jim. Just to satisfy my curiosity, though . . ."

"Ummm . . . yeah, we've started seeing each other again." He seemed mortified by the admission. "But not on company time," he quickly added. "We've only gone out a couple of times."

Somehow, that sounded like a lie. I didn't keep track of Darth's hours, but I knew for a fact that Phil practically lived at the lab, going so far as to keep a fresh change of clothes in his office closet and a toothbrush in his desk. "Sure, sure, I believe you. Just dinner and a movie now and then, right?"

"Yeah, t-t-that's all." He nodded, perhaps a little too quickly . . . and that stutter of his was better than a polygraph. "P-p-please don't let anyone know. If Jim fi-fi-fi-finds out w-w-we're . . ."

"I know, I know." And that's what bothered him the most, the chance that Jim Lang would discover that the leaders of his two rival tiger-teams were having an affair. For a chess player, that would be like finding out that the white queen and the black king were sneaking off the board to fool around. "Trust me, Slim Jim's never going to learn about this . . . or at least from me, at any rate."

Phil nodded gratefully, then his face became suspicious. "So why do you want to know?"

"Well . . ." I coughed in my hand. "You just said that you two weren't seeing each other on company time . . . and really, I believe you, honest . . . but just for the sake of conjecture, if you were seeing each other here at the lab, umm . . . would you be doing it where Samson might be at the same time?"

"B-b-buh-buh . . ." Phil stared at me as if I was his father and I had just asked if he knew how to put on a condom. And then his eyes involuntarily traveled toward the window.

While we had been speaking, without either of us taking notice, Samson had automatically gone into recharge mode. The robot had walked to the nearest electrical outlet, withdrawn a power cable from his thorax, and inserted it into the wall socket. Since Samson now spent most of his downtime in the training suite, he knew exactly where all the outlets were located.

It suddenly occurred to me that the outlets were all within line-of-sight of the suite's bedroom. The one which all of us had used when we were too tired or busy to go home.

And Samson, of course, knew how to change the sheets when asked to do so.

When I looked back at Phil, I saw that he was staring straight at me. Nothing further needed to be said: he knew that I knew, and I knew that he knew that I knew. That's another thing about highly intelligent people; no matter how smart they may be, most of them have a hard time lying with a straight face.

Phil didn't say anything. He rotated the chair to the console, where he found a spare disk, slapped it into the drive, and tapped a couple of commands into the keyboard. "Sorry you had to lose this afternoon's session," he said quietly, not looking back at me as Samson's memory buffer downloaded onto the disk, "but I think we've got a flaw in the conditioning module . . ."

"Aw, c'mon! He's just confused. He sees you and Kathy in there . . ." I saw the angry look on his face reflected in the window, but I didn't stop myself ". . . and then he sees

40

you two fighting. No wonder his conditioning is . . ."

"That's enough!" He ejected the disk from the drive and stood up quickly, shoving the disk in his trouser pocket without bothering to first put it in its case. "Th-th-this is none of your buh-buh-business, and I-I-I'd ap-ap-appreciate it if y-y-you'd k-k-k-kindly stay out of it. Samson needs to b-b-be reprogrammed. Th-th-th-that's all."

No argument either way. Phil's relationship with Kathy wasn't any of my business, and there was no doubt that Samson's conditioning module needed drastic remodification. Like it or not, our team had designed a third-generation robot which took all the wrong cues from human behavior. Kathy and Phil could fight out their problems on their own, but it wasn't right to send a robot to market whose training inadvertently reflected their love-hate relationship.

"Sure, Phil," I said. "Whatever you say."

Still not looking directly at me, Phil nodded as he headed for the door. "Th-th-that's the end of t-t-t-today's exercise," he said quietly. "I-I-I'll work on S-S-S-Sampson tonight, have it r-r-ready for t-t-tomorrow's test with D-D-D-D-D . . ."

"Sure you want to do that?" Tomorrow morning we had another test scheduled with D-team. Same routine as before: Samson comes out of the woods, offers an apple to Delilah, bows to her, offers his hand and asks if she wants him to join her on the bench. Both teams had agreed to this as a test of whether the two robots could work in unison without operator intervention. "Maybe we should ask for a delay."

Phil appeared to think about it for a moment, then he shook his head. "No," he said at last. "We'll do the test tomorrow. Between now and then, don't touch Samson. Just let me take care of this, okay?"

"Sure," I said, and he nodded and let himself out of the booth. It wasn't until long after he had closed the door behind him that I realized he had stopped stuttering. By this time, though, I had taken a seat at the console and begun doing a little work of my own.

The two R&D programs were supposed to be isolated from one another, but the seal wasn't airtight. Kathy and Phil weren't the only couple who were keeping company when no one was watching; there was a cutie on Delilah Team with whom I was cooping from time to time, sometimes sleeping over at her apartment and vice-versa. What she didn't know, though, was that I had learned her password. It was a sort-of-accidental discovery; one time we were lounging in bed together, she took a few minutes to check her company e-mail on TV, so I was able to see her password when she entered it. I had never abused that knowledge, but there's always a first time for everything, so it was with no small amount of guilt that I used my occasional girlfriend's password to gain access to D-Team's files.

It took a couple of hours of rummaging, but after a while I managed to locate a batch of reports regarding Delilah's trial runs. I wasn't surprised to discover that D-team had their own problems with their robot. Like Samson, Delilah sometimes behaved aggressively when the circumstances called for her to be friendly. The fault obviously lay in the conditioning module, yet no one—at least, not those who had written the reports; I couldn't find any from Kathy Veder—had been able to figure out what was providing negative stimuli to the robot.

But I knew. Delilah was also being trained in a suite

much like Samson's. It didn't take a rocket scientist, let alone a cyberneticist, to realize that this suite was sometimes being used by Drs. Veder and Burton for certain extracurricular activities . . . with Delilah in the same room, watching the entire time, absorbing everything. Learning all the wrong lessons about the human condition.

It could be argued either way whether Samson and Delilah truly had any emotions of their own. Were they merely imitating Phil and Kathy, or had they developed inner lives, as incredible as that may seem? Regardless of the explanation, though, their environment was causing them to sometimes behave in what appeared to be an irrational manner.

Yet love—even agape, its highest expression—isn't rational. It cannot be reduced to bar-graphs and lines of source code; once you get past pheromones, body language and casual eye-contact, there is no reason for it to happen, save for the biological imperatives to procreate, maintain tribal associations, or remain close to one's family. But love does nonetheless persist, and sometimes under the strangest of circumstances.

Were Samson and Delilah in love? Probably not; they were robots, machines with none of the aforementioned hang-ups. You could spend countless man-hours of R&D trying to resolve that question. Yet the only people who had the answer were their own creators . . . and they had a hard enough time researching and developing their own feelings toward each other.

When I arrived at the trailer the following morning, the rest of Samson Team was already getting ready for the test. Phil, however, was nowhere to be found, and neither was Samson. I paged him but he didn't return the call, and while Bob was setting up his camera and Keith was opening his first bag of Fritos for the day, Kathy Veder appeared in the atrium, walking Delilah ahead of her.

Delilah was dressed in the same ankle-length, high-collared gown she had worn the day before. Once again, I wondered what purpose it served to put clothes on a robot. It didn't seem to impede her movements—indeed, the dress had been cut so that it allowed her double-jointed arms and legs to move more freely—yet it was unnecessary to assign a gender-role to a machine. On the other hand, perhaps Darth was attempting to humanize her creation; if that was the case, it might be a good marketing strategy, yet rather futile since Delilah's spherical, nearly featureless head belied the femininity of her outfit.

Kathy stopped next to the bench, turning her back to us as she waited for Delilah to catch up. Donna hadn't switched on the shotgun mike, so we couldn't hear the instructions Kathy gave the 'bot. She pointed to the bench, and Delilah walked over to it, her feet whisking beneath the hem of her dress, until she turned and daintily sat down, once again folding her silver hands in her lap. Kathy bent over Delilah and closely examined a panel in the side of her slender cylindrical neck. I glanced at the clock. We were already running fifteen minutes late . . .

The door behind me opened, and at first I thought it was Phil. "What took you so . . . ?" I started to say until I glimpsed Keith hastily stashing his chips beneath the console. I turned around and saw Jim Lang entering the trailer.

"Mind if I join you?" he asked. As always, Jim was dressed in sandals, faded Levis and a Hawaiian shirt. In all the time I had worked for LEC, I had never seen him wear a coat and tie, not even for stockholder meetings.

"No, Jim, not at all." I recovered fast enough to not

show just how startled I was by his unexpected arrival. "We're . . . ah, still setting up here. If you want to take a seat . . . ?"

"Thanks, Jerry. Excuse me, Donna . . . it is Donna, isn't it?" Ignoring her forced smile, Jim eased past her, then settled down in Phil's empty chair. "Sorry to interrupt, but I was just curious to see how things were making out down here."

Right. Slim Jim never showed up anywhere just out of curiosity. When he made an appearance outside the executive suite, it meant that he had become aware that a project was having problems. "We're doing great, Jim," Keith said, just a little too quickly. "Just . . . uh, working out a few bugs here and there."

I looked away so that Jim wouldn't see me wince. Brilliant, Einstein. Yet Slim Jim only nodded. He gazed through the window at Kathy Veder and Delilah. "I don't see Phil," he said. "Where's . . . ah, yes, here he comes now."

I followed his gaze, spotted Phil walking through the trees on the other side of the atrium. He saw Kathy, stopped a few yards away from the bench as she looked up at him. Their eyes locked for a few seconds, and for a moment or two I thought he was going to say something to her, or she something to him. But nothing happened; he lowered his head and strode quickly toward the trailer. Her gaze followed him, and in that instant when her face turned toward the trailer, I caught the briefest glimpse of an expression I couldn't quite identify. Loathing? Longing? Hard to tell . . .

"We're lucky to have them working for us, don't you think?" Jim asked quietly.

I didn't realize he was speaking to me until I glanced his way, and saw that he was looking at me. "Oh, yeah," I replied.

"Very lucky. Two great scientists, uh-huh." And perhaps it wasn't too late to send my resume to CybeServe . . .

Phil was startled to find Jim sitting in his chair when he entered the trailer. He murmured a hasty apology for being late, which Jim accepted with a perfunctory nod, then he squeezed past the CEO to stand behind Keith. "G-g-good m-m-m-morning," he stammered as he leaned over Keith's shoulder to check out the screen. "Are w-w-w-we re-re-re-ready?"

"I'm not sure." Keith cast a wary sidelong glance in Jim's direction. "When I ran a diagnostic a few minutes ago, I found a new protocol in the conditioning module. I checked it out, and it looks like it was written last night. Do you know anything about . . . ?"

"Y-y-yes, i-i-it's a n-n-new p-p-program." His Adam's apple bobbed in his thin neck, and he seemed determined not to deliberately look at Jim Lang. "I t-t-t-think w-w-w-we're ready to pr-pr-pro-proceed."

Jim raised an inquisitive eyebrow, but said nothing as he propped his elbows on the console and clasped his hands together beneath his chin. Out in the atrium, Kathy Veder had just turned to walk away from Delilah. Phil caught Donna's eye and quickly nodded his head, and she switched on her mike. "D-Team, we're ready to roll."

"R-r-roll now," Phil said. Keith and I traded an uncertain glance. Dr. Veder was still in the atrium; she hadn't yet returned to her trailer. Keith's hands hesitated above his keyboard, and Phil tapped him on the shoulder. "Commence the t-t-t-test, p-p-p-please," he said, and Keith shrugged as he typed in the command which would bring Samson online.

"Aren't you going to wait?" Jim asked quietly.

Phil didn't reply. Instead, he closed his eyes, and his lips moved as he subaudibly counted to ten.

Something weird was going on here, and it wasn't the sort of weirdness I like. While Phil's eyes were shut and Jim was looking in the other direction, I opened a window from my menu bar and moused the emergency shut-down icon. When the Y/N prompt appeared onscreen, I moved the cursor above the Y. One tap of my index finger, and Samson would freeze like a popsicle.

Out in the atrium, Kathy Veder was almost at the edge of the clearing when Samson came marching through the trees. She stopped in mid-stride, confused and startled, and judging from her expression, not just a little alarmed. My mind's eye flashed upon a scene from *The Day the Earth Stood Still*—the robot Gort carrying the unconscious Patricia Neal in his arms—and my finger wavered above the RETURN key. Oh, no, Phil can't be that crazy . . .

But then Samson stopped. He bowed from the waist, as if he was a gentleman who happened upon a lovely young woman while strolling through the woods. Kathy's face changed from fear to amusement; she stepped aside, and Samson straightened up and walked past her.

"Oh, very good," Jim murmured. "Good object recognition."

I let out my breath and moved my hand away from the keyboard.

Samson continued walking toward Delilah. As he approached the bench where she sat, his right hand opened the cargo panel on his chest, and reached inside. At this point, he was supposed to pull out an apple and offer it to the other robot. He had gotten that part right yesterday, until he decided that slamming the apple against her head was an appropriate sign of affection. On either side of me, I could see Donna, Keith, and Bob stiffening ever so slightly.

But what Samson produced wasn't an apple, but a heart. Not the organic sort, but the St. Valentine's Day variety: a red plastic toy of the sort you might place within a bouquet of roses you send to your true love.

From the edge of the clearing, Kathy Veder watched as Samson stepped around the bench and, with grace and tenderness, held it out to Delilah.

Delilah remained still, her hands still folded in her lap, her fishbowl head staring straight ahead.

"Please," I heard Phil whisper.

And then Delilah's head moved toward Samson, as if noticing his presence for the first time. She raised her left arm, opened her palm and turned it upward, and waited.

Samson took another step forward and, ever so carefully, placed the heart in her hand.

Kathy folded her arms across her chest, covered her mouth with her hand. She was watching the robots, but her gaze kept flickering toward us, toward the window behind which Phil stood.

I glanced at Phil. He was silent, but his posture was exactly like Kathy's.

Delilah took the heart and placed it in her lap. Samson bowed just as he had done for Kathy, but he remained rooted in his tracks until Delilah raised her left hand and, in a very ladylike fashion, motioned for him to join her on the bench.

Samson took two steps closer, turned around, and sat down next to Delilah, his hands coming to rest on the bench.

Then Delilah laid her right hand upon his left hand.

And then both robots became still.

That was *almost* what they were supposed to do.

For a few moments, no one in the trailer said anything.

48

Everyone stared in astonishment at the tableau. I felt someone brush against the back of my chair, but I didn't look up to see who had just moved past me. My entire attention was focused upon Samson and Delilah, the quiet spectacle of two robots holding hands on a park bench.

"Fantastic," Jim Lang whispered. "I'm . . . that's utterly . . . my God, it's so damn real." He turned around to look up at Phil. "How did you . . . ?"

But Phil wasn't there. He didn't even bother to shut the door behind him as he left the trailer. When I peered out the window again, I saw that Kathy Veder had disappeared as well.

In fact, I didn't see either of them again for the rest of the day. A little while later, during lunch hour, I casually strolled out to the employee parking lot and noted, without much surprise, that both of their cars were missing.

"That's incredible conditioning," Jim said as he pushed back his chair. "How did you guys manage this?"

Bob chuckled as he unloaded his camcorder. Donna and Keith, two days away from their first date, just grinned at each other and said nothing. I made the program-abort window disappear from my screen before the boss noticed and shrugged offhandedly.

"Just takes the right stimulus," I replied.

If you're a robot-owner, or least one who has a Samson or a Delilah in your home, then you know the rest. After considerable research and development, and the sort of financial risk which makes the *Wall Street Journal* see spots before its eyes, LEC simultaneously introduced two different R3G models: his-and-hers robots for the home and office. They cook dinner, they wash dishes, they answer the door, they walk the dog, they vacuum the floor, they make

49

the beds and water the roses and virtually anything else you ask them to do. Sure, CybeServe brought their Metropolis to market first, but who wants that clunky piece of crap? Our robots will even carry your kids to bed and sing them a lullaby.

People sometimes ask why Samsons and Delilahs have a small heart etched on their chest plates. The corporate line is that it's there to show that our robots have a soul, but anyone who knows anything about cybernetics knows better than that. After all, that's utter nonsense. Robots are just machines, right? And who in their right mind would ever believe that a machine can learn to love?

I don't have an easy answer to that, and I've spent more than fifteen years in this industry. If you want, I'll forward your query to Dr. Phil Burton and Dr. Kathy Veder. However, you shouldn't expect an answer very soon. Ever since they got married, we've had a hard time getting them to come to the office.

Her Own Private Sitcom

Ray's Good Food Diner was located on the outskirts of town near the interstate, across a gravel parking lot from a Union 76 truck stop. The town only had 1,300 residents, so it supported only two restaurants, the other of which was a pizzeria which served up what was universally acknowledged to be the world's most indigestible pizza. This left Ray's Good Food Diner as the only place within fifteen miles where you could get a decent breakfast twenty-four hours a day.

Every Friday morning at about nine o'clock, Bill drove out to Ray's for the weekly meeting of the Old Farts' Club. No one remembered who first started calling it that, but it pretty well described the membership: a half-dozen or so men, each and every one of whom qualified for the senior citizen discount, who liked to get together and chew the fat, both literally and figuratively. There weren't any rules, written or unspoken, against women or children attending the meetings, but since no one had ever brought along any family members—their wives didn't care and their kids were all adults now and, for the most part, living away from home—the issue had never really been raised. Which was just as well; in a world where seemingly everything had been made accessible to all ages and both genders, Ray's Good Food Diner was one of the few places left where a handful of white male chauvinists could safely convene without fear of being picketed.

A grumbling row of sixteen-wheelers idled on the other

51

side of the lot when Bill pulled into Ray's. He parked his ten-year-old Ford pick-up in front of the diner and climbed out. The late autumn air was cool and crisp, redolent with the scent of fallen leaves and diesel fumes; he thrust his hands into the pockets of his Elks Club windbreaker as he sauntered past the line of cars. Even without glancing through the windows, he knew which of his friends were here just by recognizing their vehicles: Chet's charcoal-black Cadillac with the NRA sticker in the rear window; Tom's Dodge truck with corn husks in the bed; Garrett's decrepit Volkswagen hatchback with the mismatched driver's-side door and the dented rear bumper. John's Volvo wasn't there—Bill remembered that he was in Daytona Beach, visiting his son's family. Ned hadn't arrived yet, either because he had overslept or—more likely, Bill thought sourly—he was too hungover from his latest whiskey binge. Poor Ned.

The small diner was filled with its usual clientele: long-haul truckers chowing down after sleeping over in their vehicles, local farmers taking a mid-morning break from their chores, a couple of longhair students from the nearby state university. He smelled bacon and fried potatoes, heard music from the little two-songs-for-a-quarter juke boxes above the window booths: Jimmy Buffett from the one occupied by a husband-and-wife trucker family, something godawful from the one taken over by the college kids. He unzipped his windbreaker, looked around . . .

"Hey, Bill!"

And there they were, sitting around two Formica-top tables pushed together at the far end of the room: the Old Farts' Club in all their glory. Chet, Tom, Garrett . . . the regular gang, waving for him to come over and join them. A chair had been left open for him; if there was a better definition of friendship, Bill had never heard of it.

"I suppose you're wondering why I called you all here today . . ." he began.

"Aw, shut up and sit down." This from Chet, seated at the end of the table.

"We begin bombing in five minutes," added Garrett.

The same opening lines, reiterated again and again over the last—seven? ten? fifteen?—years. Friendship is also the condition when your buddies tolerate your lame jokes long after they've ceased to be funny. Or perhaps it was only a requisite of growing old.

Bill took his seat, looked around. Everyone had a mug of coffee before him, but there were no plates on the table. Another unspoken rule of the Old Farts' Club was that you ate when you were hungry; no one had to wait for the others to arrive. "Thought I was running late," he observed, "but it looks like we all got here at the same time for once."

"Nope. I've been here for a hour." Chet nodded to Tom. "He's been here almost as long as I have."

"Almost an hour," agreed Tom, studying the menu.

"I got here . . ." Garrett checked his watch. "Exactly forty-two minutes ago." Garrett was like that. "We're still waiting to order."

"You mean, we're waiting for someone to ask if we want to order," Chet said.

"Yes, this is true."

Puzzled, Bill glanced over his shoulder, scanned the room. The diner was no more or less busy than it ever was on a Friday morning; at least a third of the booths were vacant, and only a handful of people sat at the lunch counter. "So where's our waitress?" he asked. "Who's working today?"

Three men who had been nursing lukewarm coffee for

the last half-hour or more looked at each other. "Joanne," Chet murmured darkly. "But don't bother to call for her. She's in her own private sitcom."

As if taking a cue from an unseen director, Joanne suddenly appeared, walking backward through the swinging kitchen door, balancing a serving tray above her left shoulder. "Okay, all right!" she yelled as she turned around, loud enough to be heard over the dueling juke-boxes. "Just everyone hold their horses! I'm coming as fast as I can!"

In all the uncounted years he had been coming to Ray's, all the many times Bill had observed Joanne at work, he had never before seen her shout at her customers. Joanne was born and raised in this town, and started working at Ray's when she graduated from the county high school. The years had been rough on her—a low-paying job, a drunk husband who abandoned her after two years, a teenage son who dropped out of high school and was now seldom home— and long ago she had lost the looks and charm that had made her a one-time prom queen, but she was still, for guys like himself and the rest of the Old Farts, the little girl they had all watched grow up. If there were good ol' boys, then she was a good ol' gal.

Her uncustomary brashness drew his attention; the object hovering above her held it. A miniature helicopter purred about a foot above her head, its spinning rotors forming a translucent halo; as she walked past the lunch counter, it followed her into the dining room. Suspended beneath the rotors was a softball-size spheroid; a tiny, multijointed prong containing a binaural microphone protruded above three camera lenses that swiftly gimbaled back and forth.

"Oh, lordie," he murmured. "Joanne's got herself a flycam."

"Is that what it's called?" Like everyone else at the table, Tom was watching Joanne. "I knew they were called something, but I didn't know what it was."

"I call it a pain in the you-know-what." Garrett picked up his cold coffee, took a sip, made a face. "What she's doing with one here, I have no idea."

Joanne sashayed to a pair of truck drivers sitting in a nearby booth, the flycam keeping pace with her from above. "All right," she announced as she picked the plates off the tray and placed them on the table, "a western omelet with a side order of bacon, two scrambled eggs with sausage, a glass of orange juice and a glass of tomato juice. Will that be all?"

The drivers looked at the plates she had put before them. "Ma'am, I ordered a ham and bacon omelet," one said quietly, "and I think my friend here asked for his eggs over-easy with ham."

"And I didn't ask for tomato juice, either," added the other. "I wanted orange juice, too."

"We-e-e-elll!" Joanne struck a pose, one hand on an outthrust hip, the serving tray tucked under her other arm. "I suppose one of us made a mistake, didn't we?"

"Yes, ma'am, I suppose one of us sure did."

Joanne looked over her shoulder. "Ray!" she bellowed in the direction of the kitchen. "You made a mistake!" Then she pivoted on her heel, and raised her arms. "I swear," she loudly proclaimed to no one in particular (except, perhaps, the flycam), "it ain't my fault no one 'round here speaks English!"

Then she flounced away, her hips swinging with over-done suggestivity. The two drivers gaped at her. "I'm not paying for this!" one yelled at her. "This isn't what I ordered!"

Joanne ignored them. She was already advancing on the two college kids sitting in the next booth. They stared at the flycam as it moved into position above their table. "What'll you have, guys?"

One of the students pointed at the drone. "Uhh . . . hey, is that thing live?"

"Taped," she said briskly, dropping her voice for the first time. "Just pretend it's not there." She raised her voice again. "So what'll you have, kids?"

He gawked at the camera, absently combing back his hair with his fingers. The other student nervously looked back at his menu. "I . . . uh . . . can I have . . . ?"

"Son, what were you smoking last night?"

Startled, he looked up at her. "What?"

"Oh, you were smoking what." She beamed down at him. "That's new to me. I'm just a poor country girl."

"Huh? What are you . . . ?"

"Look, dudes, let me rap with you, okay?" She lowered her order pad, bent over the table to look them in the eye. The flycam dropped a few inches closer, its cameras recording everything. "I was your age once, and yeah, I used to get pretty wild . . ." She took a deep breath. "But dope is just a bad trip, y'know what I'm saying? A thing is a terrible mind to . . ."

"Huh?"

"Aw, dammit." She shook her head, glanced up at the flycam for a moment, then returned her attention to the students. "I mean, a mind is a terrible thing to waste, and you've got your whole future ahead of you."

"I . . . what?" Stammering with disbelief, the student glanced between Joanne and the hovering drone. "I . . .

hey, lady, I don't use drugs!"

"Neither of us do!" His companion peered up at the flycam. "Hey, we're straight! I swear, We're straight! Geez, we just came in here to get breakfast and . . . !"

"Think about it," Joanne said solemnly. "Just . . . think about it."

Then she was off again, heading for another table, the flycam following her like an airborne puppy. "Can we at least get some coffee?" the first student called after her.

"What in the world is that fool girl up to?" Tom murmured.

"Taping another episode of her net show." Chet watched her progress across the dining room. " 'Joanne's Place,' something like that . . ."

"But this isn't her place." Tom was bewildered. "It's Ray's. Ray's Diner. What's she doing, some kind of TV show?"

As always, Tom was behind the times. No surprise there; he was still trying to get over Bush losing to Clinton. But Bill recognized the technology; eight years might have gone by since he retired as physics teacher at the local high school, but he still kept subscriptions to popular science magazines.

Flycams were miniature spinoffs of unpiloted military reconnaissance drones. Initially intended to be used for law enforcement, only police departments were able to buy them at first, but it wasn't long before they became inexpensive enough to enter the consumer market, and now they were available at electronics stores for approximately the same price as a high-end camcorder. Early versions were remote-controlled, but later models had the benefit of newer technology. They could be programmed to automatically track someone by his or her body-heat signature and

57

voice pattern and follow them around, during which time they would record everything he or she did and spoke, with the data being transmitted to a nearby datanest. Bill figured that Joanne had probably parked the nest in the kitchen, or perhaps under the lunch counter.

"It's a net show, Tom." Chet watched Joanne perform for another pair of truckers seated at the counter. Now she was playing the coy vixen while she took their orders; she had loosened the top button of her blouse, and she was letting them get an eyeful of pink cleavage as she freshened up their coffee. The drone waited overhead, its mike and lenses catching everything. "She's got that fly-thing following her around while she works, and when she's done at the end of the day, she takes it home and makes it into another episode."

"Like for a TV show, you mean."

"The net." Chet gave him an arch look. "Don't get out much, do you? No one watches TV anymore 'cept old duffers like us."

"Hey, did anyone catch 'Miami Vice' last night?" Garrett, always the peacemaker. "They showed the one where Crockett and Tubbs . . ."

"See what I mean?" Chet waggled a finger at Garrett, cutting him off. "We're used to shows about make-believe characters in make-believe stories, but that's not where it's at anymore. Now you can go out, buy one of those things, hook it up to your DVD and your home computer . . ." He snapped his fingers. "You've got your own show."

"My wife really likes that stuff." Garrett had surrendered; no sense in trying to talk about an old cop show in perpetual rerun on a local cable station. "Every night, she sits down in the den and just searches back and forth, looking for the newest shows people have put on."

"On her computer?" Slowly, Tom was beginning to catch on. "You mean, like on . . . whatchamacallit, web sites?"

Bill nodded. "Sort of like that." He didn't add that the web sites were old tech; no sense in confusing him any further. "The net has all these different nodes, millions of them, and you can rent time there, put in your own program. Anything you want."

"Anything?" Tom's eyes widened. "Like . . . you mean . . . anything you've recorded with one of those . . . ?"

"Yes. Anything."

Yes, anything. Bill had his own desktop system, a decrepit old Mac he had been nursing along for years with mother boards and internal modems bought from online junkyards or cannibalized from CPUs purchased at flea markets. Slow as autumn sap from a maple tree, but it was enough to let him patch into the net if he didn't mind waiting a few extra minutes.

He didn't mind, although there wasn't much worth looking at, really. Too much home-made porn, for one thing; every fool with a flycam seemed to think he was king stud of the universe when he got in bed with his wife or girlfriend, and wanted to share his glory with the world. Only slightly less prevalent were the boatloads of fanatics who sincerely believed that they had stumbled upon vast conspiracies involving crashed UFOs, biblical prophecies and political assassinations; their flycams caught them standing outside military bases, government offices or ancient Egyptian ruins, delivering rants fascinating only for the width and depth of their meaninglessness.

Those shows were easy to ignore, yet there were also the ones made by ordinary people during the course of their daily lives. They modeled their shows after the TV programs of their youth—"Cheers," "Seinfeld," and "Major Dad" for the sitcom enthusiasts; "ER," "Melrose Place," and "Law and Order" for the would-be dramatists—and tried to live up to Hollywood tradition. Convenience store clerks who fancied themselves as comedians. Night watchmen thinking they were action heroes. Bored housewives staging their own soaps. Teenagers solving mysteries in shopping malls. Truck stop waitresses producing sitcoms, starring themselves in the lead roles.

Joanne disappeared into the kitchen, pausing for only a moment to carefully hold open the door for the flycam. "There she goes," Chet murmured. "Probably going to check the system, maybe put in a fresh disk, put a fresh battery in the 'cam. When she gets home, she'll look at everything she got today, edit it down, maybe add some music and a laugh track. Then she'll put in on the net. 'Joanne's Place,' staring Joanne the wisecracking waitress. Just a poor ol' country girl trying to make it through the day."

He picked up his coffee cup, saw that it was empty, put it back in its saucer. "Jesus H. Christ. And all I wanted was . . ."

The door swung open again and a lean young man in a cook's apron carried out a couple of plates of food. "There's Ray Junior now," Garrett said. "Let's see if we can get him over here." He raised a hand. "Hey! Ray!"

Ray acknowledged him with a nod of his head before he went to the two drivers who had complained about their breakfast. He delivered the re-orders and spent a minute apologizing for the foul-up, then scurried around the room, pouring coffee for other disgruntled patrons. Bill couldn't help but to feel sorry for him. Ray Junior had taken over the diner a little over a year ago when his dad retired and moved to Florida; he had done well to keep the family business going, especially on this part of the interstate where nearly every other truck stop cafe was owned by one restaurant chain or another, but he couldn't afford to lose regular customers.

"Ray, what's going on with Joanne?" Chet asked when Ray finally got to their table. "I've been here nearly a hour now and she hasn't taken our orders."

"I'm really sorry about this." Ray had fetched a cup for Bill and was pouring coffee for everyone. "I'll get her over here as soon as she comes off break."

"She's taking a break." Chet glanced meaningfully at the others. "At least the second one she's had since I've been here."

"I'll get her back here."

"You ought to fire her. She's more concerned with that damn toy of hers than with doing her job."

"Well . . ." Ray Junior absently wiped a rag across the table. "Y'know, Chet, I really can't do that. Joanne's been here for nearly eighteen years. She's like family. And . . ."

He hesitated. "And?" Garrett prompted.

Ray shrugged. "Well, y'know, we've never been able to afford so much as a billboard. All we've ever had was word-of-mouth. Meanwhile we've got competition from all the chain operations down the highway. But this show she's doing . . . well, she always puts the name of the place in the credits . . ."

"So it's free advertising," Bill finished. "You're hoping it'll draw more customers."

Ray nodded. "The ones that get popular . . . y'know, get a lot of hits . . . and, well, y'know, if it gets picked up by one of the major net servers, AOL or someone like that, then it could make us . . ."

"Famous," Chet said. "Famous across the whole

61

country. Soon you'll be taking down the old sign, put up another one." He raised his hands, spread them open as if picturing a brand-new fiber optic sign. "I can see it now. 'World-Famous Joanne's Place.' Maybe you can even sell T-shirts and bumper stickers."

"You know I'd never do that," Ray Junior said quietly.

Chet scowled. "Naw, I'm sure the notion's never occurred to you."

"Of course you wouldn't," Bill said quickly. "Thanks for the coffee, Ray. Sorry to keep you."

"On the house. Same for breakfast," he added as he moved away from the table. "I'll get her out here to take your orders."

"Hear that?" Tom said as Ray Junior beat a hasty retreat to the kitchen. "Breakfast on the house! Not bad, huh?"

"No," Bill said. "Not bad at all."

There was an uncomfortable silence at the table. "So . . ." Garret said at last. "Anyone seen today's paper?"

That was how the Old Farts usually spent their Friday meetings: discussing what they had read in the paper. Baseball season was over, so now it was time to talk football. Sometimes the subject was politics, and how those damn liberals were destroying the whole country. Or maybe it would be about what was going on in Russia, or the people who were about to go to Mars, or someone famous died last week, and pretty soon it would be close to eleven and it was time for everyone to go home and do whatever it was that country gentlemen do in their golden years. Check the mailbox, feed the dogs and cats, putter around the yard, make plans to have the kids over for Thanksgiving. Take a mid-afternoon nap and wait for the world to turn upside-down again, and hope that it didn't fall on you when it did.

"S'cuse me." Chet pushed back his chair and stood up. "Need to get something from my car."

"What did you leave?" Tom asked.

"Just some medicine. Don't let no one take my seat." He pulled his denim jacket off the back of his chair and shrugged into it as he walked past the lunch counter and pushed aside the glass door next to the cash register.

Garrett mentioned an awful murder that had occurred a few days ago in the big city a couple of hundred miles away, the one that had made all the newspapers. Pretty soon everyone was talking about it: how it had been committed, who had been arrested, whether they really done the deed, so forth and so on. Bill glanced over his shoulder; out the window, he saw that the trunk lid of Chet's Cadillac had been raised. He watched Chet slam it shut; he turned and began walking back to the diner.

"Funny place to keep medicine," he murmured.

"Huh?" Tom cupped an ear. "What's that you say?"

"Nothing. Never mind."

Chet came back into the diner, took his seat again. The rest of the guys were still discussing the murder, but he didn't seem to have anything to add; he simply picked up a menu and opened it to the breakfast page. Bill noted that he didn't take off his jacket.

A couple of minutes later, the kitchen door banged open again, and there was Joanne. The flycam prowled overhead, filming her every move, as she imperiously studied the dining room. Act II, Scene II: Joanne returns from break. Cue incidental music, audience applause.

"Hey, Joanne!" Garrett raised a hand. "Could we have a little service here, please?"

She heaved an expansive sigh (the audience chuckles expectantly), then pulled pen and order pad from her apron.

"Can't a girl get a break 'round here?" she said (the audience laughs a little louder) as she came over, the flycam obediently following her.

For the first time, Bill noticed how much makeup she was wearing: pancake on the cheeks, rouge around the eyes, red lipstick across the mouth. She was trying to erase her last ten years, at least for the benefit of the camera.

"Seems to me that's all you've been taking lately," Chet replied, not looking up from his menu. "We've been waiting over an hour now."

Joanne dropped her mouth open in histrionic surprise (*Wooo*, groans the audience) as she placed her hands on her hips. "We-l-l-l-l-l! I didn't know you were in such a gosh-darn hurry! What's the matter, Chet, you waiting for a social security check?" (More laughter.)

Chet continued to study the menu. "Joanne," he said quietly, "I've been coming here to eat before you were born. I bounced your little fanny on my knee when you were a child, and told Ray Senior that he should give you a job when you got out of school . . ."

"And if it wasn't for you, I could have been working for NASA by now!" (Whistles, foot-stomping applause.)

Chet ignored her. "Every time I've come here, I've put a dollar in your tip glass, even when you've done no more than pour me a cup of coffee. So after all these years, I think I deserve a little common courtesy, don't you think?"

Joanne's face turned scarlet beneath the make-up. This wasn't part of the script. "Well, I don't . . . I don't think I have to . . . I don't have to . . ."

"Joanne," Bill said softly, "just take our orders, please. We're hungry, and we want to eat."

"And turn off that silly thing," Chet added. "I'd like a little privacy, if it's not too much to ask."

Reminded that the camera was on her (the audience coughs, moves restlessly) Joanne sought to recover her poise. "We-l-l-l-l-l, if it's privacy you . . . I mean, if you don't . . . I mean . . . if you don't mind, I'd just as soon . . ."

"Sorry," Chet said, then he reached up and grabbed the flycam.

The drone resisted as his fingers wrapped around its mike boom, its lenses snapping back and forth. Its motor whined as the rotors went to a higher speed, and for a moment it almost seemed alive as it fought against Chet's grasp, then he yanked it down to the table.

Tom's coffee went into his lap and Garrett nearly overturned his chair as they yelled and lurched out of the way. "No! Hey!" Joanne reached for the flycam as Chet turned it over. "Stop! What are you . . . ?"

Chet pushed her aside with one hand, then twisted the drone over on its back. The rotor blades cleaved through a plastic salt shaker and swept the pepper cellar halfway across the room before they snagged against the napkin dispenser.

Bill instinctively pulled his coffee mug out of the way. "Chet, what the hell . . . !"

Then Chet pulled out from beneath his jacket the tire iron he had fetched from his car trunk and brought it down on the flycam. The first blow shattered the camera lens and broke the mike boom, and the second shattered its plastic carapace and ruined a compact mass of microchips, solenoids, and actuators. The third and forth blows were unnecessary; the flycam was already an irreparable mess.

Then he dropped the tire iron on the table and sat down. There was a long silence as everyone in the diner stared at him. Then . . .

Long, spontaneous applause from the live studio audience.

As Joanne stared at the wreckage on the table, Chet picked up his menu and opened it again. "Okay," he said, letting out his breath, "I'll take two scrambled eggs, bacon, home fries, wheat toast, and tomato juice. Please."

Tears glimmered in the corners of Joanne's eyes. "I don't . . . I don't believe you just . . . that was my . . ."

"Show's canceled, Joanne." Ray Junior, standing at the lunch counter behind them, spoke quietly. "Will you just take the man's order?"

Joanne's hands shook a little as she raised her pad and dutifully wrote down Chet's order. Then she went around the table and copied down everyone else's. Tom asked for blueberry pancakes, link sausage, rye toast; Garrett requested a western omelet, no fries or toast, and a large glass of milk.

Bill had lost his appetite; he only asked for a refill of his coffee.

Joanne snuffled a bit as she thanked no one in particular, then she turned away and marched on stiff legs back into the kitchen. No one said anything when Ray Junior came out a moment later with a brush and a plastic garbage sack. He avoided everyone's gaze as he silently whisked away the debris, then he vanished through the swinging doors.

"Well . . ." Tom began.

"Well," echoed Garrett.

Chet said nothing, slipped the tire iron beneath his chair and picked up his coffee.

"Joanne's a good kid," Garrett added.

"That she is. That she is."

"Leave her a good tip, guys. She deserves it."

"Yeah, she certainly earns her money."

"Hard-working lady."

"Damn straight. That she is."

More silence. Across the room, someone put a quarter in a jukebox. An old Johnny Cash song entered the diner. The door opened, allowing inside a cool autumn breeze; a heavyset driver sat down at the counter, took off his cap, and picked up the lunch menu. A sixteen-wheeler blew its air horn as it rumbled out of the lot, heading for parts unknown.

"So . . . Braves blew it again, didn't they?"

"Yep. That they did." Bill cleared his throat. "Now it's football season."

Green Acres

On the night of July 26, 1979, a fire breaks out in a farm supply warehouse on the 100 block of 1st Avenue North in Nashville, Tennessee. Investigators will later determine that it started by accident; old copper wiring in the hundred-year-old building short-circuited and, in turn, ignited canvas stockpiled on the second floor. Whatever the reason, the warehouse goes up fast; the four-story building is filled with inflammable material, and by the time the first fire trucks arrive on the scene, flames are rushing through its sooty windows and licking its roof.

It's clear from the beginning that the warehouse is going to be lost; all the firefighters can do is contain the blaze and prevent it from spreading to adjacent buildings on the river front. Their job is made more difficult by the weather conditions; the air is warm and humid, with prevailing winds coming from the southeast, so the smoke tends to billow out instead of going up. The firemen have donned oxygen masks, though, so they're largely unaffected by the fumes, but as the fire consumes everything within the warehouse, a dense brown fog wafts through the streets of downtown Nashville.

Only a block away is the vice strip commonly known as Lower Broad, an appropriate name since the street is lined with strip joints, porno theaters and seedy bars. When fire trucks begin roaring down Broadway toward the river, the denizens of the Classic Cat, Deemun's Den and Tootsie's Orchid Lounge get off their bar stools and wander out to see what the fuss is all about. Upon seeing that a warehouse down on the Cumberland is going up in flames, some of these drinkers, hookers and three-time losers saunter down the street to watch the show, while others simply take their beers out onto the sidewalk. It's a slow Wednesday night and there's nothing much else to do; although Lower Broad is filled with smoke, some of these upstanding citizens notice that it smells kinda good . . .

What happens next will be reported by newspapers across the world and make its way into the national folklore. Within an hour of the arrival of the first fire trucks, Lower Broad becomes the scene of a spontaneous block party. All of a sudden, people start acting up; from the most stoical bouncer to the most sour whore, big loopy grins spread across everyone's face. A twenty-year alcoholic who had once been a high-school gymnast suddenly feels compelled to do cartwheels in front of Ernest Tubb's Record Store. A hooker jumps up on the hood of a Caddy, shimmies out of her tube top and starts an exotic dance. A lapsed Southern Baptist finds a Bible and begins reading aloud from the Book of Genesis, with ribald commentary on the travails of Adam and Eve. Someone props open the doors of his custom van, slaps a Waylon Jennings tape into the stereo, and cranks up the volume; within minutes people are dancing on the sidewalks, and then in the street. The bars and strip clubs and porn theaters empty out; bartenders start giving away beer, more hookers discard their clothes and the roofs of a half-dozen parked cars become impromptu dance floors.

It's not long before Metro Police arrive on the scene. At first, the officers do their jobs, making busts for public drunkenness and indecent exposure, but after awhile they decide to let things slide. No one's getting hurt, after all, and gee, isn't it nice to see all those poor bastards happy for a change? So they hang around to make sure no one walks out in front of a moving car, and laugh when the alcoholic graduates from cartwheels to somersaults. One officer even dances with a transvestite.

At the warehouse, the firefighters not wearing respirators start losing interest in the blaze. Some become distracted and forget what they're doing; the fireman operating Pump Three switches off the feed valves when he's supposed to open them wider, while two others sit down on the bumper of a hook-and-ladder and start chatting about how much the fire resembles Van Gogh's "Starry Night." Another decides that now is a good time to call his mother to wish her a happy birthday. Only the firemen wearing respirators are able to perform their duties; this is one reason why the warehouse ultimately burns to the ground.

The following day, after the cinders have cooled and everyone involved has woken up with hangovers and bloodshot eyes, an official investigation is launched. Remarkably, the nearby hospitals have reported very few injuries: minor burns from a couple of firefighters, a few cuts and sprained ankles from the celebrants. Also, for the first time in months, no muggings, shootings, or robberies have been reported on Lower Broad. In fact, two hookers later give up their trade and go in search of straight jobs instead of jobs with straights, and the man who dropped out of church to become a drunk decides to give up the bottle and rejoin his congregation.

While everyone in City Hall is still trying to figure out what happened, someone at the fire department gets an inventory list from the warehouse owner. It turns out that the warehouse contained, among many other things, about fifteen hundred feet of rope, and that this rope was manufactured in Louisville, Kentucky, from hemp derived from *cannabis sativa,* sometimes also known as marijuana.

The Sheriff of Davidson County, upon reading the formal report submitted to him by the fire department, looks up from the loose-leaf binder.

"Marijuana?" he asks. "What the hell's that?"

Marijuana is as much a part of American history as Old Glory. Indeed, early flags are made from cannabis hemp, a fact which is not without its own irony since the word "canvas" is the Dutch pronunciation of the Greek word "kannabis." Beginning in 1619, when farmers in the Jamestown Colony in Virginia were ordered by law to sow Indian hemp seeds, *cannabis sativa* was grown throughout the original thirteen colonies as a staple crop. Everything—sailcloth, fishermen's nets, clothing, table linen, lamp oil, paint, rope—was made from hemp; as a textile, it's softer than cotton, warmer and more water absorbent, and has better tensile strength. The original draft of the Declaration of Independence was written on hemp paper; the Continental Army under General George Washington huddled within coats and blankets woven from hemp cloth while they waited out the long, cold winter in Valley Forge.

By the middle of the 19th century, cannabis was grown more extensively in the United States than cotton, and for good reason. It's more easily cultivated than cotton, especially in cool climates, and for a while it was more easily refined. All of its parts be used; the roots, buds, and leaves of the female cannabis plants were being used for the make elixirs for the relief of headaches, nausea, menstrual cramps, and other ailments. In 1850, over eight thousand hemp plantations were spread across the United States. Towns throughout the East and South were named

Hempfield, Hempstead, or Hemphill; the first families to settle the Western frontier traveled across the plains in covered wagons whose awnings were made of hemp canvas.

It was not until Eli Whitney invented the cotton gin that cannabis was replaced as the largest cash crop in America; the costs of refining cotton finally became competitive with those of cannabis. Even so, hemp remained a major agricultural product in the United States. In fact, hemp twine was commonly used to bale cotton.

At the beginning of the 20th century, although millions of acres of cannabis were planted from Virginia to California, only a relative handful of people knew that it was possible to get stoned on this stuff, and then only in the lowest tiers of American society. Mexican migrant workers in Texas and blacks in the Mississippi Delta, unable to afford anything better, learned that if you took leaves off the hemp plants you picked and rolled them into cigarettes, you could get a cheap high. But "marijuana," to use the Hispanic slang term, was considered to be a poor man's kick; smoking it meant that you didn't have enough money to buy whiskey. Segregation also meant that it was a long time before white people learned about marijuana.

In the 1930s, a short-lived effort to outlaw the cultivation of marijuana was undertaken by Harry J. Anslinger, the director of the newly-formed Federal Bureau of Narcotics. Anslinger was appointed to this job by President Hoover because his uncle-in-law, Andrew Mellon, was Hoover's Secretary of State. Mellon was the chief financial backer of the Mellon Bank of Pittsburgh, which in turn was a heavy investor in the DuPont Company. DuPont was developing artificial textiles which were intended to compete with cotton; however, the company was also aware that new processes had been recently invented which would soon make hemp cloth even less expensive than cotton. Andrew Mellon realized that DuPont's textiles would succeed only if hemp disappeared from the marketplace, so he got his in-law nephew in the new Federal Bureau of Narcotics to launch a public campaign against cannabis.

Anslinger discovered that blacks and Latinos in the deep South were smoking marijuana; since these minorities were often involved in violent crimes, he fed sensationalized, and even patently false, stories to the press that marijuana was making all those coloreds do things like laugh at white men and rape white women. As outrageous as the hoax was, it nearly succeeded; in 1937, Congress began debating a proposed Marijuana Tax Act which would effectively outlaw cannabis cultivation in the United States by taxing its growers into oblivion. It was stopped when lobbyists from various industries dependent upon cannabis made a last-minute counter-attack. Representatives from many large companies met with President Roosevelt and key members of the House and Senate and made them realize that the Marijuana Tax Act would destroy a large section of the nation's economy just when the country was struggling to recover from the Depression. Roosevelt and a coalition of Southern Democrats managed to swing enough votes to defeat the bill by a narrow margin.

Roosevelt fired Harry Anslinger shortly afterward. Then, as a concession to the hemp lobby, he ordered the Civilian Conservation Corps to plant ten thousand acres of cannabis on federal land in Tennessee and North Carolina.

It's August 16, 1969, and in a muddy farm field in Bethel, New York, more than 300,000 members of the post-war baby boom are causing an explosion of their own. So many people have traveled across the country for the

Woodstock Music and Art Fair that the New York State Thruway has been closed. The gates have been crashed, cow ponds have been turned into swimming holes, nearby woods into communal toilets. National Guard helicopters are airlifting food and medical supplies to the site, and a rainstorm has turned all these middle-class kids into mud-caked aboriginals. History will remember this moment, maybe.

Behind the teetering stage, Jerry Garcia is having a really bad day. The Grateful Dead had driven all the way from San Francisco to be one of the featured bands, but now he's wondering if it was worth the effort. First, they had to follow the Who; if playing behind Pete Townshend and Keith Moon wasn't cold-blooded murder, then being followed by Jimi Hendrix certainly is. The shower left the stage covered with puddles of rain; their equipment wasn't properly grounded, so he, Phil, and Bobby received nasty shocks every time they touched their guitars strings. Pigpen's pissing and moaning because there isn't any booze, and all these hippies have to offer is brown acid and jimson weed. The only mercy is that no one recorded them; the band refused to sign the Warner Brothers contract that would allow their set to be filmed or taped for the movie and record album rumored to be in the works. Considering that the Dead's brief performance was one of their worst, at least they won't have to be embarrassed by it later.

So Jerry wanders around backstage in search of something to take his mind off his troubles, and over there, leaning against a scaffold, is Ritchie Valens. Ritchie's the only teen heart-throb from the '50s to have successfully made the transition from rockabilly to acid rock; his hair is shoulder-length now, his Latino back-up band is hip to his idea of playing electric Tex-Mex, and his albums are doing well enough that he isn't constantly fighting his record company the way the Dead are. Jerry and Ritchie are buddies from the Avalon Ballroom days, so Jerry saunters over to see what he's doing.

"Hey, cat, what's happening?" Ritchie barely glances up from the cigarette he's rolling.

"Too little, too late."

"Caught your set, man. You guys cooked."

Jerry laughs bitterly. "If you like raw meat."

"It wasn't that bad. I mean, it could have been worse . . ."

"That's what they say about frontal lobotomy."

Ritchie looks up, catches Jerry's eye. They both know that he's being charitable. "Aw, hell, man," Ritchie murmurs, looking away. "You know what I mean. There's nothing you could have done."

"Guess so." Jerry's gaze falls on the cigarette Ritchie's rolling; it looks twisted and weird. "Hey, spare yourself the effort," he says, reaching for the Marlboros in the pocket of his black T-shirt. "Have one of mine."

Ritchie shakes his head. "Don't smoke. Not those, at least."

"So what's that?"

"Marijuana. Ever heard of it?"

Jerry grimaces. Back in his folkie days, when he and his songwriting partner were living in a beat-up station wagon and couldn't afford cigarettes, they found some discarded rope down on the wharf. Having heard rumors that hemp could be smoked, they bought a pack of cigarette papers and tried to roll the fibers into makeshift cigarettes. They puked their guts out. "Aw, no, man. Thanks anyway."

"You sure, man?" Ritchie licks the top of the cigarette paper, neatly folds it over, and offers it to Jerry. "Better than what you're smoking. In fact, I kicked cigarettes after I started with this."

"No kidding?" says a new voice. "Really?"

Some guy has just wandered by: tall, long blond hair beneath a headband, goofy grin. Mid-forties: way too old to be a hippie. When he stops in front of Ritchie, Jerry notices that the pupils of his blue eyes are dilated. Strung out on acid. Another substance Jerry's learned to distrust. Give him jimson weed any ol' day. Kinda fucks up your eyes, though . . .

"You can stop smoking if you use this? No shit?"

Ritchie nods. "No shit. Want one?" He offers the hemp cigarette to the newcomer.

"*Muchas gracias.*" The old hippie accepts the twisted cigarette, sticks its tapered end in his mouth, pats the pockets of his dirty string vest in search of a match. "Gotta light?"

Jerry finds his Zippo, flicks it to life. "Careful with that. It's not what you're expecting . . ."

"Expect nothing, accept everything. My motto." He bends down and lets Jerry light the cigarette. He takes a deep drag, exhales smoke through his nostrils. "Jeez, that's good." Then he offers his hand to Jerry. "Name's Tim. Glad to meet you."

Jerry shakes Tim's hand, then watches as he sails away. "Who was that?"

Ritchie shrugs. "Some guy from Boston. He's been hanging around back here, giving acid to anyone who wants some. Claims he's a Harvard professor . . ."

"Yeah, right." Jerry shakes a Marlboro out of his pack. Ritchie begins rolling another cigarette. How anyone could smoke hemp is beyond him. "So when are you on?"

"Right after Jimi, then I gotta find a way out of here. We've got a charter plane waiting in Albany to take us to another gig." Ritchie shakes his head. "Fuck, I hate flying . . ."

"I hear you, man." Jerry lights his cigarette and tucks the Zippo back in his pocket. "Well, I'm going to go find my guys, see if we can get out of this hellhole."

"Where you going next?"

"I dunno." Jerry shrugs. "Back to California, I guess." It's hard to keep the envy out his voice. "After today, I'm half-inclined to bag this Grateful Dead shit. Try going solo, maybe."

"Gimme a call when you get back." Ritchie drops his voice. "Carlos is talking about cutting out to start his own band. I could use another guitar player."

Out on stage, Hendrix is warping the "Star Spangled Banner" into something that sounds like a mutant invasion from space. It makes the Dead sound like a jug band. "Yeah, maybe I will," Jerry says. "Thanks."

Ritchie smiles. "Cool. Catch you later." He walks away.

Jerry takes his place against the scaffold. Yeah, he could get into working as a sideman for Ritchie. Fat chance that the Dead will ever make it big.

Just as long as he doesn't have to smoke any rope . . .

The Republicans made a stink about the government cannabis plantations in the Great Smoky Mountains, claiming that Roosevelt was trying to appease the hemp industry at taxpayer expense, but it soon turned out to be a fortunate decision. When the United States entered World War II four years later, the armed forces needed all the hemp they could get, for everything from uniforms to gun belts to parachute harnesses. Even then, it wasn't enough. After the Philippines fell to Japan and Russia was invaded by Germany, overseas hemp supplies were cut off and

America was forced to grow its own.

By the end of 1942, hemp was being cultivated across the South in record numbers and Midwest dustbowls were becoming vast plains of towering cannabis stalks. In the musical *Oklahoma!*, Rogers and Hammerstein immortalized the period with the stanza, "where the weed is as high as an elephant's eye." Seeing wartime profits, DuPont forgot its support of the Marijuana Tax Act and purchased patent rights to as many cannabis processing inventions as it could acquire. Other companies quickly followed DuPont's lead; they quickly developed efficient new means of utilizing cannabis for a wide variety of industrial and consumer products. Indeed, America felt few of the shortages that Europe experienced: printers switched from wood to hemp pulp, automobile makers redesigned car engines to run on cannabis oil, and clothing manufacturers discovered that certain cannabis strains were capable of producing inexpensive fabrics as fine as silk. The word "marijuana," along with its negative connotations, was quickly forgotten.

When the war ended, cannabis emerged as the number-one cash crop in the United States, replacing cotton as the textile of choice. It grew almost anywhere, and reached maturity much more quickly; one acre of cannabis yielded more than four acres of cotton. It was resistant to most pests and forced out competing weeds; since pesticides were virtually unnecessary, the soil in which it was planted was unharmed. It was easy to harvest, and even easier to plant. Indeed, cannabis soon became known as "the lazy farmer's crop."

Although automakers soon returned to gasoline-fueled engines as the industry standard, other industries found new uses for the hardy weed. Brake fluid, diapers, fiberboard, cement blocks, birdseed, oil paints, cosmetics, salad oil, animal feed, mulch, books, carpets, headache medicine, drapery, socks, books and magazines . . . all were made from cannabis products and by-products.

Agricultural firms incorporated the cannabis leaf in their corporate logos. Corporate representatives from Brazil, Japan and Australia were proudly shown vast warehouses of cannabis being cured before being destalked, seeded, and sent to processing plants. Members of Congress were voted in or out of office on the basis of how well they supported the hemp industry. Political candidates walked through cannabis farms in Georgia or Alabama, coats slung over their arms, ties loosened, cannabis leaves tucked in their mouths. "How high's y'all's weed, suh?" they drawled. The big scene in *North by Northwest* was when Cary Grant sought to elude a biplane by ducking into a Nebraska hemp field. Schoolchildren earned approval from their teachers by shooting up their arms: "I know, I know, I know . . . 25,000 uses!"

And it was only in the barrios and ghettos, safely segregated from mainstream America by separate-but-equal soda fountains, restrooms and motels, where cannabis told its dirty little secret. Down there, black housekeepers and Latino farmhands rolled marijuana cigarettes as they listened to race music on low-band AM radio stations.

All this changed when Timothy Leary smoked his first joint at Woodstock.

EXT.—BEACH—DAY
MEDIUM SHOT of a beautiful California BLONDE in a bikini, surfing at Malibu. THEME MUSIC comes up: bright, jingly pop-rock.
SINGER (V.O.):
It's your natural way . . .

CAMERA FOLLOWS the blonde as she comes out of the ocean and runs to her BOYFRIEND—handsome, clean-cut, affluent—who is lying on the beach. He offers THE PRODUCT to her.

SINGER (V.O.):

It's your natural style . . .

INT.—CLUB—NIGHT

CLOSE SHOT of a rock band performing in an upscale nightclub. The SAME COUPLE, now wearing stylish clothes, is seated at a table directly in front of the stage, relishing every moment. They're both smoking THE PRODUCT.

SINGER (V.O.):

It's the way you live today . . .

EXT.—STREET—NIGHT

MEDIUM SHOT of the COUPLE as they saunter down a brightly-lit city sidewalk. They pause to watch a STREET MIME doing a routine, then laugh and pretend to be washing windows with him. The BOYFRIEND is smoking PRODUCT.

SINGER (V.O.):

Make the most of it now!

EXT.—PARK—DAY

MEDIUM SHOT of the COUPLE sitting on a park bench, cuddled together, feeding ducks in a nearby pond. CLOSE-UP of the PRODUCT lying on the bench beside the BOYFRIEND.

ANNOUNCER (V.O.):

It's a whole new era for smoking pleasure . . . ERA, the natural herbal cigarette. No tar, no nicotine, no preservatives . . . only total excitement!

EXT.—DRIVEWAY—DAY

MEDIUM SHOT of the COUPLE washing a sportscar. The BOYFRIEND raises a garden hose and playfully squirts the BLONDE. She opens her mouth to catch the glistening water.

SINGER (V.O.):

It's the way you live today . . .

Make the most of it now!

CLOSE-UP of the PRODUCT lying on the front seat of the sportscar.

FADE OUT.

Timothy J. Leary was a professor of psychology at Harvard University until 1964, when he was fired because of controversial student experiments involving LSD. His dismissal from Harvard marked the beginning of a downward spiral in Dr. Leary's personal life. Emotionally fragile from his first wife's suicide, scorned by the news media as a "mad scientist," ostracized by the academic world, Leary suffered a nervous breakdown; some claimed it resulted, in part, from using LSD himself. He vanished for a few years, then resurfaced in the late '60s in Greenwich Village, where he played the role of a self-styled "acid guru" on the fringes of the New York counter-culture scene while making a paltry living as a freelance writer for *Ramparts* and *The Village Voice*.

Leary might have vanished into obscurity had it not been for his chance encounter with Ritchie Valens at Woodstock. By this time, Leary had become a heavy smoker; friends remember that he went through two packs of Camels every day, although he often claimed that he wanted to quit. While hanging out backstage at Woodstock, Leary ran out of cigarettes; unable to buy more, he was constantly bumming off musicians and roadies. Then he snagged a marijuana cigarette from Ritchie Valens.

According to *Leary!*, his bestselling 1974 autobiography, Timothy Leary quit smoking virtually overnight at Woodstock as a result of that one "joint." He smoked it down to the nub, then wandered out to the hillside and watched the bands play. Three hours later, when he finally found himself craving tobacco again, he returned to the backstage area in search of Valens. Valens had vanished by then, but fortunately he had left his sandwich bag of marijuana and cigarette papers on an amplifier. Leary found them; he rolled another joint, put the baggie and the papers in his back pocket, and returned to the hillside, where he contentedly smoked marijuana throughout the night. The following morning, while the Jefferson Airplane gave its last public performance as a band, Leary left the festival and hitchhiked his way back to New York City. Although he had ample opportunity to do so, he never bought or bummed another cigarette. He had experienced his last nicotine fit; if he was ever going to smoke anything again, it would only be marijuana.

Leary abandoned LSD as a dead-end and turned his attention to cannabis. He spent months in the New York Public Library researching the hemp industry; when that wasn't enough, he borrowed money from friends and drove his second-hand Volkswagen down South, where he spent several more months interviewing Latinos and blacks in Mississippi, Louisiana and Texas. There he learned not only that cannabis had been smoked for decades, but also that the leaves and flowertops of its female form—which contained the psychoactive tetrahydrocannabinol, or THC—had been routinely combined with its inactive male counterpart during the growth, harvest and processing stages of its industrial cultivation. Pharmaceutical companies had been using THC for years as the active ingredient in non-prescription painkillers, but poor blacks and Latinos had learned the same thing through hand-me-down folk knowledge: only the flowering hemp plants were worth smoking, while leaves from male plants were harsh and often sickening. Both were customarily harvested and processed together by the textile and paper industries, but it did no good to try smoking a shirt or a magazine, unless you burned shirts or magazines or carpets in such massive quantity that the THC values were upped considerably.

Through trial-and-error experimentation, Leary discovered that leaves from male and female *cannabis sativa* could be blended to produce a herbal tobacco substitute that was non-addictive, nicotine-free and only mildly euphoric. Not only that, but smoking this blend in the same quantities as tobacco cigarettes would effectively kill nicotine fits. In other words, it was the perfect cigarette for people who smoked, hated it, but couldn't quit.

Leary wrote up his findings as a fifty-page proposal, then went in search of backers. He avoided contact with the major tobacco companies, and concentrated instead on well-heeled hipsters whom he had met while haunting concert backstages and upscale parties. Most politely nodded and wished him good luck, but after eighteen months he managed to find eight who were willing and able to invest in his idea. With their financial backing, Leary founded the Era Cigarette Company, and with a multi-million dollar TV and print ad campaign, launched the Era herbal cigarette in May 1972.

Earth shoes. Mood rings. Hip-huggers. Black-light posters. "The Sonny and Cher Show." Era cigarettes. All these things were hip during post-Vietnam America, when everyone was groovy and even congressmen sported long sideburns. For about six months, Era was enormously popular; even people who had never smoked before tried them, just so they could say they had. In a very short time, Timothy Leary went from being a washed-up ex-Harvard prof to "Doctor Tim," the hippie entrepreneur who was a regular on the Dick Cavett show.

Then, just as quickly, Era cigarettes fell from grace. Smokers complained of drowsiness, bloodshot eyes, and uncontrollable fits of hunger. Hairdressers said that they could always tell whether customers smoked Eras because their hair would be frizzy, full of split ends. Those who bought Eras to wean themselves off tobacco often said that the herbal substitute made them crave cigarettes even more than before. And finally, people began to gradually admit that, no matter how cool or trendy they might be, Eras tasted like shit.

In early 1973, Congress outlawed cigarette advertising in the broadcast media. When the fun-loving Era Couple vanished from TV screens, sales plummeted. Leary met with the company board of directors; after two days of argument, they decided to retrench and regroup. Era would be taken off the mainstream market and instead sold it in tobacco shops and health-food stores, where consumer demographics showed there were still enough buyers to keep the product afloat.

The remarketing strategy succeeded. Era vanished from grocery shelves and cigarette machines, but it didn't become extinct; it fit into a specialized market-niche, comprised mainly of people who actually liked its earthy taste and somnambulant buzz. So Era continued to sell a few hundred thousand cartons a year, which was just enough to keep the investors happy and Doctor Tim stocked with whatever bathtub hallucinogen he was experimenting this week.

Then a warehouse in Nashville burned down, and everything changed.

The appointments secretary to the First Lady walks into an anteroom on the second floor of the White House. "She'll see you now," she says to the pudgy young man sitting on a couch.

Al Costello, Assistant Director of the DEA, puts down the issue of *National Review* he's been skimming for the past two hours and follows the secretary into the adjacent office. The First Lady is seated behind her desk, talking on a phone. She raises an imperious finger as she swivels her chair away from him. The secretary shows Costello to an armchair in front of the fireplace, asks him if he wants coffee, then disappears.

Costello waits nervously while the woman behind the desk—by some accounts, the second-most powerful person in the United States—winds up her conversation. He stands up as the First Lady crosses the office to extend her hand. She's much smaller than she looks on TV; the taut skin of her face is strangely artificial, as if molded from wax.

She's just taken a seat across the butler's table from him when the secretary reappears, carrying a china service engraved with the Presidential seal. She pours coffee for him before vanishing again. The First Lady doesn't take coffee; Costello decides to let his go cold. Her smile is polite but her blue eyes are cool. He's been waiting five weeks for this meeting; now he's got five minutes.

Costello begins with a brief rundown of the facts. The use of cannabis as a narcotic is rapidly escalating across the country. Although hemp is legally grown in all fifty states, no one ever believed that its female parts (she raises a hand to her prim mouth and coughs) . . . that is, the leaves from seed-bearing plants (a faint nod), would ever be used as a recreational drug. However, the incident in Nashville last year has caused cannabis to gain widespread popularity. There are reports that "marijuana," as it has become widely known, is penetrating the mainstream as a . . .

Yes, yes. The First Lady is a trifle impatient. I read the newspapers. Why is this of interest to the President?

Trying to hide his nervousness, Costello picks up his coffee. It's gone lukewarm. She stares at him when he slurps it, her eyes following his hand when he returns the cup to the table. Yes, ma'am, I'm sure you do. Since the President has spoken out against illegal drug use and you yourself has made this an important item of your agenda, we at the DEA were hoping . . . that is, we would like to request . . . that you aid us in a public crusade against hemp smoking.

Her eyes don't blink. In what way?

The DEA has developed a public-affairs program which would target young people, particularly those in high school and college, where demographics show that marijuana has made the greatest impact. It would warn them that use of cannabis can lead to acute mental illness, loss of primary motor skills, hair loss, sexual impotence (cough, glare) . . . pardon me, loss of reproductive ability . . . even death. The program will revolve around a slogan—very simple, easily understood—which would be put on posters, T-shirts, billboards and so forth, and also be used in a nationwide TV and radio campaign. What we need is a prominent public figure to introduce the slogan in such a way that it would seem like a spontaneous remark.

The First Lady's face remains neutral.

"I see," she says at last. "And just what is this slogan?"

"Just say no."

The First Lady blinks. "Just say what?"

"Just say no."

"Just say no *what?*"

"Just no."

"No?"

"*No.* Just no."

"No what?"

"*No!* Just say no! That's all. Just . . . say . . . no."

The First Lady stares at him. "That's the stupidest thing I've ever heard."

An hour later, over pizza lunch in the food court of the Old Post Office mall, Costello reiterates this incident to a friend who works as a legislative aide to a North Carolina senator. The aide smiles and chuckles, and finally laughs out loud when Costello professes his belief that the First Lady was stonewalling him.

Of course she was, he says, stirring his half-empty soda with a straw. I wish you would have told me about this before you went over there. I could have warned you.

Warned me about what?

The aide shakes his head. Ever heard the name Joseph Templeton? He's CEO of Pacific AgriCorp, the largest hemp grower on the West Coast. Close personal friend of the President and a major campaign contributor. You just went in there with a campaign which would put him out of business. Jeez, you're such a schmuck.

At the next table over, a businessman lights an Era. The two men watch as he settles back in his chair and blows a luxurious smoke ring. So that's it? Costello asks quietly. People keep smoking this stuff?

The aide smiles. Don't sweat it, he says. We've already got people working on it.

Marijuana entered the American mainstream just when

the nation's political sails were beginning to tack to the right. Two decades of social experimentation were being called into question; where liberal doctrinaire had reigned supreme, conservative objections were quickly gaining ground. The economy was suffering because industry was overregulated. Schools were bad because students weren't being taught traditional subjects. Crime was rising because criminals weren't being prosecuted. Women were getting uppity, minorities were getting too much power, and the poor were poor because they wanted to be poor; no one had shown these people the error of their ways.

It had to be somebody's fault. Can't be yours or mine, so it must be someone else's.

Someone driving on the Los Angeles freeway during afternoon rush took a wrong left turn, slammed into another car which hit another car. The pile-up caused a ten-mile traffic jam and sent four people to the hospital. Highway patrolmen discovered a pack of Eras on the dashboard of the first car. The driver had been smoking marijuana.

Productivity at manufacturing plants across the country drastically falls in the last six quarters. Line workers show up for work later than usual, take more breaks, call in sick more often. Quality suffers; consumers begin buying more retail goods from foreign sources. A well-publicized study shows that more than half of the blue-collar employees report smoking marijuana.

SAT scores are down. High school students across the country are failing college admission exams in record numbers. Teachers complain that discipline is falling. Questionnaires show that many students have started smoking marijuana; if they can't find them in local tobacco stores, then they sneak into local hemp fields late at night. The ones with the seeds are the good stuff.

Johnny Carson has Timothy Leary on his show. Doctor Tim lights an Era to show that there's nothing wrong with his product, then cracks up in front of six million viewers when Johnny shows him his mismatched socks.

A commercial airliner crashes in Colorado, killing all seventy-six passengers and six crewmembers. No marijuana is found aboard, but an investigative journalist from the *Rocky Mountain News* discovers that the flight engineer smoked marijuana at a Halloween party twelve days earlier.

The *Washington Post* publishes a story about an eleven-year-old boy, safely anonymous, who claims to be a heroin addict. The child commits robberies to feed his habit. He says he got started by smoking marijuana at age seven. City child-welfare officials fail to find this child, and there are dark rumors that the story is a hoax, but the story makes the national wires and the reporter receives a Pulitzer.

It's in *Newsweek*. It's in *Time*. It's on the five-o'clock news and the six-o'clock news and the ten-o'clock news. "Nightline" devotes an hour to the Marijuana Menace; Ted Koppel pits Doctor Tim against Surgeon General C. Everett Koop, and one of them isn't under the influence. Two weeks later, Leary announces that he's moving to Switzerland. Better ski conditions.

Polls show that seventy-two percent of Americans want marijuana to be outlawed; only thirteen percent are aware than marijuana is derived from cannabis, and less than eight percent know that hemp is the largest cash crop in the United States.

The First Lady makes an appearance at a Washington drug rehabilitation center. "Just say no," she says, and a new sound bite is born. Cotton growers and synthetic textile manufacturers soon become the largest contributors to the President's re-election campaign, and congressmen running for reelection soon receive heavy donations from their PACs.

In June, 1984, five years after the Nashville warehouse fire, bipartisan bills are introduced on the floors of both the House and Senate to outlaw the cultivation, processing, and production of *cannabis sativa* in the United States.

By coincidence, it just happens to be an election year.

Lloyd Pullman's sitting on the front bumper of his pickup truck when the County Sheriff arrives. He drops his cigarette and stamps it out under the sole of his workboot, but doesn't stand up as Bill Von Norstand gets out of his cruiser and saunters over to him, pulling up the seat of his pants.

"Morning, Lloyd."

"Morning, Bill. How's it going?"

"Fair to middlin'. You?"

"Could be better."

It's almost nine o'clock. The July sun isn't halfway up the sky, and heat is already beginning to rise off the dirt road running past the west side of Pullman's farm. Blue hills rise in the distance beyond ten-foot stalks of Kentucky hemp. The spring was nice and rainy, the first months of summer moist and hot: the best growing season Pullman's seen in years. His plants should be twenty feet high by Labor Day, just in time for harvest . . .

Pullman scuffs the toe of his boot on the ground. He has to stop thinking like that.

"Yeah, I imagine so." Sheriff Von Norstand looks uncomfortable. He pulls off his mirror shades and wipes their lens on the front of his uniform shirt. The walkie-talkie hooked to his uniform belt chatters; distant voices vying for his attention. Bill ignores them. "I'm really sorry about this,

Lloyd. If there was any other way . . ."

"Not blaming you. Ain't your fault."

Von Norstand seems relieved. He and Pullman have known each other all their lives; they grew up together in Dolores, went to the same schools, played on the high school basketball team, double-dated for the '67 Senior Prom. After Lloyd graduated from Kentucky Tech and Bill came home from 'Nam, they returned to Dolores. Many of their friends had long since packed up and left, but they wanted to settle down and raise families. This is the best place in the world.

Bill reaches into his back pocket, pulls out a folded sheaf of typewritten paper, creased in the middle from where he's been sitting on it. "Well, let's get it over and done with," he murmurs unhappily, straightening out the papers with his rough hands. "I think I'm supposed to read you some stuff . . ."

"Don't bother. I know what it says already." Lloyd's already received a draft of the same form, along with countless manila envelopes containing even more forms, from half a dozen federal and state agencies. He had read countless times, often late at night at the kitchen table after Margie and Louise had gone to bed, sometimes while making his way through a six-pack of beer. The ones he had to sign, he had already sent back. This is the last one: the one that counts.

The Sheriff looks relieved. "Good. Didn't want to do it anyway." Still, he stares at the forms, as if afraid to look his oldest friend in the eye. "God, Lloyd, if there was any other way, I swear . . ."

"There isn't, so just shut up about it." Lloyd's voice is uncustomarily harsh. "You're not making it any easier, so cut it out."

From down the road, the dim mutter of an approaching truck. Dust rises from somewhere just out of sight. Lloyd stares that way for a moment; when he looks back again, he sees that Bill has put on his sunglasses again.

"You're not going to give me any trouble about it this, are you?" Bill asks. His voice is neutral.

Lloyd gazes past his own reflection, straight into the invisible eyes of the man who introduced him to Margie when he was still dating her. "You know me better than that," he replies softly. "Now take off those cheaters."

Bill drops his head in embarrassment. "Sorry." He takes off the mirror shades, tucks them into his shirt pocket below his badge. "Been hard on me, too. Suppose you heard what happened last week with Joe McNeil . . ."

McNeil's another hemp farmer on the other side of the county. Younger man, newcomer to Dolores; moved here from Arkansas just twelve years ago. Nice guy; sings in the choir at Bill's church. When Bill came to see him, McNeil refused to sign the papers; he tore them up, argued with Bill, then threw a punch at one of the guys from the truck. Bill had to take him away in handcuffs. McNeil's now serving a sixty-day sentence in the county workhouse, and there's talk that the D.A. may be pressing state and federal charges.

"I'm not that way," Lloyd says, and he isn't. The last thing he wants is to have Margie bring Louise down to jail to visit her old man. The truck is in sight now, a distant speck between barbed-wire fences. "Let's just get it over with."

Bill places the papers on the hood of Lloyd's truck, flips to the last page, smooths it out with his hand, then unclips a Bic pen from his pocket and hands it to Lloyd. Lloyd takes one last look at the field, then he signs his name, enters his Social Security number and dates it.

Two generations of hemp farming, gone like that.

Bill has just signed his own name to the form when the truck comes to a halt behind his cruiser. The truck is grey, and has U.S. Department of Agriculture decals on its doors. The front bumper sports a peeling Van Halen sticker. Four young men climb out: mid-twenties, beards and long hair, early beer bellies. White trash kids, hired to do the dirty work. Rock music blasts from the radio until the driver cuts off the engine. They stretch and polish off paper cups of 7-11 coffee, then the driver shuffles toward Bill.

Bill turns away from Lloyd. He meets the driver halfway, hands him the paperwork. The crew chief scans the forms, murmurs something to Bill. Lloyd can't hear what they're saying and could care less. The crew chief takes the paperwork back to his truck and stashes it under the front seat. One of his men is taking a piss on the shoulder of the road; he zips up when the boss whistles for him, then ambles to the rear of the truck. The others follow. They've got a long day ahead of them.

Lloyd's already climbing into his truck when Bill catches up with him. "You sure you don't want to watch?"

Lloyd glances in his mirror. The kids are already unpacking their flame throwers. They're supposed to wear air masks, but he doubts any of them will put them on. Fringe benefits.

"Naw," he murmurs, slipping the key into the ignition. "Why bother?"

Bill nods. "So what are you going to do now?"

"I dunno." Lloyd starts up the truck. "Haven't decided yet. See you 'round, Bill."

"So long. Take her easy."

Bill taps the truck's roof and Lloyd drives away, heading

down the road toward the state highway. Soon as he's out of sight, he steps on the gas. He's running late for an appointment for a farm realtor in Lexington.

He glances once in his mirror, and quickly looks away when he spots a thick brown plume rising from his property. Some of that smoke must have gotten into his eyes; a couple of miles down the road, he pulls over to dry the tears from his eyes.

The Marijuana Prohibition Act of 1984 succeeded where the Marijuana Tax Act of 1937 failed.

Because it didn't distinguish between the strains of *cannabis sativa* which contained THC and those which didn't, all varieties were criminalized. That subtle point wasn't lost on the legislators who wrote the act; they were merely acting on the advice of the special-interest groups who wanted hemp out of the way. The net effect was the same. Sixteen months after President Reagan signed the act into law in a Rose Garden ceremony, cannabis ceased to be the largest cash crop in the United States.

Era cigarettes disappeared from the shelves of tobacco shops and health food stores. Some store owners, believing that the new law wouldn't be strictly enforced, attempted to sell their remaining stock under the counter; when FBI agents and undercover cops began making busts, though, even that gray market ceased to exist. The Era Cigarette Company declared bankruptcy; a short time later, Timothy Leary discovered that the U.S. State Department had revoked his passport, making it impossible for him to return to his native country. By then, he had been diagnosed with cancer; at least in Switzerland, he was able to legally purchase marijuana to ease his pain.

That was only the beginning. Airline pilots reported

seeing vast columns of smoke rising from farm fields in every corner of the United States, from New England to Southern California. In parts of the rural South and Midwest, smog alerts were issued where none had ever been before. Parents were warned to keep children indoors, windows were kept shut and people could be seen wearing surgical masks on the streets.

The prohibition became a media scare. A favorite plotline of made-for-TV movies was someone committing robbery, rape and/or murder after using marijuana. *Deadly Weed* had its villain peddling shanks of hemp rope in school playgrounds before he's caught by a plucky young housewife and a folksy old detective; it was, of course, Based On A True Story. A popular far-right TV commentator decried "mary-jew-wanna"—no one missed the allusion in his mispronunciation—as a sinister plot to destroy the United States of America; several tobacco stores that once sold Eras had their windows smashed or painted with swastikas. A self-described "former marijuana addict" published a bestselling memoir about her years as a junkie, complete with lurid descriptions of being forced into prostitution just so she could buy another pack of Eras.

As hemp farms across the country were sold, foreclosed or abandoned, a domino effect began to set in. Hemp companies were forced to purchase new equipment which would process raw cotton instead of cannabis; many chose to simply declare bankruptcy. The pharmaceutical industry suddenly found itself without a major source; nonprescription painkillers became expensive, and cancer and AIDS patients found themselves deprived of nonprescription painkillers that they once depended upon. Paper costs skyrocketed when printers found themselves having to switch to wood pulp; vast tracts of forestland were clear-cut on a scale never before seen, and the publishing industry went into turmoil as the price of newspapers, magazines and books rose faster than reader demand. Several publishers went out of business altogether.

Clothing, cosmetics, housepaint, engine lubricants, livestock feed, construction materials, electrical insulation, baby laxatives . . . suddenly, a lot of commonplace things became much more expensive, and less people were able to buy them. By 1990, inflation and unemployment pushed the United States into a recession.

Yet, although cannabis had been outlawed, the Marijuana Prohibition Act didn't eradicate cannabis. Congress might have just as well attempted to repeal the law of gravity in order to help the space program. Even after every hemp plantation in the country had been torched or sprayed, uncultivated cannabis still grew wild along roadsides and in meadows. It was a weed, after all; it was pernicious, tending to grow wherever its seeds found ground. When the media scare died down, when people began to realize that a hand-rolled joint wouldn't drive you insane and that you couldn't get high by smoking an old T-shirt, an underground market developed that no propaganda campaign could stop. Outlaw farmers cultivated marijuana in backyard gardens and forest clearings; when some were raided by cops or DEA agents, others moved indoors, cultivating it in attics and cellars. Stop people from growing marijuana? Sure. Right after you stop them from growing tomatoes and carrots.

Organized crime tried to move in, and for a while it used marijuana as a means to introduce customers to harder drugs. In worked in the inner cities, yet even the Mafia couldn't control all the little victory gardens springing up across the heartland. You can't sell something that people have learned to grow for free. Country mice taught city mice a few tricks, but by then there were millions of hard-core drug addicts dependent upon heroin, cocaine and crack.

The marijuana prohibition lasted until 1998. And then, something happened.

"If I had a second chance, I probably would have inhaled . . ."

The President of the United States, seated on a stool before a MTV studio audience.

The tape freezes just as the audience breaks into laughter and wild applause.

A dozen men and women are gathered in a sitting room on the second floor of the White House. It's another late-night policy session: empty pizza boxes and soda cans are scattered across the tables, everyone has their ties loosened. The President is wearing a cardigan sweater and jeans; he shifts uncomfortably in his armchair.

"Not one of my best moments, is it?" he asks.

Some chuckle; a few wince. The young aide holding the VCR remote shakes his head. "Actually, Mr. President, I disagree. I believe that this was a defining moment in the campaign."

Several people protest loudly, but the aide raises his hand. "Yeah, yeah, I know . . . the Republicans jumped all over it, and the opposition used it in their attack ads. But it didn't lose us the election the way everyone thought it would. In fact, if anything, it helped solidify our lead in the polls, and we've got the numbers to prove it."

"Prove what?" This from a cabinet undersecretary leaning against the fireplace. "George, that tape's thirteen months old. It's ancient history. What are you trying to get at?"

The aide glances at the President. He's steepled his fingers together in front of his mouth, saying nothing, listening intently.

"What I'm getting at," he replies, "is that I think we've stumbled onto something, and that's how unpopular the Marijuana Prohibition Act has become among the rank-and-file voters."

Silence. "Are you suggesting that we move to repeal the act?" someone quietly asks.

He shrugs. "Sort of, yes."

Groans from around the room. "The churches will cream us!" the undersecretary snaps, flapping a hand dismissively. "The Christian Coalition . . . !"

"The Christian Coalition threw their weight behind first Buchanan, then Dole." The aide remains calm. "Look where it got them. Forget 'em. Look at the facts . . ."

Everyone's paying attention now. "The act has been on the books for thirteen years now, and look where it's gotten us." The aide begins ticking off his fingers. "It's hurt the economy. It was a major driver behind the last recession and put a lot of people out of work. Many companies either have had to shut down or had to retool from the ground up. We've spent hundreds of billions of dollars trying to enforce the law and millions of people have been sent to jail, but you can still walk two blocks from here and buy a joint on the street. Organized crime has used the marijuana black market as a gateway to hard drugs that we could wipe out if it didn't exist . . ."

"Got any numbers to back that up?" The President's voice is soft, but it draws every eye in the room. The President always asks for statistics when he's interested in something.

The aide nods. "Plenty, sir, but even they're not the

most significant ones. My people have checked several different polls taken on this issue, and the average is that . . ."

He picks up a legal pad next to his chair, flips back a page. "Twenty-two percent of the country wants the act repealed, thirty-seven percent favors deregulation, and sixteen percent favors decriminalization with broad-based controls. Twenty-two percent wants the law to stay unchanged. Eight percent are undecided."

He looks up from the pad. "That means less than one in four wants marijuana prohibition to remain as is. Almost everyone else thinks it's a crock."

Someone in the back of the room whistles. Low murmurs from around the room. "I dunno," one senior advisor says, straightening her skirt. "This might not go down on the Hill."

"Somehow, Martha, I just knew you were going to say that." Everyone laughs; the aide leans forward to rest his arms on his knees. "I've got word from the House that a bipartisan group of six dems and four pubs are prepared to cosponsor a deregulation bill if we come on board. Three dems and two pubs in the Senate are ready to introduce the same measure on their side of the Hill if we go first."

Silence. Everyone looks at each other.

"Names," the President asks.

"The man wants names . . ." The aide flips to the next page then sitting, reads the names of senior congressmen and senators from both sides of the aisle in either house. Everyone gasps when he gets to a Republican senator who wouldn't agree with the President on the time of day. "Nobody's on the record yet," the aide finishes, "but they're committed in principle. They're waiting for the nod from here."

The cabinet undersecretary scowls. "For the record," he mutters, "I'm utterly opposed to this proposal." He shifts his legs as if to rise.

"Your objection is noted," the President says, giving him a cold look that says that his resignation would be welcome if tendered. The undersecretary remains seated; he stares down at his lap.

The President glances at his watch and takes a deep breath. "Folks, it's getting late, and my daughter wants help with her homework. Let's table this until next week, all right?"

Everyone stands up to stretch. A couple of people rummage through the pizza boxes in search of an untouched slice. The President starts to head for the door. Then, almost as an afterthought, he steps over to the aide.

"Are you sure you've got numbers for all that?" he asks very quietly. The aide smiles; the President nods. "On my desk, tomorrow morning."

"Yes, sir. They'll be there." The aide watches as the President heads out the door, then picks up his legal pad. It's going to be another all-nighter in the Old Exec, but he doesn't care.

God, this is why he loves being a policy wonk. Every now and then, you get a chance to do something really cool.

On the morning of December 1st, 1998, the President of the United States signed the Omnibus Cannabis Deregulation Act. He performed the ceremony in the company of several dozen senators and representatives from both parties; when he was through, he handed his pen to Timothy Leary's widow. Then he went outside with his family to light the National Christmas Tree.

The new law was not forged without bloodshed. Indeed,

it was the most fiercely debated subject of the last few years. Dozens of congressional sessions were held to debate the act; thousands of hours of testimony were given before various subcommittees. Lobbyists supporting and opposing the measure ran up enormous phone bills and spent countless hours in hotel rooms and airplanes. Dire political threats were issued by both sides, followed by counterthreats. Two large demonstrations, pro and con, were held in the Washington Mall. Polls were made, and then more polls. Every magazine and newspaper in the country weighed in with their opinions, ranging from the thoughtful to the banal. Woody Harrelson brought a potted hemp plant onto the Letterman show and Pat Robertson told his audience on the "700 Club" that Jesus opposed marijuana decriminalization. Rush Limbaugh went berserk for fifteen months straight before he suffered a stroke in the back seat of his limo. For the first time in recent memory, the abortion-rights issue took a back seat on the national agenda.

When everything was done, and all the necessary compromises were reached, marijuana prohibition came to an end in the United States.

Industrial hemp was once more allowed to be grown, albeit under strict Department of Agriculture guidelines. So was THC-potent marijuana, but under strict FDA regulations, and only by specially licensed farmers. Marijuana could be legally sold in states, counties and municipalities where it wasn't expressly prohibited by local law; even so, federal law placed it under much the same restraints as liquor. It could only be distributed and sold by licensed retailers, couldn't be legally purchased by anyone under the age of 21 and couldn't be sold through automatic vending machines. Federal and state taxes chased the price of a pack of twenty marijuana cigarettes up to thirty dollars in some areas. The law banned its use by military and civil-service employees, and allowed private companies to mandate drug tests on a discretionary basis; it also allowed law enforcement agencies to automatically revoke the licenses of anyone suspected of driving, flying or operating heavy machinery while under the influence.

The new law yielded mixed results. Many people who had been curious about marijuana tried it for the first time, and thus marijuana use soared for a couple years. Then, much to the surprise of those who had predicted social anarchy, it plummeted just as dramatically. Many people just didn't like its effects, or they found beer was cheaper. Many who liked marijuana quit once they discovered that it could cost them their jobs; in many occupations, being able to pass a urine or hair-analysis test became as necessary as having a high-school diploma. Those who persisted soon discovered that marijuana, much like tobacco or alcohol, carried its own social stigma. Good dates don't show up at the door with bloodshot eyes; a gentleman or lady doesn't suddenly forget your name before a goodnight kiss. "Are you stoned or just stupid?" turned out to be a much better put-down than "Just say no."

On the other hand, there were positive effects. Cancer, AIDS and glaucoma patients found their symptoms easier to tolerate, and some reported their illnesses going into remission; as a result, medical labs were able to turn their attention to discovering permanent cures.

The price of paper dropped. Thousands of new magazines were launched, and millions of new books put in print, once publishers were no longer dependent on new or recycled wood pulp; for the first time in years, it became possible to buy a newspaper for fifteen cents, a magazine for seventy-five cents, or a paperback for a buck. Stephen King was so happy, he published four new novels in one year.

Old-growth forests, and everything that lived in them, were left alone. Owls and eagles were soon taken off the endangered species list. Clearcutting became a travesty of the past when even the chopsticks in Chinese restaurants became made out of hemp fiber. Less acreage was being devoted to cultivating feedstock for farm animals; this in turn meant that more food was able to be grown at less expense and with less ecological impact. Greenpeace went back to saving whales.

So forth and so on. To be sure, the world's problems weren't solved overnight because of an ugly weed. Yet they became a bit easier to handle, and when the 21st century finally arrived, everyone was a little more happy, the future a little more bright.

And the best was still to come . . .

As she does every morning, Louise Pullman starts the day with a stroll through the greenhouse, not so much to check the crop as to admire her handiwork. Like her father and grandfather before her, Louise is a hemp farmer, and she's proud of her heritage.

First she looks in on the baby plants whose seeds were removed from the incubator and planted on the greenhouse's east side a couple of weeks ago. Snug in moist beds of compost and mulch, their tiny leaves regularly spritzed by the irrigation pipes above their raised tables, the sprouts are coming along nicely. Louise checks the automatic timer to make sure that the sprouts aren't receiving too much water, then moves on.

Next are the more mature plants, each about four feet high, planted tightly together so that they'll produce strong, fibrous stalks as they grow taller beneath the fluorescent infrared lamps suspended from the ceiling. Like most of the cannabis being cultivated in the greenhouse, these plants are mainly males with only one female planted every four feet or so. Louise steps off the pathway to gently push through the plants until she reaches one of the females; it's bushing out nicely, and when she gently squeezes the bract of one of its buds her fingertips come away with a resinous brown stain. She smiles as she gently strokes the leaves, then moves on with her inspection.

Finally, Louise reaches the full-grown plants: rows of magnificent, sapling-size giants nearly thirty feet tall, whose tops nearly graze the light fixtures far overhead. One of her assistants has mounted a ladder to prune leaves from one of them. He looks down to wave good morning to her, as he does, he accidentally drops his shears. Louise waits until the scissors fall to her, then lightly catches them in her hand. The assistant climbs halfway down the ladder so that Louise can hand them back to him; when he does, she notices a few leaves sticking out of his chest pocket. She gives him a silent look of admonishment, which he returns with a sheepish, red-faced grin. Louise decides to take it up with him later; she's in too good of a mood right now.

She's halfway toward the high gray wall that marks the greenhouse's west side when her wristcomp chimes softly. Louise stops, raises her left wrist, smiles to herself as a reminder appears on the tiny screen.

Ah, yes. She smiles to herself: once every two weeks, one of her favorite times rolls around again.

Louise taps the earpiece of her headset, murmurs something into it, then reaches into her breast pocket to pull out a pair of dark glasses. Another hemp farmer pushing a wheelbarrow of mulch puts down his load to do the same as, far above them, past the irrigation pipes and light fixtures, there's the faint sound of motors coming to life.

Arching her back a bit, Louise looks directly upward, watches as the metal shutters that have shielded the greenhouse's thick glass dome slowly retract into the walls. For a moment, she can see only pitch-black darkness; then a bright shaft of light from the newly risen sun lances into the vast circular greenhouse.

And then, as polarized sunlight washes across acres of marijuana, she sees a white-flecked blue-green orb hanging almost directly above the lip of the converted lunar crater.

Gazing up at the distant Earth, Louise once again remembers her childhood home. It's a long way from Tranquillity Station to Dolores, Kentucky; many things have changed since the day her father lost the family farm. But the best revenge comes to those who are patient . . .

Humming a sweet old song, Louise saunters past rows of towering hemp. When she gets off duty, she'll use a little satellite-time to give Dad a call. Just to tell him that she loves him, and that everything's okay.

Missing Time

The facts, simply put, are these: on the morning of Wednesday, September 25, 1996, the Mayor of the city of Worcester, Massachusetts, left a downtown restaurant after a breakfast meeting with several of his political supporters and began walking back to his office. Between 8:16 a.m. (and thirty-one seconds) and 8:16 a.m. (and thirty-two seconds), he vanished from the face of the earth.

This is what occurred during that single second of missing time.

When he disappeared, the Mayor was alone. The restaurant was located only five blocks from City Hall, so he had decided to leave his car in his reserved parking space and stretch his legs a bit. Breakfast had filled him up a bit more than he expected, though, and he had walked less than half a block before he found himself regretting leaving his wheels behind. Therefore, when a dark blue Ford mini-van pulled over to the curb and the gentleman behind the wheel asked Hizzoner if he wanted a lift, the Mayor didn't hesitate.

Why should he? The driver had called him by his first name, after all, so he obviously knew him. He was a well-dressed, clean-cut man about the same age as the Mayor; Hizzoner pegged him as a West Side businessman whom he had met at a fundraiser or a Chamber of Commerce luncheon. And he certainly looked familiar (although Hizzoner couldn't recall the man's name for the life of him). And, just to clinch the issue, there was a bumper sticker from the Mayor's last election campaign on the mini-van's rear bumper; as a professional politician, Hizzoner knew the risks of snubbing a voter, unintentionally or otherwise. He was, after all, a man of the people.

So Hizzoner opened the passenger door and climbed in. He slammed the door shut, pulled the lap strap across his waist as the chest restraint automatically slid across his front, and had just turned to the driver and was about to offer a sheepish apology for having forgotten his name when there was:

(a sudden lurch)

(an abrupt sensation of falling)

(a high-pitched whine)

(a dazzling flash of white light)

and then his vision cleared, and the Mayor saw that the city had disappeared.

It was one of those rare moments in which Hizzoner was caught totally speechless.

"Relax, Mister Mayor," the driver said. "You're in no danger, I assure you."

Nothingness lay beyond the van windows: white-on-white limbo, as if they were suspended in the middle of a blank sheet of paper. Yet it wasn't entirely without form or substance; from time to time, something faintly rippled across the void, like hot air rising from a summer sidewalk. And although he no longer felt as if he was falling, there was a subtle sensation of movement, like he was in a small boat bobbing down a gentle country stream.

Hizzoner clutched the armrest of his seat. "Whu . . . what . . . how . . . what . . . where . . . ?"

"It's very simple," said the driver. "You're in a chronospace transfer vehicle. A time machine, if you wish

107

to use an archaic term, although it's not entirely accurate. You see . . ."

But the Mayor had seen and heard quite enough, thank you. He was having a psychic snap. He had been working too hard; the stress of his job had been building up, and now . . . well, this was definitely a sign that he needed to visit the doctor. Or take a good, long vacation. Or both. He snapped open the lap strap, hastily tugged the chest restraint over his shoulders, and flung open the door . . .

The driver frowned. "That's not a good idea."

Hizzoner ignored him. He extended his right foot out of the van, then stopped. There was nothing beneath the sole of his shoe. Nothing except the white void.

Breathing hard now, he reached into his suit pocket, found the receipt from the restaurant he had just left. He wadded it up and tossed it out the open door.

It fell, and fell, and fell, plummeting into the pale abyss until it diminished to a tiny yellow dot that finally vanished. Hizzoner watched it until he couldn't see it anymore.

"Whu . . . where did it go?"

"When did it go, you mean." The man sitting beside him remained smiling and implacable. His hands moved across the dashboard controls (which, Hizzoner now saw, resembled nothing he had ever seen in a Ford showroom) as he studied a screen where the speedometer would normally be located. "I'm tracking it, though, so it should emerge . . . ah, there it is. Want to go get it? The City Comptroller might want it for his records, after all."

The Mayor swallowed and numbly nodded his head. "Close the door, please," the driver said, and once Hizzoner had done so, the stranger typed commands into a keypad on the steering column. Past the windshield, the ripples began to form complex whorls and shapes, like oily water washing across a pane of warped glass. "It's just as well you did that," the driver continued, "because it gives me an opportunity to explain things a bit . . ."

There is a place (he told Hizzoner) that exists between the third and forth dimensions, one which belongs to neither but connects both: the spacetime continuum, or chronospace. Unlike either the third or forth dimensions, chronospace is nonlinear; it is more vast than the universe, because it contains countless numbers of parallel universes, its boundaries limited only by unlimited possibilities. One can best visualize chronospace as an immense block of Swiss cheese; each hole in the cheese is a different universe, and the tunnels connecting the holes are passageways between the universes. This chronospace transfer vehicle, conveniently disguised as a Ford mini-van, is capable of traveling down these tunnels, and therefore slipping between one universe and another. Don't try to understand how it works—just accept it, okay?

Hizzoner nodded and said nothing. He didn't understand, and didn't want to. All he knew was that he needed to see a doctor real damn soon.

Outside the windshield, a world gradually solidified and reformed, like a blurred TV image coming into focus. There was a sudden jolt, another flash of light . . .

The CTV stood in the middle of a meadow surrounded by trees tinged with the first colors of autumn. Off in the distance were sloping hills. It was early morning, and everything was still, save for a breeze that rippled the tops of the high grass.

"You can get out now," the driver said. "Your receipt should be somewhere nearby."

Hizzoner looked at him. The driver nodded reassuringly.

Hizzoner reluctantly opened the passenger door and stepped out of the mini-van. There was a fresh coolness in the air, much like that which he had left behind. Birds sang and mosquitoes burred across the meadow, but otherwise everything was silent.

The driver joined Hizzoner as he walked around the vehicle until they found, just a few feet away, the wadded restaurant receipt nestled in the high grass. It was moist with dew. Unfolding it, the Mayor read what he just had for breakfast: French toast, two slices of bacon, orange juice and coffee.

"Where are we?" the Mayor asked, his voice trembling.

"Worcester, Massachusetts," the driver replied. "September 25, 1996, at 8:16 a.m. We haven't moved an inch from where I picked you up."

Hizzoner opened his mouth, but the driver raised his hand before he could speak. "No, of course this isn't the city you know. In fact, it isn't a city at all, as you can plainly see. In this frame of chronospace, humankind never evolved at all. We're the only people on this entire planet."

He loosened his tie and sat down on the van's rear bumper, just above the campaign sticker bearing Hizzoner's name. "This is one of the more radical deviations from what you'd consider . . . um, the normal universe. There's countless other probabilities, all coexisting in different frames, each the result of large and small deviations in their individual histories. In one frame, this place is a radioactive wasteland . . . you died here, as a teenager, when the Soviet Union launched a nuclear first-strike against the United States after it refused to remove its missiles from Cuba in 1962. In another, Worcester is a small town across the river from Shrewsbury, and you're a local drunk who picks fights in bars and spends his nights in jail. And in yet another, you're an assistant to Mayor Abbie Hoffmann, who's held office since 1980 and . . ."

"Okay, okay, I get it, I get it." The last notion was too horrible to contemplate. "So what's the deal here? I mean, what are you trying to prove, huh?"

This was the sort of desk-pounding bluster that had brought Hizzoner to power, starting back when he was a young, iconoclastic City Council member. It worked well in City Hall when TV cameras were trained on him and reporters were present; in the middle of an autumn meadow, though, it was an inefficient protest. His constituents were birds and insects; the driver was unimpressed. He folded his arms across his chest and gave his passenger a benign smile.

"I want to show you some things," he said, and lifted a hand when the Mayor started to object. "No, no more alternatives to your present. They might amuse you, perhaps, but that's all they'd do, and I haven't undertaken this effort only for your entertainment. I wish to show you something much more meaningful."

Hizzoner stroked his mustache as he looked askance at the driver. "The future?"

"There're many different futures." The driver shrugged. "I was thinking of a date in particular . . . this very same day, but twenty years from now. September 25, 2016."

"So which . . . um, frame do you want to show me?"

The driver raised three fingers.

"Am I . . . I mean, am I part of them?"

The driver slowly nodded.

"But then you'll take me back, right? Back to, I mean . . ."

"Where we started? Of course. I have to. One mustn't upset the balance."

"Why? I mean, why are you doing this?"

An enigmatic smile. "That would be telling. Of course, if you'd rather have me leave you here . . ."

"No!" Hizzoner shoved the receipt back in his pocket. "Okay, let's go . . . but make it quick. I'm a busy man."

"Yes, you are indeed." The driver stood up. "I wouldn't dream of wasting a moment of your time."

The CTV re-emerged exactly where, although not when, it had entered chronospace: the same block of the same street where the driver had picked up Hizzoner. In fact, the street looked so much the same that the Mayor almost opened the door to get out. Now was a good time to make a run for it . . .

"I wouldn't do that if I were you," the driver said. "In fact, you might want to lock your door." He touched a button on the dashboard. "Forward, slow."

On its own, the mini-van began rolling down the street, heading in the direction of the Common. As it moved, Hizzoner got a closer look around. It was recognizably Worcester, but things had changed. Tall stacks of garbage were piled high on sidewalks that were cracked and buckled; almost every storefront they passed was boarded up, with lewd graffiti spray-painted on the plywood; the stores that were open had permanent security grates covering their windows. The few cars parked on the streets were battered wrecks; one of them was raised on cinderblocks, its tires missing and its windows shattered. Two teenagers were using crowbars to pry one of its doors off; they were the only people in sight.

"Oh my God," Hizzoner murmured. "What happened here?"

"I suppose you could say that you did," the driver replied.

112

They took a left turn onto Front Street. Here, in the Common, they found more people. Camped out in raggy tents and lean-to shelters in the shadow of City Hall were scores of men and women; dirty and hard-eyed, they huddled in front of sooty cookfires fed by trash and the remains of the trees that once grew here. The Galleria was gone; behind a sagging chain-link fence lay only a blackened, burnt-out hulk.

"What do you mean, I happened here?" Hizzoner demanded.

"Perhaps I'm being unfair," the driver said. "A city doesn't crumble solely because of one man. The decisions of many people ultimately led to this. However, the decline began with policies made during your administration . . ."

The public library was shut down, its windows as boarded up as any of the businesses that had once operated in the city center. The driver stopped at the next intersection to allow a six-wheeled National Guard APC to trundle past; sitting on its hoods were two soldiers in heavy riot gear. "First, money for public education was reduced, so schools were closed. Then public housing was curtailed, so more people were put out on the street. The sanitation workers went on strike, so they were fired and no one was hired to replace them. Then the police department's budget was cut back, until no new cops were being hired and most of the remaining force caught the blue flu . . ."

"I've done none of these things!"

"No, you haven't . . . not yet, at least."

A loud popcorn sound from somewhere nearby: full-auto gunfire. Hizzoner instinctively ducked in his seat and the driver told the mini-van to go a little faster. Two National Guardsmen dashed across the street ahead of them, their rifles held at ready. As the van turned right on Main, the

Mayor saw that City Hall was encircled by razorwire fence. Across the street, the Shawmut Building was abandoned, its windows broken out.

"Anyway, Worcester is now considered one of the three worst cities in the United States," the driver continued. "Anyone able to leave moved out a long time ago. Most of the industries have relocated elsewhere, so the unemployment rate stands at forty percent, and what's left for those who have stayed are mainly service jobs. No newspapers, no local TV stations, only a couple of radio stations . . ."

"Forget that! What happened to the tax base?"

"Ah, the money. I was just getting to that." The driver took the wheel and steered the mini-van down Main. "When no one wanted any new taxes and demanded that the existing ones be reduced, the tax base gradually dried up. The state granted the city about thirty million dollars for a downtown redevelopment project which you and some of your supporters insisted would attract visitors and make new jobs. Everything was sunk into this project, and when it went ten million dollars over budget, the City Council voted to raid the treasury to make up for the cost overruns. For the sake of the city, of course."

They took a right turn, drove three blocks and came to a stop in front of what had once been a parking lot across from the boarded-up Centrum. Here was the first new building Hizzoner had seen in their drive through downtown Worcester: a sleek, lopsided oval with mirrored windows, barricaded behind ten-foot concrete walls patrolled by the first policemen Hizzoner had seen during this tour. A lovely structure, a diamond in the rough; above its locked revolving doors was a sign:

WORCESTER AQUARIUM

"That's where all the money went," the driver said.

"They used to have some trained dolphins, but one night some street people broke in and . . . well, I understand they found the carcasses in the park two days later. But the piranha collection is still safe."

Hizzoner stared at the pride and joy of Worcester for a few moments. Then he turned to the driver. "Does it get any better than this?"

The driver smiled. "Yes, it does . . . but not in this frame."

He touched the keypad, and once again the CTV disappeared into the white void.

They dropped out of chronospace into the same block where the Worcester Aquarium had been located. Once again it was a parking lot, yet now it was filled with futuristic cars; cables ran from their hoods to small turrets. A smiling young woman in a uniform waved them into the lot; the driver rolled down the window and handed her a plastic card; she scanned it with a bar-code reader, then politely directed him to the nearest vacant space.

"You can get out now," the driver said to Hizzoner. "In fact, you'll have to. No autos are allowed past this point."

Hizzoner climbed out of the mini-van and nervously followed the driver as they walked back toward the city center. He anticipated gunfire, burned-out buildings, piles of garbage, armed soldiers on the sidewalks . . .

And saw nothing of the kind. Electric trolleys quietly slid along recessed rails between broad pedestrian walkways where cars had once crept in gridlock. Main Street was lined with cement planters containing small trees; the tables of sidewalk cafes were occupied by relaxed people enjoying breakfast. Bicycle racks were placed in front of nearly every doorway. Every storefront was open, and there wasn't a se-

115

curity grate in sight. A police officer dinged the bell of his ten-speed to get them out of the way; as he rode past, Hizzoner noticed that there was a taser in his holster instead of a service revolver.

The streets were spotless. The air was fresh and clean. For the first time in his life, Hizzoner smelled autumn leaves instead of exhaust fumes in downtown Worcester.

"Oh, my God," the Mayor murmured. "What happened here?"

"You didn't," the driver said.

There was a faint murmur from the sky. Peering up past new skyscrapers, he spotted a large blimp cruising far overhead. "That should be the eight-thirty commuter from Boston," the driver said, checking his watch. "You've got regular airship service here, eight times a day, for those who haven't been able to move out here. There's also rapid-transit, of course, but . . ."

"People commute here from Boston? C'mon . . ."

"Oh, yes . . . from Boston, Springfield, the north county cities. Jobs at Medical City, Tech Central, the universities and retail centers. High standard of living, low crime rate . . . Worcester's the most desirable place to live in Massachusetts. In fact, it's considered one of the best cities in the country. Imagine that."

The Common was crowded with children; a vast, green playground lay behind City Hall, which looked as if it had been scrubbed only yesterday. Old men played shuffleboard where winos once slept; songbirds nested where only pigeons had once dared to tread. The Galleria was gone, replaced by a hotel-entertainment complex.

"What do you mean, I didn't happen?" Hizzoner asked.

The driver tsked. "Tragic accident. One day you came out of your office, started to walk down the stairs. You didn't notice the sign that the stairs had just been mopped. You slipped, hit your head, fell down fifteen risers . . . sorry, Your Honor, but you never regained consciousness."

He stepped aside to let a bicycle pass. "Anyway, your sudden demise meant that a special election had to be held in your district. There were many contenders, but the person who won was a young man in the his mid-twenties. He had grown up here, and believed in a Worcester that didn't look like the one everyone else had accepted as status quo. He had fresh ideas, and over the next two decades, one small step after another, he brought about these changes. Of course, he had friends who shared the same vision . . ."

"Who is he?"

"I don't think you ever met him." The driver pointed to a familiar window on the top floor of City Hall. "But he's up there now. Want to meet him? Not that you have much in common, but . . ."

Hizzoner turned and stalked back down the street. His face was burning.

"Maybe another time," the driver murmured.

When the CTV rematerialized from chronospace again, it arrived on the same street where a parking lot existed in one frame and the Worcester Aquarium in another. Once again, it was September 25, 2016, but when the driver made the same circuit through the city center, Hizzoner had to look hard to perceive any difference from his native frame.

The streets were crowded with cars, and there wasn't a bicycle to be seen. Some of the storefronts had different facades, but they were in recognizable buildings; they were no new skyscrapers and the Shawmut Building was still the tallest building in town. The Galleria was intact, but its windows were boarded. The public library was open; it looked empty and disused. The marquee over the Centrum was empty. Homeless people loitered on the sidewalks. There were no National Guardsmen in the Common, but its fountains were dry. City Hall was as grey as ever.

Hizzoner rolled down his window and took a deep breath. Worcester still smelled like Worcester.

"Nothing's changed," he finally said.

The driver nodded. "No, not really. Oh, there's a couple of new shopping centers out in the suburbs. The city has a triple-A baseball team. The *Telegram-Gazette* and *Worcester Magazine* have gone entirely electronic and don't publish a paper edition any more . . . but, no, there has not been much change here in the last twenty years."

Hizzoner looked up at his window in City Hall. "Am I . . . ?"

"Still in office?" The driver laughed. "Of course not. You retired around the turn of the century, took a job at Clark University teaching political science. The next mayor followed your footsteps just as you had laid them."

The van cruised down Main Street, passing office workers hurrying to their jobs, bums looking for handouts, pigeons pecking at crumbs. "He took no risks, took no chances, and when he was voted out of office, he was replaced by yet another mayor who has done exactly the same. Every Tuesday night the City Council convenes in its chambers and goes down the docket. They pass petty ordinances, bicker over minor proposals, and waste time with the same internecine politics that have preoccupied every City Council for the last three or four decades. Nothing is gained and nothing much is lost. Everyone plays it safe. But every day another young man and woman swear that they're moving out as soon as they can. Very often, they manage to do so, and when they do, they seldom come back."

The driver pulled over in front of a boarded-up Mechanics Hall. "Is this what you want?" he asked, turning to look at Hizzoner. "I know that a mayor can't change things all by himself, but he's supposed to be a leader . . . that's in his job description. If you can advocate change, then do so. If you can't, then get out of the way. But the future isn't about following polls or patronizing supporters. It's about taking risks, taking . . ."

"Okay, all right. You've made your point." Hizzoner took a deep breath. "You've given me a lot to think about, but isn't it about time you took me home?"

The driver stared at Hizzoner for a full minute. "You are home, your honor," he said quietly. "You never left."

He told the CTV to drive. It entered a quiet side street and disappeared into the labyrinth of time.

At 8:16 a.m. (and thirty-two seconds) on the morning of Wednesday, September 25, 1996, a blue Ford mini-van dropped back into existence. The only witness to its near-simultaneous disappearance and reappearance was a custodian who happened to be emptying the contents of a garbage can in an alley Dumpster. He blinked, looked again, and marched back into the side entrance, swearing to himself that he needed to stop watching science fiction movies.

Hizzoner looked around before he opened the passenger door. Everything looked exactly the same. He found the door latch, opened it, swung one leg out. He glanced at the driver, who silently nodded in confirmation, then he stepped out of the mini-van. This time, there was pavement beneath his feet.

He let out his breath and looked back at the driver.

"Just one more thing," he said. "You look kind of familiar, but . . . well, you never told me your name."

The driver smiled and held out his hand. "It's been a pleasure to meet you, Your Honor. My name's Ray."

Hizzoner looked harder at the other man.

His jaw dropped.

He slammed the door shut, and stood trembling on the deserted sidewalk as the blue Ford mini-van with his campaign sticker on its rear bumper pulled away from the curb and moved down the street. It turned the corner and vanished from sight.

The Mayor continued his stroll back to City Hall. Four and a half blocks gave him time to think about many things. By the time he reached the familiar granite steps, he was already considering plans for the future.

First, they would start with an aquarium . . .

Graceland

1. ". . . strange days, it seems . . ."

"I miss me gold tooth," Keith said.

He was sitting on the edge of the oak stage, his bare legs dangling over the bamboo-slat front. The Mersey Zombies were taking a break during the sound check. A couple of Titanthrop stagehands were making themselves busy, checking the electrical cables for burn-throughs in the fish-skin insulation and rearranging the massive stacks of speakers. In the sound booth, located in the middle of the open-air amphitheater's seating area, the King was haranguing some luckless techie about the recurrent feedback problems from the mikes; they couldn't hear what was being said, but the King's ring-encrusted forefinger was jabbing back and forth and the techie's head was alternately nodding, shaking, nodding, shaking, as if keeping time: yes sir Elvis, no sir Elvis, yes sir Elvis, no sir Elvis . . .

"You miss your tooth." Sitting next to Keith, his bare back resting against a monitor speaker, John lit a limp joint with a firestarter and sucked the smoke into his lungs. "So what? I miss my glasses . . ."

" 'Coo, you always looked like a fairy with them on . . ."

"I most certainly did not," John croaked. He held in the toke for a second, then slowly exhaled. Behind them, Sid was sullenly practicing the opening riffs of "Anarchy in the U.K." on his bass. Brian was nowhere in sight, as usual. "And just for the record, I never believed that story about

121

how you busted your mouth after you drove a Caddy into a Holiday Inn swimming pool . . ."

"It wasn't a Caddy," Keith insisted, "it was a bloody Lincoln Continental, and I did so break out me front tooth, when I climbed out of the water and slipped on the deck while running from the coppers . . ."

"Yeah, yeah. We've heard the whole sodding story many times." John passed the joint to Keith. "And I don't look like a fag with my glasses on. I loathed those contact lenses Epstein used to make me wear . . ."

"Heard from him lately?"

"Not since he joined the Dowists . . . Besides, Yoko liked the glasses . . ."

"Oh, for God's sake, man, when are you going to stop talking about your old lady?" Keith picked up one of his drumsticks and idly scratched his sunburned back with it. "I mean, you're getting more pussy than Frank Sinatry . . ."

"Lord!" John looked at him sharply. "Is Sinatra here?"

Keith shrugged. "Not that I've heard. It's just a line I picked up from one of the Yanks." He took a quick hit off the joint and passed it back to John. "Pigpen told me that one," he gasped. "Or maybe it was Lowell . . ."

"Okay, so I get laid regular." John gazed dismally at the rows of empty bamboo benches in front of the stage. He absently reached beneath his kilt and scratched. "But I miss the missus, all the same," he said softly. "She was a good woman. Good singer, too."

Keith made a face, but wisely kept his mouth shut. They were both quiet for a moment, listening to Sid as he struggled through the bridge of "God Save the Queen," the punked-out version that the other three members of the Mersey Zombies refused to play during their shows. Keith cocked his head toward the kid. "I mean, you think young

Mr. Ritchie there misses Nancy?" he asked softly. "The bloody wench was nothing but poison. Even she showed up here two months ago; he told her to shove off or he'd stick her again . . ."

Sid's head jerked up. "I did *not!*"

John looked over his shoulder at him. "Easy lad," he said. "The Moon was only joking."

Sid wasn't satisfied. He unplugged his guitar, hauled the strap over his shoulder, and threw the instrument down on the stage, startling one of the Titanthrops. "You geriatric old farts make me want to vomit," he muttered as he stalked toward the curtained door leading to the backstage area.

"Then go vomit," Keith called after him. "Just make sure you don't do it in your lunch pail again. *Ah-hahahahaha!*"

Keith's maniacal laugh was one of the few traits that endeared him to John. He shook off the lingering memory of his wife's face as he reached over to pluck the joint from Keith's fingers. "He doesn't miss Nancy," he said, "but I think he does miss riding the old white horse."

"Just as well. The shit killed him in the end." Keith frowned, pensively tapped his drumsticks between his legs. "Come to think of it, so did all that booze I was putting away . . ."

"You both bought it within weeks of each other, as I recall . . ."

"Yeah. So we did." The wicked smile reappeared on his homely face. "But at least I managed to get old before I croaked. The kid, now, he was barely old enough to shave . . ."

"Hope I die before I get old . . ." John sang.

"Roger was full of shit and so was Pete. Ox didn't say

123

enough to be full of shit . . ."

"S'truth. Way I felt about George."

"*Ah-hahahahahahaha!* Lord love a duck . . . or a bass player!" Keith reached up to touch his youthful, undamaged front teeth. "But I still miss my front tooth, you know. It was quite classy. The birds thought it had sex appeal. You reckon I might find another one from . . . ?"

"Hey! What're y'all think you're doing up there?"

John and Keith looked up at the sound of the baritone, Southern-accented voice. The King was stalking down the aisle from the sound booth, clapping his hands for attention. "Shit," John murmured, discretely stubbing out the roach behind him.

"I thought I told you!" the King bellowed. "No drugs while we're working!"

Keith looked at him blandly. "But we're not working, mate," he said in a maddeningly mild tone of voice. "We're having tea." He pointed up at the midday sun. "See? It's tea time."

The King's face became livid. "I don't see any tea up there, son. All I see is that goddamn mari-hoochie I told you not to smoke during rehearsal. Now you get Sid and Brian back up here and you make sure you play your asses off tonight, 'cause we got a riverboat coming in this afternoon, now do you hear me?"

"Who's the headliner?" John asked.

"The other band!" the King yelled. "And they're gonna headline all week because you English assholes can't get your shit together and an American band can and I don't like your attitude and I think y'all play like a bunch of English queers and I don't give two shits if you were one of the Beatles . . . !"

"Frankly," John interrupted, "neither do I."

124

That shut him up, but John couldn't resist twisting the knife a little more. He cleared his throat as he rested his chin in the palm of his right hand. "Tell me," he inquired, "are you *still* blaming me for your movies?"

The King scowled at him but said nothing; he was never good for a comeback. Keith hid his bemused smile behind his hand. "Goddamn fucking English eel-suckers," he finally muttered as he turned and began stalking back toward the sound board. "Think you invented rock 'n' roll . . ."

Sunlight reflected off the letters embroidered in semiprecious stones across the back of his redfish vest: TCOB. Taking Care of Business. John watched the King walk away, feeling somewhat sad for him. A couple of years ago, when Elvis started managing them, he still had his just-resurrected slim body and handsome face, a sexuality reminiscent of his vintage years. Now he was becoming an obese wad again, only worse than before; he had let his hair grow out, and his mammoth ass stuck out from beneath his kilt. Worst of all, he had developed into a mirror image of his old manager, albeit without the Colonel's redeeming qualities. And he couldn't sing worth a damn. But he was the King of Graceland; if you didn't want to be a dragonfisher, a farmer or a slave, then you played by his rules.

"He was a lot more fun before he died," Keith whispered.

John popped the roach into his mouth and chewed on it thoughtfully, savoring the burnt-herb flavor on his tongue. He stood up, giving the drummer a rough slap on the shoulder. "We were all more fun," he replied. "C'mon now, mate. Back to the grindstone."

"Rock 'n' roll," Keith murmured.

2. ". . . long live rock . . ."

The island was known as Graceland.

Thirty years after Resurrection Day, it was the only place in the new world where live rock could be heard, and its existence was largely due to Elvis's considerable influence. Through the course of many high-level trade agreements, the enlistment of a handful of loyal Titanthrops, a couple of years of seeking out resurrected musicians, and (so it was rumored) at least a dozen translations, Elvis had managed to establish a small colony a hundred miles up-River from Parolando, an undiscovered bit of dirt and rock where two unclaimed grailstones lay. Not unexpectedly, he decided to call the island Graceland. This was how it was listed on the riverboat charts, the name by which it was known to the hundreds of thousands of Valleydwellers who had heard of it.

Graceland had only one industry: rock 'n' roll, played live and loud. Elvis had been canny enough not to put his bands upon riverboats to tour up and down the great river; there were too many uncivilized places where his groups could lose not only their grails and hard-won equipment, but also their lives. Instead, he settled an island and sent out word that two supergroups performed there six nights a week, eight months a year, and let everyone come to him. Tickets were bought at the dock through barter: whatever Graceland's inhabitants needed—fishmeat, cloth, refined metals, tools, open grails, new firestarters, precious and semi-precious stones, riverdragon products, liquor and cigarettes, groupies (especially groupies)—were gained in trade for a week's admission into the stockaded amphitheater.

Each week, another riverboat landed at the dock, un-

126

loading a hundred-odd passengers who had bartered their way up-River or down-River to Graceland. They surrendered their goods at the dock, then went to the cabins on the island's lee shore where the visitors' grailstone lay. Admission to Graceland was for exactly a week, with admission to the amphitheater coming extra. However, since all weapons were confiscated at the dock by the Titanthrops and the accommodations were pleasant, few minded the cost. It was the closest many of the resurrected could get to having a vacation in the new world.

Of course, Graceland had its own dues to pay. Not only did the surrounding river-nations have to be constantly bribed to keep them from contemplating invasion, but all the amphitheater belongings—from the electric guitars to the relatively sophisticated sound equipment to the upstream hydroelectric generators that powered everything—had been custom built by the inhabitants of Parolando and New Bohemia, who in turn received the lion's share of Graceland's gate receipts. There were few creature comforts available to the permanent inhabitants as a result; however, as the King was known to frequently observe, it beat hell out of working. If picking one's fingers to the bone each night on crude copper strings couldn't be considered working, that is . . .

There were two regular house bands on Graceland, alternating sets every night during concert season. One was the American band, the Wonder Creek Revival: Lowell George on lead vocals and rhythm guitar, Duane Allman on lead guitar, Berry Oakley on bass, Rod "Pigpen" McKernan on harmonica and keyboards, Dennis Wilson on drums and—when she was sober enough to take the stage—Janis Joplin as guest singer. The Creeks had a laid-back Marin County sound that appealed to most of the Valleydwellers, and it was easy to relate to "Proud Mary" or "Watching the River Flow."

The Mersey Zombies, on the other hand, were at an inherent disadvantage. Given the mixed heritage of the Beatles, the Rolling Stones, the Who and the Sex Pistols, the quartet could manage a few numbers that were palatable to the average Valleydwellers, but their sound was more geared toward guitar-driven British hard rock, which seemed to be unsettling to most of their listeners; songs like "Cold Turkey" and "I'm So Bored with the U.S.A." didn't have much to say to an audience far removed from either heroin or Uncle Sam. And then there were contradictory reputations of the two bands. If Janis went incoherent and mumbling off into a bluesy ramble, there was always her old boyfriend Pigpen to back her up. But the Mersey Zombies had a nasty rep for on-stage bickering, backstage fistfights and short sets, and Sid couldn't be restrained from spitting into the front rows when people began to jeer.

More than a few times, Elvis had been asked why other resurrected rockers couldn't be hired. The King usually mumbled one of his usual excuses—"good idea, buddy, I'll work on it" or "we're straightening out the contract, y'know"—but the fact of the matter was the musicians who had been found during his long talent search were the only ones who still considered themselves to be music people. Jimi Hendrix was still alive, but he now lived in Soul City, where he played an occasional duet with Robert Johnson; no one who didn't live in the African-heritage nation-state had ever heard them perform. Hank Williams and Patsy Cline were married and owned a farm downstream, as did their nearby neighbor, the Big Bopper. Ronnie Van Zandt and Steven Gaines were dragonfishermen; Buddy Holly and Ritchie Valens co-owned a small airship company flying out of New Bohemia. Bob Marley was rumored to be a revolutionary, secretly traveling along the Rivervalley to infiltrate and foster rebellion within slave-nations wherever he and his gang of Rastafarians could find them. Bon Scott was a hopeless dreamgum addict without a grail, squatting wherever he could and begging for the basic necessities in whatever village would accept him.

And no one knew what had happened to Jim Morrison . . . if, indeed, he had truly died in Paris when everyone thought he did.

3. ". . . please to introduce myself . . ."

Shortly before sundown, the grailstones delivered dinner with all their usual sound and fury. Once the audience removed their grails, the Titanthrops opened the wood gates of the amphitheater and allowed the newcomers inside the stockade. Now, beneath the torchlight surrounding the seating area, a hundred of the resurrected were sitting on bamboo benches, waiting for the first band to come on stage. The summer-evening breeze carried mixed odors— fried fish, lichen wine, tobacco and marijuana—along with the low buzz of voices, impatient whistles and handclapping. The sounds and smells of rock 'n' roll . . .

"Ten minutes to curtain, John."

John let the curtain fall back into place; he had parted it a half-inch to peer out at the audience from the backstage area. He turned to look at the skinny young woman who had quietly come up from behind him.

"Already beat you to it, love," he said. She blinked in apparent confusion; he pinched a fold of the curtain. "See?"

Mary West Wind blushed and looked down at the floor,

embarrassed at having not caught the awful pun. John flashed her a smile to show that he didn't mind and she relaxed. Mary West Wind had been a San Francisco flower child until six tabs of particularly nasty LSD had dispatched her to strawberry fields forever. Here on Graceland, she served as stagehand and permanent groupie-in-residence to both house bands. She was so sweet and innocent, though, that none of the rockers—not even Sid in his most repugnant moments—had the heart to seduce her. John was completely aware that she had a crush on him in particular.

"The King told me to ask you to find Brian," Mary said meekly. "I mean, I know where he is, but I can't . . . I mean, I shouldn't . . ."

John sighed and rubbed his eyelids. His vision was now perfect, but he still missed his glasses. Like Keith and his rotten gold tooth. "I know, I know," he murmured. "Bloody damn . . . I shall go track down our errant stone."

He began walking away from the curtain, Mary stepping aside to let him pass to the short flight of steps leading to the dressing rooms. On sudden impulse, John paused, leaned over, and gave her a peck on the cheek. "Always stay the way you are, dear," he whispered in her ear, and Mary blushed again as he hopped down the stairs.

Backstage was a long wooden shed, partitioned into individual dressing rooms and a larger "green room" located just behind the stage entrance. The members of the Wonder Creek Revival were gathered in the green room, waiting for their nightly gig. Duane was practicing licks on his unplugged guitar, Berry, Lowell, and Pigpen were playing poker, Dennis was catching a nap on the couch in the corner and Janis, as usual, was getting drunk. Like John, all wore simple kilts, sandals and redfish shirts or vests. The days of elaborate stage outfits were long gone, along with stretch limos, Dom Perignon in chilled buckets, five-course catered meals, crystal punch bowls filled with cocaine and contract riders stipulating that five pounds of M&Ms had to be available with all the red ones removed. On the other hand, also missing were the usual backstage hangers-on: overdressed radio jocks with their photographers, ready to accost you while a camera flashed in your face so that a self-serving picture could be published in the next issue of *Billboard*; record reps hovering in the corridors, hand-grabbing and shoulder-hugging, trying to hustle another sleazy deal; fawning winners of local record-store contests with copies of your worst album, babbling inanities while you tried to make your way to the bathroom; and, of course, the groupies with their mall hair and blowjob lips, eager to fuck a rock star so they could write it all down in their memoirs, or at least make their boyfriends insanely jealous.

All things considered, John was only too happy to see the end of all that posturing and pretense. What was left was the music, pure and simple, like a neglected rose garden that had been cleared of broadleaf vine and chokeweed. Some things, though, had remained much the same . . .

He passed through the green room and walked down the hall to the dressing rooms. Sid was in his room, apparently passed out on a cot, his bass propped against a wall. John stuck his head through the door, put his fingers between his lips, and whistled sharply. "Wakey, wakey, you killer junkie! It's showtime!"

Sid's eyelids fluttered. "Fuck off, you fuckin' ol' hippie," he muttered from the depths of his dreamgum stupor, but John was already striding down the hall, passing a short side-corridor leading to the back door. He heard voices down the hallway, but didn't pause to look. Probably the King, raising hell with someone else about some real or imagined transgression . . .

The door to Brian's room was shut. John stopped and pressed his ear against it; from within, he could hear faint gasps of pleasure. He grinned; Brian was getting his customary pre-show lay. Different girl each night; all he had to do was scout the nearby camp until he found a bird who wouldn't mind getting screwed by the man who taught Mick Jagger how to sing. If it weren't for the fact that all Valleydwellers had been made sterile on Resurrection Day, Brian could have probably populated an entire village with his illegitimate offspring . . .

Enough was enough, though. Time to go to work. John took a deep breath, then reconsidered the urge to shout. Instead, he gently rapped his knuckles against the door, then pinched his nostrils between thumb and forefinger. "Telegram for Mr. Jones!" he called in a nasal voice.

An exasperated sigh and a feminine giggle from the other side of the door. "Coming!" Brian shouted.

"I'm certain you are," John replied. "Five minutes."

"See you in four and a half." More muffled laughter.

"Very good, sir." John didn't have to worry about Brian making it to the stage; it was always Sid who gave everyone trouble. Next, to find Keith; from farther down the hall, he could hear the hyperactive ratta-tat-tat of drumsticks against a chair. Keith was wired and ready to go. Now, if only he hadn't destroyed his dressing room again . . .

As he turned to walk down the corridor, John was startled by a hard tap on his shoulder. He jumped a half-inch off the floor, then spun around to find a massive, hairy shape filling the hallway.

John sagged against the wall, laying a hand against his

chest. "Oh . . . Billy, it's you," he gasped. "You scared the life out of me, mate."

Billy was one of the Titanthrops who worked on the island. Although the bands rarely had any problems with audience members sneaking back to the dressing rooms uninvited, Elvis insisted upon having a titan as backstage security. Billy guarded the rear door that John had just passed. No guest list was necessary; if Billy was told a name—as Brian did every night—then Billy would remember that name for weeks. And if someone tried to con or muscle their way into the dressing rooms, they were usually treated to a flying lesson over the stockade wall.

"Thorry to interrupth you," Billy said in his usual deep-throated lisp, "but there'th thomeone at the door who inthith upon theeing you."

Billy looked annoyed, if only because he had to bend almost double to keep from banging his huge skull against the ceiling. John sighed; rock stardom was dead in the afterlife, but it still didn't prevent zealous fans from seeking an autograph at exactly the wrong time. "Tell them I'm about to go onstage and I'll see them after . . ."

"He'th rather thee you now," Billy persisted. Before John could respond, he added, "He'th from the Church of the Thecond Chanth, and he thaid he knowth you from back then."

He paused, then added in a low voice. "He thaid it wath important. He thaid hith name was Jim."

John looked askance at the titan. "Jim? I don't know anyone named . . ."

He stopped. For a long moment, John stared at Billy, deciphering what he had just said. When it struck home, his first impulse was to yell for Keith and Brian . . . hell, not just them, but for Duane and Pig and Janis and Mary West

Wind and anyone else who remembered the magic, anyone within earshot who remembered the Lizard King . . .

"Pardon me," he said, then he ducked beneath Billy's right arm and slowly walked toward the intersecting hallway. Behind him, he heard the nervous rattle of drumsticks, a woman's faint cry of orgasm. All around him, there was sound: the twang of Duane's guitar strings, someone laughing at an old joke, the faraway clapping of hands by an audience waiting to see the rejuvenated legends of their youth. John broke into a trot . . .

He stopped at the crossway, stared at the open door. Torchlight from outside illuminated a robed figure, standing half-seen just outside the door.

No call to him, though. No gesture of recognition, no familiar all-fucked-up amble down the hall to meet him. Only a monkish figure in severe brown robes, hornfish helix draped around his neck. And within the dark pit of the hood, the barest glimpse of a familiar face, first seen long ago in Toronto when they were sharing the bill.

"Jim?" he whispered. "Jim, is that you?"

"After the show, John." The voice was very quiet, but it was still the same unmistakable voice. "Back here when you're through."

The figure then melted into the shadows, allowing the door to slowly swing shut again.

John stared at it until Keith goosed him with one of his drumsticks and reminded him that the crowd was waiting. For the first time since anyone in the band could remember, John was late coming on stage.

4. ". . . no future for you . . ."

The Mersey Zombies set lasted an hour; to nobody's great surprise, least of all John's, it was a lame performance.

John had long since learned that the intrinsic problem with the band was that, because of the all-star lineup, everyone expected to hear their favorite Beatles or Stones or Who or Pistols songs. However, there were many differences between each band member's sensibilities that could not be easily paved over by the fact that they were all British rockers; it was like expecting Nat King Cole and Jimi Hendrix to successfully collaborate because they were both African-American musicians. While it was perfectly possible, for instance, for Keith to hammer out the nuclear-attack percussion of "I Can See For Miles," John had trouble singing the lyrics; although John and Brian were perfectly happy to perform "Ruby Tuesday"—the only song their respective groups ever had in common—Keith would almost fall asleep at the drums and Sid would make I'm-so-bored faces at the audience. John would all but give up keeping time with Sid on "Anarchy in the U.K.," Brian made weird faces at the bassist's guitar-thrashing, and Sid barely tolerated Brian's woodwinds during "You Can't Always Get What You Want." The only song in which the whole band meshed was "Helter Skelter," even though it was clear from the audience reaction that this particular song was still associated with Charles Manson; even while the band kicked out the jams, too many faces in the crowd looked as if four giant cockroaches had suddenly crawled onstage. Manson and his killers had ruined that song for all eternity, literally.

It was only when the other three members left the stage to allow John to sing "Imagine" as the finale that the audience seemed to wake up, even sing along with the final refrain. This was not unusual; that particular song struck a chord among Valleydwellers, who'd found themselves in a world without borders, countries or flags. When it was over, John stood up from the makeshift piano to rousing applause; he bowed once, then gratefully strode off the stage.

A party was already in swing in the dressing room. Keith was arm wrestling with Duane; Brian had joined a conversation with Janis, Berry and Dennis; Sid lurked quietly in the corner, glaring at everyone with once-fashionable punk contempt. John walked past them, completely unnoticed; he stopped by his dressing room to put his guitar on the bed, then stood for a few moments, gazing indecisively at the fish-skin packet of joints that lay on a table. "What the hell," he murmured, then picked a joint out of the packet before leaving the room and heading back down the corridor toward the rear door.

Billy was minding his post, sitting on an enormous oak stool next to the open door. The titan stood up as John approached. "He'th thill waiting for you," he rumbled. "I athked if he wanted to come back to your room, but he didn't want to."

"It'th . . . oops, sorry . . . it's okay, Billy." The Titanthropic lisp was rather infectious. "I'll talk to him outside." Billy nodded and stood aside; John patted his hairy forearm as he stepped out the door.

The wooded area behind the stage was dark, illuminated only by a couple of flickering, half-spent torches that marked the way to the outhouses. He could hear the rhythmic hand-clapping of the audience as they urged the second band to come on stage. John's eyes, unaccustomed to the gloom after the bright lights of the stage, sought the shadows.

"Jim?" he called softly. "Hullo? Jim?"

The robed figure he had seen earlier detached itself from the shadows beneath an oak tree. "Here," a quiet voice said from beneath a raised hood.

John took a step forward, then stopped, uncertain. "If that's truly you," he said, "then let me see your face."

There was a moment of hesitation, then the figure's hands moved within the dark folds of the robe and lowered the cowl. He stepped forward into the light, revealing himself to John.

It was Jim, all right, but not the Jim he remembered. His dark hair no longer reached his shoulders; instead, it was cut very short, almost monkishly. The face was still starkly handsome, but the familiar mannish-boy glower had completely vanished, leaving behind only a neutral, almost beatific expression. By all accounts, Jim had died overweight and bloated, his innate sensuality stolen by liquor and drugs. Now he was rejuvenated, but as a cloaked figure standing in the half-light, as if materialized from one of the William Blake poems that had so influenced him as a UCLA art student.

"You've changed a bit," John said.

Jim's heavy-lidded eyes blinked. "We were never close, John, so how would you know I've changed?" He raised his arms, his sleeves falling back from his hands. "Perhaps this is how I've always been."

John chuckled. "I never saw you wearing *that* on the cover of *Rolling Stone*." Jim only stared at him, unamused. John held up the joint he had grabbed before leaving the dressing room. "Care to join me for a little smoke?" Jim said nothing. "Don't do drugs anymore, hmm? How 'bout we go out and find some girls to ball, then?" Again, no reply. "Well, why don't you just go out there and flash 'em your dick, just for old times' sake?"

Jim's eyes shut for a second, as if to control himself. "I'm beyond such things now," he said. "But, yes, you're right. I have changed."

"So I noticed." John stuck the joint between his lips, lit it with a firestarter and sucked in the ragged-tasting smoke. In one life, a man's wearing ass-tight black leather jeans and French silk shirts; the next, he's decked out in sackcloth and ashes. Figures. "Did you hear the show?" he asked, exhaling through his nose.

"I heard."

"Not exactly a rave review." John cocked his head toward the door. "Hey, why don't you come in? I'll reintroduce you to the other band. Most of 'em think you didn't make it over, but I'm sure they'd be willing to let you sit in. At least you do better justice to 'Light My Fire' than they do."

The slightest flicker of a smile. "Perhaps . . . but I no longer sing."

"Really?" John started to take another toke, but suddenly felt foolish. He bent down to snub out the joint, then tossed it away. "What a waste." He paused, looking in the direction of the discarded joint. "Y'know, I don't think I ever told you this, but you were good. Really, really good. I was even a little envious of your voice. And some of the things you wrote, particularly your poems . . ."

"That's not why I've come here, John."

"Then why the hell have you come here, Jim?" In exasperation, John folded his arms across his chest, staring back at the disciple. "Come to stand by and laugh at the fool who's still singing 'Day Tripper' five nights a week?"

"I'm not laughing at you."

"Jesus! You sound like a bloody priest!" Fed up with the

138

conversation, John impulsively turned around, began to stalk back toward the door. He was almost inside—Billy, half-rising from his stool, was about to get out of his way— when he turned around again. "Of all the people in the world," he snapped, thrusting a finger at the robed finger, "I would have expected at least *you* to be honest!"

Jim's face remained impassive, but for a brief instant there was irritation in his eyes. "I have said very little to you," he said quietly. "So far, you've done most of the talking."

They stared at each other for a few moments. Through the door, John heard a shouting match—"you fuckin' fucked-up fuck-off, why can't you handle a simple fuckin' song like . . ." and "bugger off, you bloody sod"—Sid and Keith, from the sound of it, having another post-show quarrel. In a few minutes, they would be trying once more to flatten each other's noses.

"Billy, break it up, please," John murmured without looking over his shoulder. He heard the stool scoot back as Billy maneuvered his Buick-size body through the door. Unless Sid unwisely attempted to kick Billy in the nuts again, the squabble was as good as settled. John hesitated, then walked back to where Jim was patiently waiting for him.

"So talk, then," he said.

5. ". . . this is the end . . ."

Long after midnight, John lay in his tent, gazing up the ceiling pole. Mary West Wind was fast asleep next to him, the bedsheets curled around her nude body. Out of sheer impulse, he had brought her back to his tent after the show;

they had made love in a frantic, almost adolescent sort of way, yet despite her fervor she had fallen asleep almost as soon as she had climaxed. John felt almost relieved; he didn't feel like talking, just as, indeed, he had felt a strange detachment from her even in the middle of their throes. They had used each other for their own purposes; she had finally fucked the sexy-looking guy on the back sleeve of *Meet the Beatles*, and he had found temporary surcease from the dark thoughts in his mind.

Now he lay naked atop the blankets, listening to the cool breeze, remembering another night in a different lifetime.

Getting out of the car with his wife, the boxed tape of that day's studio session under his arm. The usual crowd of autograph-mongers and fans hanging around the front door of the Dakota. Walking down the sidewalk, Yoko passing in front of him, heading into the open archway of the building. Feeling pleased with the day's work, looking forward to playing with his young son before going to bed.

A young man's voice, calling from somewhere behind him: *Mr. Lennon?*

Turning, seeing a shadowed figure in combat stance barely five feet away, aiming a pistol directly at him.

A moment of confusion, wanting to say something . . . then muzzle flashes, loud gunfire, the horrible force of bullets slamming into him . . .

Twisting backward, pain lancing through his body, mind numbed by what's just happened, not believing what just happened. Staggering toward Yoko . . . Christ, he's been *shot!* . . . collapsing to the sidewalk, saying something he can't remember to his dear wife as the doorman rushes toward them . . .

Ambulance sirens, voices shouting, policemen all around, cold concrete against his back. A glimpse of the

young man, standing on the curb, calmly reading a paperback. Being loaded on the stretcher. Nausea, weakness, a
sense of passing from time and space. *Do you know who you
are?* the disembodied voice of a cop asks softly, just before
the end . . .

Well, constable, at least I think I do. I mean, it was right
there on the tip of my tongue just a few minutes ago, right
before some deranged asshole shot me. I once shook hands
with the Queen, and I'm pretty positive that I've played
Shea Stadium, if that's what you're asking. But if you'll
only give me a few minutes, I'm sure I can give you a correct answer. Umm, you wouldn't mind making that multiple choice, would you?

"Not very bloody funny," he whispered to himself.

We can't allow you to continue, Jim had said. *You're much
too dangerous* . . .

Without really thinking abut it, John slowly slipped his
legs over the side of the bed. The soles of his feet came to
rest on the coarse wooden boards of the tent platform, and
for a few moments he peered into the darkness, listening to
Mary's breathing . . .

We've been given a chance, don't you see? Jim's voice had
almost been pleading. *We've been brought here by the an-
cients, every one of us from time immemorial, to achieve personal salvation through our individual actions. We can still find
grace with God, John, but only if we give ourselves the
chance* . . .

Through the darkness, he could hear the River. Downstream, somewhere nearby, dugout canoes were stealthily
making their way toward Graceland, paddled by Second
Chancers who had been waiting for this hour, when everyone on the island would be sound asleep.

But you and the others have revived the old ways. You

141

brought technology to this island where only life-sustaining grailstones had once existed, and you use it to preach evil. You've brought back idol worship, debauchery, lust of every kind . . . all those things I myself once practiced before the resurrection . . .

John bent over, picked up from the floor the kilt that Mary had torn from him. He stood up and slid it around his waist, his eyes searching among the various objects resting on tables and chairs around the tent—spare clothes, his grail, a carved wooden tobacco box and other handmade ornaments given to him by fans, his guitar—until they found a long, flat thing in the corner.

I had hoped you might join us, but I see that's impossible. All I ask now is that you receive my testimony, and understand why we've done what we shall do, why I've led them here . . .

John picked up the dragonfish knife, sliding it out of its scabbard. A dim, reddish glow was reflected off its polished surface.

Rock must die, John . . .

Through the open tent-flap, he saw a sudden blaze of firelight from the amphitheater.

You must accept this . . .

"Bloody hell I will," John whispered. Clutching the knife, he strode out of the tent.

Already there was shouting from the campsites, cries of surprise, anger, shock, desperation. He could see people emerging from their tents, staring in disbelief at the bonfire that had erupted from the stage area. Now there were new, smaller fires: the backstage shed, the speaker stacks, the sound board, all being set ablaze by distant robed figures who had scaled the stockade walls and were now torching the amphitheater.

A rush of heat against his skin. Through the trees, he

glimpsed audience members moving toward the stockade. From somewhere not far off, there was an agonized scream, suddenly cut short as a knife found the throat of a Second Chancer.

"John?" Mary called from behind him. "John, what's going on?"

John ignored her. Somewhere in the heart of the inferno, Jim was out there, torch in hand, igniting precious sound equipment, acoustic baffles, his own crude but irreplaceable piano. The technology of music, deemed the source of all evil by a group of fanatics.

Jim must have known that he would die again tonight; he'd all but told John what he'd intended to do, and John had attempted to escape the blunt reality of his threat by taking home a sweet little hippie chick. If you smoke enough pot and fuck long enough, you can avoid coming to grips with anything. When it came right down to it, he had always been a world-class champion at avoiding responsibility.

No more. Not when something he loved was being destroyed.

Mary was still calling his name as he took a few more steps into the night, the palm of his hand sweating against the handle of his knife. Jim was somewhere in there, waiting for him. Find the fucker. Grab him by the neck. Slash his goddamn throat . . .

Do you know who you are? the nameless policeman asked again.

John stopped. He felt his knees buckle as he sagged to the ground.

He remembered the Cavern Club. He remembered the Royal Albert Hall. He remembered the first American tour, the teenage girls who sobbed over a patch of ground he'd walked across. He remembered going to India while Epstein was dying. He remembered falling in love with Yoko. He remembered the final rooftop performance with the lads just before he called it quits. He remembered the bed-in demonstration against the Vietnam War, and the countless other protests against war and violence. He remembered Julian's birth, and Sean's. He remembered the one and only time he'd met Jim before today, backstage in Toronto when the Plastic Ono Band and the Doors had been the headliners.

He remembered writing a song about how it was okay to give peace a chance.

"Good lord," he whispered. "What am I doing?"

He didn't remember dropping the knife. Indeed, he didn't remember much else until Keith sat down next to him on the dew-soaked grass, lit up a joint and offered it to him.

6. ". . . with a little help from our friends . . ."

"Haven't seen anything like this since we played the pubs, eh, mate?" Keith said dryly. John looked up from the joint, shook his head. "Not exactly the proper sound," he went on, "but it's got a good beat and you can dance to it. *A-hahahahaha.*"

For once, his laughter was forced. John continued to stare silently at the burning amphitheater. Firelight cast long shadows from the trees, silhouetted figures rushing back and forth past the stage; the air smelled of burning wood. The Titanthrops had managed to muster a bucket bridge from musicians and bystanders, but it didn't look like it was doing much good. Graceland was well on its way to becoming history; it would take more than the King's charisma to rebuild it. Keith picked up the knife John had dropped and toyed with it, almost as if he was considering a quick round of mumblety-peg.

"You could have stopped him, y'know," he said quietly. John looked sharply at him. "I mean, I saw you two out there having a chat, so I suppose you must have known what was going to happen."

"Not worth killing him."

"Hmm, got a point there. But why didn't you at least let on to the rest of us?"

"Didn't think he really meant it. Not until it was too late." John thought about it a moment, then shrugged. "Not sure it would have made any difference. Elvis would have thrown 'im off the island, but that wouldn't have been the end of it. Even if we had stopped him this time, he would have just returned." His gaze returned to the flames. "This way, the arseholes got what they wanted. They won't be back again."

"Right." Keith stuck the knife in the ground between his legs, then took another hit off the joint and offered it again to John. John looked at it for a second, then pinched it out of the drummer's fingers. "Well, I suppose it makes a daft sort of sense . . ."

"You're not going to tell anyone, are you now?"

Keith exhaled and scowled at him. "What do I look like, a narco?" He shook his head. "But what makes you think there's going to be a next time?"

John *tsk*ed, letting the joint burn between his fingers. "Here, mate. You should know better than that. You can't kill rock 'n' roll that easy." He stubbed the joint out on the ground. "I mean, you can ban it from school and burn all the Beatles records you want and let all the holy rollers carry on about how it's the devil's music and so on, but it's a tough beast to knock off." He waved a hand at the fire. "So they torch a stage. Big hairy deal. We can always build another one. Rock 'n' roll will never die."

"If you say so." Keith picked up the joint again, straightened out the bend in the paper, and carefully relit it. From somewhere far off, they heard another terrible scream. John wondered if it was Jim . . . "Next time, though, you wonder if we can get Elvis to sing?"

John smiled as he watched the smoke and flame rising into the first light of dawn over the endless River. "Only if he gives me back my glasses."

"Yeah, right. And me gold tooth . . ."

"Now don't start with that gold tooth shit again."

Jake and the Enemy

I heard this story from Marty Gould, back when he was the manager of Lang Electronics' domestic services division and I was working as a tech writer at the corporate headquarters in Westboro. I can't say we were the closest of friends, but we were pals nonetheless, and we often got together for lunch at the company cafeteria.

Late one morning Marty called to ask if I wanted to grab some chow, and since there was nothing else on my schedule I said sure, meet you in a half-hour. By the time I arrived, he'd already parked himself at a table and was on his first cheeseburger. Lunch for Marty was two cheeseburgers, a side-order of onion rings, a bowl of baked beans, and a slice of apple pie with a scoop of vanilla ice on top, with a jumbo Coke to wash it all down. Needless to say, he had a formidable appetite; I think you can imagine what size trousers he wore.

So we talked about this and that—how hard it was to get Red Sox tickets, the best seats in Fenway, so forth and so on—as he ploughed through his buffet and I nibbled at my cottage cheese and fruit salad, and then he snapped his fingers as if he suddenly remembered something. "Hey, by the way," he said, "I think you need to update the owner's manual . . . specifically, the section on canine interaction protocols."

"The what?" Like a lot of people in cybernetics, Marty's first language was geek, with English as his second tongue. "You mean, how to teach 'bots how to deal with dogs?"

147

"Uh-huh." Marty picked up a napkin and wiped his mouth. "My service reps have been getting some customer feedback lately. Seems we're having trouble in that area."

"For which model?"

"L-1012b . . . Companion Model IIB."

The Companion Model IIB was our second-generation household robot, LEC's bestseller on the commercial market until we introduced the Samson and Delilah series a year or so later. "That's part of the self-tutorial protocols. Check the index . . . I think it's listed under 'Pets.' "

"No, no, I don't mean that." Marty took a sip off his Coke. "We've looked at the book, and it's the usual stuff. Distinguishing dogs from humans, avoiding them when they're in the way, how to feed and clean up after them, that sort of thing. My service reps need something different . . . how to teach a robot to defend itself from a dog."

Now that was something no one had ever asked me before. The owner's manual is the first step in dealing with a problem, or at least it should be. I've spent countless hours making the book as clear as possible, though most of the time the customer hasn't read the book. Five minutes on the phone with tech support usually takes care of the problem; if they can't help, then a service rep makes a house call. Therefore, if the service division people come back to the tech writers, there must be an unprecedented situation.

"Defending itself from a dog?" I asked. "What do you mean, a watchdog or something?"

"No. Just a mutt." Marty took a sip from his Coke. "Lemme tell you what happened . . ."

About two months earlier, a gentleman by the name of Dwight J. Lawrence in upstate New York purchased a LEC

Companion IIB. According to the customer survey card he mailed back to the company, Mr. Lawrence purchased the 'bot from a retail electronics store in Albany as a birthday gift for his wife Jeanne. The card disclosed that the couple had an annual household income of $50,000-$75,000, both were college-educated professionals—Mr. Lawrence was an English professor at a nearby junior college, Ms. Lawrence a nurse-practitioner at a local hospital—and they owned the usual assortment of home appliances: two computers interfaced with a smart-house network, wallscreen broadband TV, DVD/CD/DBS home entertainment system, even an electric can opener. They had no children, but they raised chickens in the back yard. And they had a pet . . . a dog, as it would turn out.

Originally named Six Of Eight by the animal shelter from which he was adopted, Jake came from a large litter brought in by someone who'd discovered his best friend had been knocked up by someone else's best friend. A short-haired, medium-size dog with light brown fur and white spots on his muzzle, chest and paws, he looked like a cross between a boxer and a lab, with perhaps a little German shepherd and pit bull thrown in. In short, your typical all-American mutt.

The Lawrences lived in a two-story farmhouse out in the country. Every morning at six o'clock, Jake woke up, stretched, then sauntered downstairs to the glass door leading to the back porch; two short barks, and the house would open the door to let him out. Once he'd done his business, Jake would come back in for his morning Milk Bone, given to him by Ms. Lawrence while she made toast and cereal for herself and Mr. Lawrence. He'd follow Mr. Lawrence out to the chicken coop and watch him scatter feed for the birds and gather any eggs they'd laid.

After his family left for work, he'd laze around the front yard for the rest of the day. The town didn't have any leash laws, but the Lawrences' one-acre property was surrounded by a electronic fence designed to keep him from straying from home. It didn't matter much to him, because there were plenty of squirrels to chase and birds to watch, and every so often one of the neighbor dogs would drop by for a visit.

He was always waiting in the driveway when Ms. Lawrence returned late in the afternoon, and he'd bound out to greet Mr. Lawrence when he came home. A good round of ball in the backyard, then Mr. Lawrence would make dinner for him; if he hadn't chewed up any shoes or dug holes in the flower bed, perhaps there would be some table scraps for dessert. In the evening he'd sit with Ms. Lawrence and let her rub his belly while they watched TV in the den, or he'd keep Mr. Lawrence company while he graded papers. Another quick trot outside before bedtime, then he'd accompany the master and mistress upstairs and curl up on the floor beneath their bed, getting up now and then to patrol the house and make sure everything was safe. He luxuriated in a regular schedule which didn't place any demands upon him, and took pride in the fact that he was special.

Life was good.

Then, one day when he was about a year and a half old, everything changed.

When a white van rolled into their driveway early that evening, he greeted the driver with short happy yaps, and circled him and Mr. Lawrence as they unloaded a large cardboard shipping carton and brought it inside on a hand truck. Ms. Lawrence was surprised by this unexpected delivery; Jake stood nearby while the service rep and Mr. Lawrence opened the box in the kitchen, pulling away styrene packing material and plastic wrapping. The service rep pulled out a remote; a brief discussion with Mr. and Ms. Lawrence, then he said something to the remote.

A peculiar double-beep; lights flashed from within the box. Then something rolled out into the kitchen, and that was when Jake met the Enemy.

This, of course, was the 'bot Dwight Lawrence had bought for Jeanne. She had complained for some time that she never had enough time to clean house, make dinner, or do laundry (or, indeed, take care of Jake); buying a household robot was his birthday gift to her. Somewhat resembling R2-D2 from the *Star Wars* movies, the Companion IIB stood three feet tall, with a rotating upper turret containing its sensory array; it moved on a set of independently-mounted tandem wheels that enabled it to climb stairs, and it contained two double-jointed arms that could telescope two feet in any direction. It was voice-activated, and its fuzzy-logic systems and 100k MIPS onboard memory allowed it to understand plain-English verbal commands.

Ms. Lawrence was delighted, and Mr. Lawrence was proud, but the moment he saw the 'bot, Jake's ears went flat against his head, his tail between his legs, and he growled.

"That happens a lot." Marty was working on his onion rings, dabbing them in a paper cup of ketchup. "Most dogs don't like these things. Cats freak, too, but after awhile they either avoid the 'bots completely or just get used to them, just like they get used to the vacuum cleaner or the kid's RC toys. But dogs . . . they're different. My people hear this all the time. Nine times out of ten, they hate 'bots from the git-go."

"That's weird. I've never heard that before." I'd taken back my tray and fetched a cup of cappuccino from the serving line. "You'd think it would be the opposite."

"You got any pets?" I told him that I kept some tropical fish, and Marty shook his head. "Fish don't count. They're wallpaper with mouths. Look, I've had both dogs and cats, and lemme tell you, cats are dumber than rocks. Don't get me wrong . . . they're cute, they're friendly, they're fun to have around . . . but when it comes to I.Q., they're vastly overrated. Dogs have more on the bean, especially mutts, and from what I've been told, Jake was one smart puppy."

"And Jake didn't like the new 'bot."

"To put it mildly, no."

Jake cautiously approached the robot. He sniffed it; the 'bot moved toward him and the dog quickly backed away. He bared his teeth, gave it his most vicious bark; the robot stopped, but didn't retreat as it should have. The service rep and Mr. Lawrence whispered something to each other, then the driver gave the remote to Mr. Lawrence; he turned his back, murmured something into the remote. The robot rolled forward.

"Hello, Jake," the robot said, its voice an imitation of Dwight's. "Can we be friends?"

Jake cocked his head, raised his ears. It sounded like his master, yet it obviously wasn't him; it didn't carry his scent, nor did it walk on two legs. Therefore, it couldn't be his master. He slowly circled the newcomer, his head half-bowed, regarding the thing with suspicion as its turret rotated, tracking his every move.

He growled, barked at it again. The robot remained where it stood. "Hello, Jake," it said again, this time its voice soothing and androgynous. "Can we be friends?"

It knew his name, yet it offered none of the body-signals Jake recognized. It didn't submit, nor did it retreat. Jake was confused. And it was close to his food and water bowls, which irritated him even further. So there was only one thing for him to do: assert his territory.

Jake stepped closer to the robot, raised his hind leg and peed on the floor.

"No!" Ms. Lawrence grabbed him by the collar, hauled him away. "Bad dog!" she snapped, then her hand came down, once, twice, three times, swatting him hard against the rear end. "Bad, bad dog!"

Jake yelped, and when she let go of his collar he bolted from the kitchen. Hurt and humiliated, followed by the coarse laughter of the ones he loved most, Jake dashed upstairs and into the bedroom, where he squirmed beneath the bed, the Bad Dog place where he always retreated when he'd been punished.

He remained there for the rest of the night. After awhile, he heard the van leave, and at first he thought the driver might have taken the weird thing with him, but then he heard it rolling around the house, its strange voice saying things he couldn't understand, Mr. Lawrence and Ms. Lawrence conversing with it in a way he'd never been able to do. Frightened and ashamed, he didn't come downstairs to watch TV. No one scratched his ears or gave him a belly-rub; he licked his butt and that made him feel a little better, but not much.

Jake finally went to sleep, yet for the first time since he moved into this house, he didn't feel safe and secure. He was no longer alone. There was something else here, and he didn't like it one bit.

"Y'know, I read somewhere that the intelligence of a

full-grown dog is about the same as that of an average four-year-old child." Marty had finished his cheeseburgers and onion rings, and now he was eating his beans. That was the way he ate, one item at a time. "The same vocabulary . . . about thirty to fifty words . . . and much the same emotional range. So if you've got a dog, you're in effect dealing with a little kid. Tantrums, jealousy, a limited understanding of what you mean . . ."

" 'Bots are smarter than that." I sipped my cappuccino. "We can program them to understand up to three thousand . . ."

"Uh-uh." Marty shook his head. "Talk to the AI boys sometime. 'Bots can respond to fifty thousand words . . . a little more or less, depending on which language they're using . . . but they don't understand a single one of them. You can teach a robot to say, 'I love you,' but it doesn't mean anything more to it than saying, 'I'd love a beer right now, go get me one.' But if you hug a dog and say 'I love you,' pretty soon it learns what you mean."

"Yeah, okay. What are you getting at?"

"Look . . ." Marty covered his mouth, burped, went on. "Robots are capable of mapping an entire house and remembering exactly where everything should go. They can recall the correct placement of dinner table settings, how to load and unload a dish washer, where the linen is stored and when the sheets should be changed, the perfect recipe for veal orange, when you want your morning coffee or your evening glass of wine, how to recite a favorite poem . . . but there's no emotional or intellectual depth to these things. It's all just memory, action and reaction. A mouse is smarter than a robot, when it comes right down to it. And as I said, dogs have the intelligence and emotional range of a small child."

"And this means . . . ?"

Marty smiled. "If a dog went to war with a robot, who do you think would win?"

Over the course of the next two days, Jake studied the Enemy.

He avoided any direct contact with the robot, carefully remaining just out sight whenever it was in the same room with him. It was a weekend, so Mr. and Ms. Lawrence were home during much of the day; they devoted considerable time and effort to tutoring their new acquisition, with Jeanne leading the 'bot through the house, demonstrating household chores one step at a time, while Lawrence followed close behind with the remote in one hand and the owner's manual in another. Once the 'bot learned a particular routine, all it took was a verbal command—"make the bed," "do the dishes," "mop the floor," "answer the door," and so forth—for the robot to perform it.

The more the robot learned, the more Jake envied it. The greatest frustration of his life was that he was unable to control his world. His forepaws were suitable for walking, running, scratching his muzzle and grasping a bone while he gnawed at it, yet although he knew how to open the refrigerator or turn a water faucet, he was unable to do so. The robot did these things with ease; its arms would extend, telescope, bend, and four-fingered claws would do whatever needed to be done. The first time it performed a task, perhaps there would be an accident—a glass would be broken, a bedsheet dropped at the wrong time, a picture frame put back in the incorrect position after dusting—but after Ms. Lawrence carefully demonstrated the correct procedure, the 'bot would remember these things and execute them flawlessly the next time. And Mr. and Ms. Lawrence would be pleased and say things which sounded good, and the robot would say "Thank you," and Jake, hiding behind a table or just around the corner, would hate the Enemy just a little bit more.

The worst was when Ms. Lawrence taught the robot how to feed him. Jake had always enjoyed this time of day, for that was when his family offered tangible evidence that they loved him. The purr of the can opener, the addition of a cup of dry kibble, the placement of his plastic bowl on the kitchen floor with a couple of gentle words in French—*bon appétite*—which Jake didn't understand—were all part of a daily ritual. And now, even this changed; the robot selected a can of Alpo from the cupboard, opened it, poured its contents into his bowl, adding a scoop of dry food, and put it on the floor, all with a mechanical precision that guaranteed that his dinner would always be delivered exactly at five p.m., not a minute earlier or later. Jake was so outraged he refused to eat, yet he was hungry and eventually he surrendered to the inevitable. He ate without much pleasure, and ten minutes after he was done, the robot inspected his bowl, then picked it up to carry it to the sink. Mr. and Ms. Lawrence watched this with delight, oblivious to the fact that Jake had slunk away, his tail drooping to the floor.

Monday morning came around, and as usual Mr. and Ms. Lawrence left for work. Now Jake found himself alone with the Enemy. At first he thought that, once his family was gone, the robot would simply come to a standstill; to his horror, it became even more active. It constantly roamed the house, cleaning, gathering, straightening, its random clicks and beeps signaling its arrivals and departures. Jake moved from one room to another to avoid it, yet he soon discovered that all his private places—the dark hole beneath the bed, the little crawlspace behind the den couch, the warm spot beneath the living room window where he liked to sun himself—were all subject to invasion. More than once, he bravely stood his ground, snarling and barking at the Enemy as it approached, yet the 'bot simply ignored him and came through. It never collided with him, but neither did it go away and leave him alone.

No place was safe except the outdoors; for some reason, the robot never left the house. Jake curled up beside the chicken coop and dozed for awhile, yet it was early November, and when he awoke the wind had shifted to the north and the sun had disappeared behind thick grey clouds. Cold sleet started coming down the sky, driving him back inside, and almost as soon as the porch door closed behind him, the Enemy was right behind him, buzzing as it wiped up his muddy paw prints, beeping in alarm as he shook himself on the living room carpet. Rain patted against the upstairs windows as he huddled beneath the bed, yet the robot appeared a few minutes later, insistent upon cleaning up after him.

This went on, day in and day out, during which Jake found himself spending precious little time with his family. The Enemy had become the center of attention; when Mr. and Ms. Lawrence were home tinkering with the 'bot, teaching it to do new tricks for their amusement, Jake was an annoyance, a sloppy, tongue-wagging nuisance which got in the way of this sleek, clicking thing that could wash dishes, remake the bed, and even play chess. More than once, Mr. Lawrence tried to make Jake become friends with it, yet he seemed equally amused when Jake bared his teeth and growled at the 'bot, never realizing just how much the dog loathed the Enemy. And the belly-rubs became less frequent, the cuddles and ear scratches the exception rather than the rule.

As time passed, though, Jake gradually began to notice

certain things about the robot. When it went through the house, it did so in a discernible pattern, following a preset routine. First it would clean the downstairs rooms, then it would go upstairs, then it would come back down and continue its daily chores. When it straightened up each room, it always returned items to a particular position; for example, if a decorative vase on a living room shelf had been moved more than an inch in any direction, the 'bot would make sure that it was returned to its proper place. It could command the porch door to open, yet it never went outside itself.

And although it was capable of climbing the stairs, it did so very slowly, with great difficulty. Jake could sprint up and down these same steps in less than a second, yet it took nearly five minutes for the robot to get from the first-floor landing to the top of the stairs, pausing on each riser to regain its balance.

It was in this way that Jake perceived a means of retaliation.

Late one morning after Mr. and Ms. Lawrence were gone, Jake patiently waited at the top of the stairs. He lay on his stomach with his head between his paws, listening to the Enemy as it moved from room to room, until at last it appeared at the bottom of the staircase and began to trundle upward, its tandem-mounted wheels rising over each step. Watching it, Jake was reminded of a squirrel with a broken leg, desperately trying to hobble to the nearest tree before he leaped upon it and snapped its neck. It was much the same trick, really; wait until your prey comes close enough, then strike without mercy.

The robot had just reached the top of the stairs when Jake lunged. He raised his forepaws, smacked the Enemy square in the center of its barrel-like chest. The Enemy toppled backwards and began tumbling down the staircase. It beeped and clicked frantically as its right arm hit a wall and snapped off, then there was a sharp crack as one of its turret lenses shattered. The robot smashed against the landing, then rolled over and lay against the floor. Its upended wheels burred for another minute or so, its remaining arm thrashing back and forth, then there was a sharp beep and its diodes went dark.

Jake waited until the robot was still, then he came the rest of the way down the steps. He stopped to give it a sniff, then he raised his leg and urinated upon it. Then he trotted away and went into the living room for the first undisturbed nap he'd had in over a week.

The Enemy was dead. Life was good.

"Wait a minute," I said. "How do you know the dog pushed the 'bot down a flight of steps? Even I know the Model IIBs are unstable in climb mode . . . that's why we've red-flagged that page of the manual."

Marty smiled. "You want the long answer or the short answer? The short answer is that when our service rep came out to take the 'bot in for repairs, he found paw prints on the front panel. It was raining earlier that day and the dog was outside for awhile, so it was just like finding fingerprints at a crime scene."

"Did he tell the clients?"

"Oh, yeah. That's his job." Marty shrugged as he picked up his fork and attacked his slice of apple pie. "They didn't believe it, of course . . . wouldn't believe it, really. Not their dog. He's not smart enough to do something like that. But our guy knew better, and therein lies the long answer."

"I'm not following."

"My people have seen this sort of thing before. Dogs get-

159

ting pissed off at 'bots, pushing them down stairs and so forth . . ."

"Oh, c'mon. I'm having a hard time with this . . ."

"You don't believe me? C'mon over to my office and I'll let you read some of the field reports I've received. I've got a whole folder full marked 'Dog Attacks.' They piss on 'em, crap on 'em, chew their wheels, grab their manipulators and drag 'em around the room. One got knocked off a tenth floor apartment balcony. We even heard about three stray dogs who managed to chase a Groundskeeper Model III off the country club golf course it was grooming and into the parking lot where it got nailed by a car. You can't tell me that was an accident."

Marty was grinning as he said this. "The robots never see it coming, of course. For them, dogs are just one more body-heat source that has to be avoided. 'Bots don't feel anything toward dogs, but dogs hate 'bots, and in the smarts department your average mutt has the 'bot out-classed by a thousand to one. Our service reps know this, so they've modified certain protocols to even the odds."

"You mean the intruder defense system."

"Uh-huh. Works most of the time." Then he shook his head. "But our friend Jake was more devious than we expected."

For a week, Jake thought he was free.

The morning after the robot suffered his unfortunate accident, the white van returned. The service rep gave Jake a biscuit and scratched him behind the ears, inspected the inert 'bot and had a short conversation with Mr. and Ms. Lawrence, then he put the damaged robot in the back of his van and drove away. Mr. Lawrence must have been told that Jake was responsible, for as soon as the van was gone he swatted Jake on the rump and scolded him. Jake pretended to feel guilty, but deep inside he was as happy as the first time he killed a mole. By evening, all was forgiven; he was curled up with Ms. Lawrence in the den, and for the next several days life returned to normal.

Yet just as Jake was about to forget about the Enemy, late one afternoon the van pulled into the driveway, and he was startled to see the driver unload his foe. It looked just the same as it had when he pushed it down the stairs, without so much as a scratch. Once again the driver gave him a biscuit, but this time Jake dropped it from his mouth; there was a hollow sensation in his stomach, a coldness against his fur that had nothing to do with the coarse wind that blew snowflakes against the window. He stood at the other end of the living room and watched in horror as the Enemy came back to life; it beeped and clicked, its turret rotating back and forth, its arms unfolding to telescope outward.

Again, the service rep had a brief discussion with Mr. and Ms. Lawrence, only this time they kept looking in his direction. He heard his name mentioned, and a couple of times they laughed, and Jake went along with the joke and wagged his tail, yet there was something in their voices and facial expressions which left him ill at ease. And meanwhile the Enemy, the damned Enemy, stood between them, miraculously resurrected and ready to make his life miserable once more.

Well. What worked once would surely work again.

The following morning, Jake waited until his family left, then he began following the Enemy as it recommenced its chores. As before, the robot followed a set pattern, beginning with its kitchen duties and continuing through the rest of the ground-floor rooms. Jake patiently stalked it just as he would a chipmunk he'd spied scurrying near the wood pile, and when the robot had finished cleaning downstairs, Jake dashed past it and ran upstairs.

His tongue lolled from his mouth as he lay on his belly and waited for the 'bot to make its way up the steps. If the fall didn't kill it this time, Jake could always finish it off while it was on its back. Those arms could always be pulled off, for starters.

The Enemy reached the top of the stairs, and Jake leaped to his feet. The robot's turret swiveled toward him. Its voice snapped: "Jake! Stop!"

Jake understood, but he wasn't about to obey. He hurtled toward the robot, sprang forward . . .

A low-voltage electrical charge surged from the robot's arms. In all his short life, Jake had never felt pain like this before: a flash of cold heat flashed through his muzzle, making the roots of his teeth scream with agony, causing his fur to stand on end. He yelped as his muscles convulsed, and suddenly he felt himself punched aside as if struck by an invisible hand.

He hit the wall, slid to the floor. Stunned, he managed to stagger to his feet, but now he was in utter terror; his bladder emptied itself as he bolted away from the robot, leaving behind a trail of urine as he ran into the bedroom and took cover within the Bad Dog place beneath the bed.

Whimpering, he peered out from beneath the covers, watched the Enemy as it followed him into the bedroom. He squirmed to the other side of the bed, and when he was sure that he was far enough from the robot that it wouldn't shock him again, he scurried from beneath the bed and ran downstairs.

From his hiding place behind the den couch, Jake licked himself and listened for the Enemy. For the rest of the day he remained there, dreading its return, yet the robot never came near him again. Morning became afternoon; the Enemy came back downstairs, and Jake trembled as it briefly passed through the den, yet the robot made no moves in his direction. After a long time, the kitchen cupboard opened and closed; a few minutes later, the can-opener made its purring noise, and shortly after that he heard his bowl being placed on the kitchen floor. Yet it wasn't until he was sure that the Enemy was no longer in the vicinity that he crept from cover and carefully made his way to where dinner awaited him.

After a few days, Jake regained his courage. The Enemy had to go; it was no longer merely a rival, but now a clear and present danger, and he stalked it relentlessly, following it from room to room. Yet whenever he came close, no matter how quietly he sneaked up on it from behind, the 'bot would somehow sense his approach. Its turret would revolve in his direction and its claws would extend. "Jake! Stop!" it would shout, and Jake knew that if he moved any closer, he would get another electric shock. And so he'd back off, and the 'bot would resume whatever it was doing.

So. He couldn't attack the Enemy. Not directly, at any rate. That meant he had to figure out another means of driving it from of his home.

The Enemy liked order. Indeed, the Enemy lived for order. Jake observed that, if he moved any object in the house from one place to another, the next time the 'bot came through the room, it would immediately notice the change and move that object back to its proper place.

Winter had come; the leaves were off the trees, the days shorter and colder. Once every now and then snow would fall from the sky and blanket the front and back yards. When this happened, Mr. Lawrence would take a shovel from the garage and clear the driveway, yet often several days would go by before he'd do the same for the back porch. Jake knew how to walk through deep snow, yet the Enemy had no legs. Indeed, the Enemy never left the house; unlike Jake, who'd been trained from puppyhood to open and shut the back door by barking at it twice, the 'bot was apparently incapable of doing so.

It didn't take long for Jake to put these things together.

One morning after the Lawrences left, he waited in the living room for the Enemy. He sat silently and watched while the 'bot wiped and cleaned and set things straight in its methodical fashion, and when Jake was sure that it was out of shock-range yet could clearly see what he was doing, he walked forward, picked up a wooden nut bowl from the coffee table, and began to carry it away.

The robot ceased operating the vacuum cleaner. "Jake! Stop!" it demanded, but he didn't obey. Still carrying the bowl in his mouth, he trotted into the kitchen, then stopped near the back door and waited for the Enemy to follow him. When the 'bot was close enough, he dropped the bowl and barked twice. The door slid open, and Jake snatched up the bowl and dashed out onto the back porch.

The Enemy hesitated at the door, and for a moment Jake thought he might have guessed wrong. But the 'bot wanted the bowl back; it had to be returned to the coffee table. So it slowly crawled over the door's recessed runner and rolled out into the unshoveled snow that lay six inches deep upon the back porch.

It moved three feet, then it got stuck.

Jake immediately dropped the bowl, then ran past the robot and back into the house. The robot's wheels were still churning in the snow as Jake barked twice again. The door slid shut, and now Jake was inside and the robot was outside.

The Enemy remained outside for the rest of the day, unable to move, incapable of opening the door by itself. To make matters worse, shortly after midday the snow began to fall once more. Jake stood by the back door, his tongue hanging from his mouth, as he watched fine white powder slowly collect upon the Enemy's turret and rise around its sides. He could hear its beeps and clicks and whirrs through the glass, yet after awhile even those stopped, and it wasn't long before its diodes darkened and it went dead.

Jake didn't feel one bit sorry for it. Going hungry for a little while longer was a small price to pay for liberation, and he didn't even mind the spanking he received when Ms. Lawrence came home to find the robot stranded on the back porch and Jake curled up asleep next to the back porch. He wondered how she had figured out what he'd done, until he saw her dig the nut bowl out of the snow.

The next day the white van returned. As before, his friend the service rep gave him a biscuit and scratched his ears; unlike Mr. and Ms. Lawrence, he was highly amused. And then the Enemy was taken away, and once again life was good.

"That's when I heard about this." Marty had finished dessert, and now he was sitting back in his chair, the soda clasped in one hand. Lunch hour was over, but neither of us had to get back to the office quite yet, and he was plainly enjoying his story. "Up until now, my guy in Albany was taking care of it by himself, but when he learned that the mutt lured the L-1012b out on the porch . . ."

"Hold it right there." I raised a hand. "Look, I'm not saying you're putting me on, but . . ."

"You don't believe me, do you?" Marty grinned. "I don't blame you. Couldn't believe it either, and I've heard 'em all. But like I said, I've got his report in my files. So when they brought the Lawrence's robot in for repairs the second time, I personally drove out to Albany to check on the situation. We downloaded the 'bot's memory into a computer and went through it minute by minute, and . . ."

"It happened just that way?"

He shrugged, slurped his Coke. "Just that way. We were laughing our butts off. Of course, the clients weren't happy about it, especially when it turned out this wasn't covered in the extended service agreement. Just to be fair, I told my people to fix the 'bot free of charge, then I called the family and told them to instruct the robot how to open and shut the back door."

"And that solved the problem?"

Marty shook his head. "No, not quite. Jake had one last ace up his sleeve."

As soon as he was adopted, Mr. Lawrence taught Jake to stay away from the chickens. Jake went half-way with his master on that one; he never killed any of the Rhode Island reds his family raised, yet when Mr. and Ms. Lawrence weren't around he saw nothing wrong with wiggling through the gate and chasing the birds around the pen. The plump little hens were fun to run down, and after awhile Jake learned a neat trick. So when the white van brought the Enemy back a second time, he knew exactly what to do.

When the hens were cornered, their natural tendency was to fall down on their backs and raise their clawed feet defensively. Either that, or they'd huddle into themselves, tuck their heads beneath their wings and wait to die. When they did the latter, Jake found that it was possible to clamp his mouth around them and pick them up; he was always careful not to bite too hard, and the chickens themselves

166

were too frightened to give much resistance. Once he had one of them outside the pen, he'd let them loose, then chase them around the back yard. The best part about the game was that Mr. and Ms. Lawrence never figured out how the birds got loose; they simply figured that the chickens managed to squeeze out through the gate, never suspecting that the dog had anything to do with it.

Three days after the Enemy returned, Jake waited until his family left and the Enemy started cleaning the house. Once it had gone upstairs, he let himself out through the back door, then entered the coop. It was a cold morning, so the chickens were in their henhouse, huddled upon the straw nests they had built on the wire-frame shelf. They squawked when their nemesis came in, but they were too cold to put up much of a fight. Jake picked one at random and carried it away. A few minutes later, he came back and got another one, and then another one after that.

When the 'bot came back downstairs, its infrared sensors detected the presence of three unfamiliar body-heat sources; one in the kitchen, one in the living room and one moving around the front hall. The 'bot's turret turned back and forth; it simply didn't recognize the chickens, and there was nothing in its protocols that allowed for such an anomaly. Yet they clearly didn't belong in the house, so therefore they had to be removed.

As it moved toward the nearest chicken, though, it flapped its wings and hopped up on the kitchen table, overturning an antique milk bottle filled with flowers. Water dripped onto the floor as the hen stalked across the table, bucking in distress. The 'bot immediately rushed to the sink to find a sponge, and in doing so startled the second chicken that had come in from the hallway to investigate. Seeing the second chicken, the 'bot reprioritized its tasks

167

and moved to capture the bird, but it escaped through a doorway into the living room.

So now there were two chickens in the living room, and one of them had left some droppings on the floor. The 'bot had three emergencies: (1.) clean up the mess in the kitchen, (2.) clean up the mess in the living room, (3.) capture the chickens. And within moments, a fourth job was added to the list when a chicken jumped on a bookshelf and knocked over Mr. Lawrence's collection of toy soldiers.

This was the beginning of a very long day. And all Jake had to do was stand back and watch the fun.

By the time Ms. Lawrence returned home, the house was in shambles: broken pottery and glassware strewn across the floor, feathers and chicken crap all over the furniture, overturned lamps, wadded carpets, pecked walls and chair legs. Three bewildered chickens strolled around the house, ignoring both the dog hiding beneath the bed and the 'bot standing motionless in the den, error codes flashing across its display panel.

Jake woke up from his nap, yawned and stretched, and came downstairs just in time to see Ms. Lawrence come back from the chicken coop. She stared at him for a long time, and for a few moments he wondered if he was going to get spanked again. Then she sighed, opened the kitchen cabinet and pulled out a can of Alpo, and it was then that he knew that he had won.

The following day, the white van returned. This time the service rep didn't give Jake a biscuit or an ear-scratch, but that was okay; Jake sat in the driveway and watched while the defeated Enemy was carted away for the last time. Then he trotted back into the house and went to his favorite sunspot in the living room, where he curled up and took a nap.

Life was good.

★ ★ ★ ★ ★

"Anyway, so the Lawrences got rid of their 'bot." Marty carefully sorted out the trash into the garbage and recycling bins, then slid the tray into the rack. "It was still covered by the warranty buy-back plan, so they received a partial refund. Someone called Dwight Lawrence a week or so later and asked if he wished to reconsider, but he told 'em he'd already used the money to buy his wife a nice new watch."

"And the dog? Jake, I mean?"

Marty paused by the register to get a toothpick. "Still there. I called myself, just out of curiosity, and had a chat with Mr. L. He and the missus knew the dog was unhappy with having a 'bot in the house, but they kept hoping that things would work out. The thing with the chickens was the last straw. When that happened, they knew one of them would have to go. So . . ."

"I'm glad they made the right choice." Then I realized what I'd just said. "Not that . . . I mean, I wish they'd kept the 'bot, but . . ."

"No, no, I know what you're saying." Marty sucked on his toothpick as we walked down the corridor to the elevators. "A robot is just a household appliance, when it comes right down to it. We build 'em as well as we can, but only a fool would trade a good dog for something that amounts to little more than a walking can opener. And that's what happens in ninety percent of the cases we've seen. If the dogs don't get along with the 'bots, then the owners ditch the 'bots and keep the dogs."

There was a framed ad poster for the Companion Model IIB in the hallway next to the elevator. Marty punched the button, then turned to study the poster. "Anyway, that's our problem. We've got a war between dogs and robots. Until the AI boys build a robot that can outsmart a dog, we need to find a way to stop losing customers. The way I figure it, we start with the owner service manual."

"How about informing customers not to buy 'bots if they own a dog?"

"Funny. That's funny." Marty peered at me. "Whose side are you on, anyway?"

"I dunno . . . whose side are *you* on?"

Marty grinned as the elevator doors opened. "The side that's winning," he said quietly. "Until then, I'm just collecting a paycheck."

I stepped inside, touched the button for my floor. We all do our jobs; we make ourselves as comfortable as we can, and push back the odds a little more every day. And in that way, life is good.

Warning, Warning

The first interstellar expedition was doomed from the beginning. Not because of inadequate technology—the starship itself, with two decks of living space within its elegant saucer-shaped hull, used a revolutionary hyperdrive as its main propulsion system—but because of lack of forethought. Yet the mission planners were so intent upon colonizing an Earth-like planet that lunar-based telescopes had discovered, against all odds, in orbit around Alpha Centauri that they didn't take into full consideration all the variable factors, not the least of which was the high possibility of human error.

First, there was the foolishness of sending forth a single family. Someone failed to read J. B. Birdsell's paper, "Biological Dimensions of Small, Founding Populations" (*Interstellar Migration and the Human Experience,* edited by B. R. Finny and E. M. Jones, University of California Press, 1985) which pointed out that a self-sustaining colony of less than a hundred people was clearly impossible. Yet the starship had only been designed to hold six passengers, who would be sealed within cryogenic freezing tubes during the four-and-a-half years it would take the ship to reach its destination. Budget cutbacks were held to blame for the fact that the ship wasn't made bigger, yet the mission planners could have selected a more evenly matched crew: three single men and three single women, or even three married couples. A family of five, with one unattached male, may have been psychologically stable, yet it also se-

171

verely limited the gene pool, and a lot of off-color jokes were made about the possible parings among the three children and the ship's pilot.

But that wasn't the worst of it. A covert action operative from a hostile nation—Iraq? North Korea? Libya? to this day, no one knows for sure—had managed to become part of the mission support team as one of the prelaunch checkout physicians. Shortly before the starship left Earth, the agent successfully penetrated the security cordon surrounding the launch pad and entered the spacecraft. A guard discovered him within the ship, but the agent killed him; his body was later discovered in a Dumpster near the pad. The saboteur then reprogrammed the environmental control robot to destroy the ship's major systems six hours after, yet his luck ran out when he was caught aboard at liftoff. So now the starship had an extra passenger, which put an extra burden on its overdelicate inertial guidance system.

Panic-stricken, the saboteur revived the family and the pilot from suspended animation, but not before the robot severely damaged the guidance systems and destroyed the radio transmitter. The vessel's hyperdrive, now without adequate c-cube control, propelled the vessel out of the solar system; no one aboard was sure what happened next, but somehow they found themselves in another part of the galaxy. It was only merciful intervention on the part of the family matriarch which prevented the pilot from jettisoning the phony doctor from the airlock, yet the saboteur—clearly mentally unstable from the beginning, and now a full-blown paranoid-schizophrenic—attempted twice to kill members of the crew before the ship was forced to crash-land on a desert planet.

The members of the expedition tried to make the best of

their dire situation. The youngest child, who was something of a protégé despite his youth, reprogrammed the robot so that it was no longer homicidal, while his father and the pilot explored the immediate area surrounding the crash site and his mother and two older sisters successfully set up a base camp. For a time, they regained the semblance of a model nuclear family as they set upon the task of repairing the ship and making it flightworthy once more.

Yet the saboteur had become increasingly psychotic. When he wasn't talking aloud to the robot or hoarding food rations, he was still scheming to murder various members of the expedition. Soon it became too much for them to bear. After a whispered conference with the father, the pilot drew a laser pistol from the ship's weapons locker, escorted their unwanted guest a couple of miles from the base camp and, behind the shelter of a large boulder, shot him dead. The saboteur was buried in a shallow, unmarked grave; to the end, no one knew his real name.

The execution of the phony doctor, albeit necessary, had a bad effect upon the expedition's morale. Until this point, the older daughter had been sexually attracted to the pilot, which had been anticipated by the mission planners and approved by her father and mother. Afterwards, she became increasingly aloof, not only from the pilot (who in turn became frustrated and angry when his advances were coldly rebuffed) but also her parents and siblings. Meanwhile, the planet gradually revealed itself to be unrelentingly hostile, even as the expedition members became less wary of their alien surroundings.

The older daughter was the next to die, when a sudden earthquake dislodged a massive boulder and caused it to roll down a steep escarpment beneath which she happened to be standing. The pilot was the sole witness to her death; in the weeks that followed, he fell into a state of acute depression. Nearly a month later, he was caught by surprise when one of the sixty-foot-tall cyclopean giants who prowled a nearby valley found him while he was tending to a remote weather platform; his remains were discovered the following day, or at least those which hadn't been devoured.

Fighting against shock and grief, the rest of the expedition redoubled their efforts to repair the starship and leave the planet, yet the odds were now clearly against their favor. The next to go was the younger daughter. When the son made a desperate attempt to launch a handbuilt SOS rocket into space, it exploded in the high atmosphere and came down as a fireball which incinerated his sister. Instead of punishing him, though, his parents decided to put him back in cryogenic suspension. Two of their children had perished already, and now they feared for the life of their young, reckless son.

Perhaps they made the wisest decision, for it was only three days later that they were caught in a freak electrical storm caused by the planet's erratic climate. They were attempting to cover the small hydroponic farm when the father was struck by lightning attracted to the metal tarp pole he happened to be holding at that instant; he died instantly of electrocution.

In the end, the mother fought a solitary battle to preserve what little was left of her family. With the assistance of the robot, she managed to get the starship back into operational condition, yet when the time came for her to leave the nameless planet upon which she had been marooned, she found herself unwilling to leave the graves of her husband and first-born children. Perhaps this was misplaced loyalty; perhaps she had simply gone insane herself. Most likely she believed that the expedition had been jinxed from the beginning, and that by remaining behind she would remove the curse. Whatever the reason, she programmed the robot to launch the starship back into space. When the starship lifted off, she was huddled beneath a flimsy tent near the graves of her family, watching as it rose into the monochrome sky.

Once the starship was in orbit above the planet, the robot did its best to plot a return trajectory to Earth, based upon the slender evidence given by unreliable astrogational readings and fragmented data from the onboard computers. This task took almost an hour. Once the return course was set, the robot returned to its bay on the ship's lower level, from which it would periodically emerge, once every month or so, to check the ship's status during the seventy-six years it would take for it to return to Earth.

Within a cryogenic tube on the ship's upper level, the sole surviving member of Earth's first interstellar expedition remained ageless, frozen in suspended animation. Yet his subconscious mind stayed active; in a perpetual state of R.E.M. dream-sleep, he imagined surreal fantasies in which his family, along with the pilot and the saboteur, was not only alive and well, but also encountered strange beings from a thousand worlds. Extraterrestrial circuses and intergalactic traders, space hippies and space bikers, frogheaded princes and carrot men, jungle planets and mouthless invaders from the fifth dimension—all utterly alien yet comforting in their simplicity.

The dreams of a young boy, lost in space.

The Fine Art of Watching

"Two hours, Blue. Are you sure we're in the right place?"

Mr. Coffey was having a bad morning. Through my earpiece I could hear the impatience in his voice, as cantankerous as a child who had been made to sit in the car while Mom and Dad went shopping. This was the second time Ed had asked that question in the last half-hour, and the question was just as pointless now as it had been thirty minutes ago. Either we were or we weren't, and if we weren't, I'd have some hard questions of my own.

I glanced up from the guide book I had been pretending to read for the last couple of hours, gazed across the Getty's front plaza toward the tram station. A digital clock above the awning read 11:59. A short distance down the monorail track I could see the tram itself, slowly moving up the hill toward the museum.

"Stand by, Green," I murmured, ducking my head a little so that none of the handful of people loitering around the plaza would observe me talking to myself. "Red, are you in position?"

"Affirmative, Blue," Michaela replied. Her voice was very quiet in my ear, and I resisted the temptation to glance behind me to make sure. Wide concrete steps led up from the plaza to a broad promenade directly in front of the art museum. Michaela would be sitting on a semi-circular bench beneath a shade tree, also pretending to read something while she kept an eye on me from about forty feet away. She was a trained professional, so she knew how to

remain innocuous while on stake-out. Or at least so I had been told; this was my first field operation with her as a partner, and her reliability was only one of many questions in my mind.

The electric tram had reached the top of the hill, and now it silently moved past the blue casement windows of the auditorium building as it approached the station. I closed the guidebook and tucked it beneath my arm as I stood up from the bench and sauntered toward the snack kiosk in the center of the plaza. Futuristic and dazzling white in the California sun, the J. Paul Getty Center sprawled across a west L.A. hilltop like the Acropolis of Athens as reimagined by a Hollywood set designer; I wondered how many scenes for made-for-TV science fiction movies had been filmed here. In the far distance rose the Hollywood Hills, dun-colored desert mountains overburdened by the terra-cotta homes of movie directors and rock stars. I couldn't see it from where I stood, but the surveillance van was somewhere up on an undeveloped ridge overlooking the San Diego Freeway, parked on a service road off Sepulveda Boulevard where Mr. Coffey would have a clear line of sight down upon the Getty. If I stood close to the wall at the southern end of the plaza and waved my arms, Ed might be able to see me if he was peering through the telescopic lens of one of the cameras he kept aboard the Spookmobile.

Yet Mr. Coffey wasn't watching us that way. Or at least he shouldn't be. I stopped in front of the kiosk, looked up at the menu board above the counter, and raised my hand to cover my mouth as if I was about to cough. "Green, where's the flycam?"

"Look up. I'm repositioning now."

Raising my hand against the bright midday sun, I glanced upward just in time to catch a glimpse of a small, swift form as it purred overhead, whisking about sixty feet above the plaza as it moved from the flat rooftop of the restaurant building to the roof of the auditorium. If anyone else had spotted it, they probably would have mistaken it for a hummingbird, yet no one paid any attention save for the Hispanic lady standing behind the counter. She gazed at me curiously, perhaps wondering if I was ever going to visit the museum or simply hang out in the plaza and drink iced latte all day.

"Can I help you?" A vaguely worried smile. I had visited her little bistro twice already. Behind her, the tram was coasting into the station.

"Umm . . ." I made a pretense of studying the menu as I watched the tram. It glided to a halt within the narrow groove of the station platform; a moment passed, then its doors slid open, and I could hear a recorded voice politely telling its passengers to watch their step as they left. Yet each of its cars was only half-full; it was a Tuesday morning in late October, well past the height of the California tourist season, and although you still needed to make advance reservations, the Getty wasn't as popular as it normally was during the summer months just past.

Nonetheless, quite a few people got off the tram which visitors took from the underground parking garage at the bottom of the hill. Unless you happened to work here, it was the only way to enter the Getty. Still making a show of examining the menu board—did I want latte, espresso, cappuccino, chi or just a plain, ordinary Diet Coke?—I stepped to one side to get a better view of the tram while still keeping the kiosk between me and the platform. Out of the corner of my eye, the counter lady lost interest in me and turned away. There's something about L.A. which lends itself to people with short attention spans.

Earnest-looking art aficionados, pony-tailed Hollywood yuppies, UCLA students toting daypacks, Asian tourists, beautiful young women with expressions of perpetual boredom and legs slightly shorter than a giraffe's, all tanned from afternoons spent in Malibu and dressed in the loose-fitting, open-necked pastels which are Southern California's contribution to global fashion. Sallow of complexion, dressed in a charcoal business suit, I suddenly became aware of how much I stuck out. Not good for covert work. I was unknotting my tie and slipping it off from around my neck when I spotted our primary target, one of the last passengers to disembark from the tram.

"Black is here," I whispered, the bone-convection mike concealed within my sunglasses picking up my words as clearly as if I had spoken them aloud.

"Copy that, Blue," Mickey replied. *"I see him."*

A short, slightly overweight man just past sixty, with longish dark hair recently turned silver, Black wore a tan sport coat and a black cashmere mock-turtleneck. He had a rolled-up magazine beneath his left arm. If he was nervous in any way about what he was doing, he was very good at not showing it. He strolled out from beneath the station awning, paused briefly to glance around the plaza—I ducked back behind the kiosk and counted to five—then began to saunter toward the stairs, following the crowd as it headed toward the museum.

"I've acquired Black," Mr. Coffey said.

"Keep him in sight. I'm following." I waited until he was on the stairs, then I slipped out from behind the kiosk and picked up his tail.

Okay, freeze-frame. Let's take a minute to find out who the good guys are and who are the bad guys.

Black was Jack Edgar, Ph.D., a senior biochemist employed by a large pharmaceutical corporation which made its headquarters in Long Beach. About three months ago, his company was caught by surprise when one of its chief European rivals, a biotech firm in Italy, suddenly announced a process for producing tPA—tissue plasminogen activator, a kind of blood anti-coagulant used by hospitals for treating heart attacks—which was remarkably similar to one which Dr. Edgar's division had been developing for several years. All at once, its lead in bringing a valuable product to market was imperiled, along with several hundred million dollars in R&D money and potentially ten times as much in long-term revenues.

It looked very much as if someone at Company A was selling secrets to Company B, but in order to successfully prosecute a patent infringement suit against the Italians, Company A had to prove that its tPA process had been stolen. That's when Company A called Company C—Falcon Associates, Ltd., which specializes in handling such matters, with great discretion and at a considerable price.

After ten weeks of investigation, Dr. Edgar had emerged as our prime suspect. As a major player involved the tPA project, he had complete access to everything at his company's research labs. Furthermore, he lived beyond his apparent means; in the last few months, he had abruptly traded in his four-year-old BMW for a new Porsche and had moved from a condo in Redondo Beach to a nice hilltop house in Sherman Oaks. Of everyone working at Company A whom we checked out, Edgar most closely fit the profile of an insider selling corporate secrets for cash.

Yet no one could figure out how he was getting the material out the door. To its credit, Company A had long since enacted tough—some might say draconian—security measures which were meant to insure that its crown jewels stayed safely locked away. Visitors were never allowed to enter the research facilities, and everyone who worked there had to sign in and sign out at the front-door guard station. No paper files were permitted to be taken home, and the guards inspected everyone's briefcases, shoulder bags and satchels before they were allowed to leave the building at the end of the day. Phone calls were monitored, computer files were encrypted upon creation and all e-mail was filtered through online censors who inspected every single memo for proprietary information.

Nothing Dr. Edgar had done while he was employed by Company A had ever raised a red flag, yet when our people examined company security records, they noticed an odd thing. On the last Tuesday of each month, Dr. Edgar would leave the office around mid-day to go somewhere. He simply signed out at about 10 a.m., then would reappear at the lab by around 2 p.m. He did it so quietly that no one at his company noticed his absence, yet nonetheless there was always a four-hour gap in his monthly schedule which he had never explained to anyone.

Last month, after he had made one of these little disappearances, one of our operatives paid a visit to his office shortly after the company closed for the day. Again, nothing he had left on his desk, in his file cabinet or in his computer appeared suspicious. Even the little dunking bird which watered itself at the glass upon his bookshelf had no secrets to tell. Yet our operative was nothing if not thorough; she upended the trash can next to his desk and searched every piece of litter which fell out onto the carpet. And lo, what did she find but the two torn halves of a car pass for the Getty Center, time-stamped for 11:40 that very same day.

We used our usual resources—namely, sweet-talking and

bribery—to check the Getty's guest-reservation list through the past twelve months, and it turned out that Dr. Edgar had visited the place on the last Tuesday of every month, always at the same time. Counting mid-day traffic time on the 405 from Long Beach to West Hollywood, and it all fit together: Dr. Edgar had established the Getty as a regular rendezvous point.

And that's where my team and I come in.

So here's Black, Dr. Jack Edgar, trooping up the polished white steps of the Getty, just one more Angelino in search of a little high culture to enliven an otherwise dull day, blissfully unaware that he's being shadowed by two spooks and something that looked like a toy RC helicopter. Yet he was a cautious man. As he got closer to the top of the stairs, he paused again to look around. I made no sudden moves, but simply drifted a little to the left so that I remained in his blind spot. I couldn't see Mickey, which was good because it probably meant that Black couldn't see her either. A tiny shadow flitted across the steps; that was Ed's flycam, making like a sparrow as it flew from the auditorium to the curved edge of the museum's flat roof.

Black noticed none of this. Pulling his magazine from beneath his left arm, he idly swatted it against his thigh as he continued walking up the steps to the promenade. I was still forty feet behind him, though, so I lost sight of him as soon as he left the stairs.

"I've lost Black," I murmured.

"Got him, Blue." Through the crowd, I caught a glimpse of Mickey as she stood up. A slender woman of average height, with long blond Botticelli hair tied back in a dark blue bow, she wore wide-frame sunglasses and a calf-length black dress with a long slit up one sleek thigh. Subtle, she

was not; if she had been surrounded by lingerie models, I still would have noticed her. I had questioned her appearance earlier this morning before we left the hotel, telling her that she needed to learn how to melt into a crowd, but she had smiled and given me the benefit of a small observation: when the average guy spots a good-looking woman in a crowd, he tends to immediately look away. A quick size-up and that's it; unless the woman in question makes direct eye-contact, most men tend to be shy around alpha females, instinctively sensing them as being too threatening. Hence, according to her, a well-dressed woman is the perfect camouflage.

I don't know whether this was something Mickey figured out on her own or if it was the product of Mossad training—it sure didn't sound like any CIA tradecraft I'd ever learned—but I wasn't going to argue. If the tail was blown because she had been spotted by the target, though, you could bet I'd take away her Lord & Taylor catalog once we returned to Washington.

"He's entering the museum," Coffey said, and I quickened my pace, trying not to appear in a hurry as I half-jogged up the remaining steps. *"Stay on him, Red."*

No answer from Mickey. She was probably too close to Black to risk voice contact. I reached the top of the stairs just in time to see her strolling toward the glass doors of the museum. Ten feet in front of her, Black was just then entering the building. The door shut behind him, and Mickey was on him.

So far, so good . . . but then I saw something new.

A guy with curly blond hair, wearing a blue windbreaker, sitting on a semi-circular bench in front of a rock fountain. He was watching Black, and when he walked into the museum, he folded his brochure and stood up to follow him.

Black's contact? I couldn't be sure, but he was behind Mickey and she hadn't spotted him. I raised my hand as if to clear my throat. "Stand down, Red," I said softly. "He's mine."

Mickey heard me; she stopped just before she reached the door, turned to glance sharply in my direction. Out of the corner of my eye, I could see the dude in the windbreaker casting a curious glance in our direction. Damn it, now we were attracting attention to ourselves. Even if Black wasn't looking back to see if he was being followed, there was a strong chance that his contact might.

"Hey, what's going on down there?" Mr. Coffey demanded.

No time to explain the situation to either of them. I put a big, sheepish grin on my face as I marched toward her. "Honey, I'm so sorry," I exclaimed, taking her by the arm and stepping her away from the door. "I didn't see you get off the tram."

Mickey caught on. "I didn't see you either," she said evenly, forcing a smile of her own as I gave her a quick buss on the cheek. "I was about to go in by myself."

Behind us, the last few people from the tram were entering the museum. Curly didn't pay any further attention to us as he fell in among them. I gave Mickey a hug, whispered in her ear: "Stay here and cover the door, I'll call if I need backup."

"Blue, this isn't the game plan," Ed snapped. *"What are you doing?"*

Mickey wanted to ask the same thing, but she couldn't. She gave me a go-to-hell look as she stepped back. "Excuse me," she said, forcing sweetness into her voice, "but I think I need to powder my nose."

"Okay," I replied. "I'll meet you back here." She glared

at me through her sunglasses, then she turned and strode away.

That little public tiff may have saved our cover, but it also cost us valuable seconds. When I entered the museum's air-conditioned foyer, Black was nowhere to be seen, and neither was Curly. The uniformed security guard standing just inside the door gave me the eye as I hastily glanced around. Nearly everyone who had entered the museum was heading for the ground-floor galleries, but a few were walking up the circular staircase leading to the second floor. I had to take a chance, so I chose the stairs.

The second floor was a maze of cool, silent rooms with polished parquet floors and track lighting suspended from the high ceilings. Every step I took seemed to echo off the aquamarine walls no matter how quietly I tried to walk.

An art museum. Man, what a perfect place for a contact. Everyone is looking at the stuff on the walls instead of each other, yet the place is so quiet a ballerina in practice shoes would sound like a soldier stomping through in winter boots. Black might be an amateur, but he had picked his rendezvous site like a pro.

I moved quietly from one room to the next, my hands folded behind my back, trying not to look as if I was in a hurry. The photosensitive lenses of my sunglasses had cleared, and now I could see the artwork clearly. Here, I found the late Italian Renaissance: Mantegna's *Adoration of the Magi*, Bartolommeo's *The Rest on the Flight into Egypt*, Dossi's *Mythological Scene*. No sign of either Black or Curly, so now I drifted into the next room to check out the Dutch masters: Rembrandt's *The Abduction of Europa*, Steen's *The Drawing Lesson*, Van Dyck's *Thomas Howard, 2nd Earl of Arundel*. A couple of Russian tourists got a little too close to Rembrandt's portrait of St. Bartholomew before a security guard appeared from nowhere and politely moved them away, but by then I was heading for the room filled with stuffy English and French portraits.

Still no Black, and now I was getting the lousy feeling that I had made the wrong decision. I paused in front of Jacques-Louis David's *The Sisters Senaide and Charlotte Bonaparte* and cleared my throat again. *"Red, go in and check the ground floor."*

Nothing but static. Damn! I should have known better. Our communications link was being relayed through the Spookmobile; however, since Coffey was parked way the hell over there, its low-watt radio signal couldn't penetrate the museum's thick granite walls. This was the reason why Ed hadn't parked the Honda SUV in the underground garage beneath the Getty; not only did he need to have a clear fix on the flycam, but he also needed to be able to receive signals from our headset radios, and that would only work if we were all out in the open. Although he and Mickey were still able to talk to each other, I was now out of the loop.

And I'd lost Black.

Fighting down panic, I quickly left the room. Through the doorway was a circular corridor leading around a central atrium well. California sunlight washed through a skylight in the ceiling far above. Muttering obscenities beneath my breath, I marched around the atrium to the next gallery, walked through the door . . .

And nearly collided with Dr. Jack Edgar.

"Uhp . . . excuse me."

"No problem." Dr. Edgar stepped aside without so much as a second look, went back to examining the painting on the wall next to the door.

Now we were with the French Impressionists of the late

19th century. I tried not to do a double-take as I sauntered past him, heading for Cezanne's *Still Life with Apples* on the opposite side of the room. There were a couple of other people in the gallery, closely studying Manet's depiction of a Parisian street on the morning of Bastille Day. Behind me, Dr. Edgar continued to savor Monet's conical wheatstacks with the first snow of winter upon them.

We circled the room for the next few minutes, Black and I, our backs turned to one another, stalker and prey. After a few moments the other visitors left the room, heading for another gallery, leaving him and me alone among the company of masters. He moved to the Cezanne and I went to check out the Manet. In the foreground was a one-legged man in a blue coat, hobbling on crutches down the Rue Mosnier; somehow, I knew exactly how he must have felt. Black idly tapped the folded magazine in his hand against his leg as he went to inspect another Monet and I chose that moment to shift my attention to the handsome young lovers in Renoir's *La Promenade*.

I was just beginning to realize how subtly Renoir had utilized light and shadow when I heard Dr. Edgar leave the room. I counted to three, then glided after him, keeping him in sight as he moved into the next gallery. I was about to follow him through the door when I saw him approach an enormous canvas which took up one entire wall: a vast parade down a European street, dozens of people in odd costumes—clowns, witches, a skeleton in a top hat, a man dressed like a cat—passing before a reviewing stand, with a laughing cardinal in a miter leading the procession and a uniformed marching band not far behind. A scarlet banner overhead read "Vive La Sociale." A colorful and very strange work of art; it vaguely reminded me of the album cover of the Beatles' *Sgt. Pepper's Lonely Hearts Club Band.*

Standing by himself in the room, Black stared at the mural for a long time, transfixed by its cryptic beauty. I hung back, lingering just outside the door, allowing Dr. Edgar that moment alone with this weird masterpiece.

After a couple of minutes, he glanced one way over his shoulder, then the next. I quietly moved back one step, avoiding his wary gaze. When I looked back again, he had moved to the plaque on the wall right of the mural, apparently to read the description of the piece.

He was now holding the folded magazine in front of him. As he studied the plaque, he seemed to be absently curling it within his hands, yet as I watched closely, his right hand traveled to its back cover and did something I couldn't quite make out.

Was he removing something from the magazine?

Behind me, a pair of slow footsteps were entering the room in which I stood: a young couple, keeping quiet conversation as they wandered through the museum. I moved a little away from the door, pretending to examine the nearby Manet while I kept an eye on Dr. Edgar.

Then, in a moment which passed so quickly I might have missed it if I hadn't been watching him so keenly, his right hand moved to the plaque. He gently stroked its top edge with the tips of his fingers, barely seeming to touch it . . . then his hand fell back to his side and, after another second or two, he stepped away from the wall.

Black gazed at the mural for another minute. A furtive smile briefly stole across his face. I'd seen that sort of smile before, in the years when I had worked in Nairobi for the CIA; in that instant, I knew that he had made his drop.

He turned and walked away from the huge painting, once again idly tapping the magazine against his thigh. On his way out of the room, he paused next to the door; another quick look around, then he pulled out a small piece of chalk and made a tiny, almost unnoticeable white mark on the doorframe.

I waited until I heard his footsteps fade down the corridor, then I entered the gallery.

As much as I wanted to rush straight to the plaque, I had to restrain my curiosity; a roving security guard chose that moment to walk through, briefly giving me the eagle-eye as I stood before the mural. Through the doorway on the far end of the gallery, I caught a glimpse of Black sauntering through the next room, no longer interested in any of the art displayed on its walls. Mickey would pick his trail as soon as he left the museum. I waited until the guard had disappeared into the room I had just left, then I walked over to the plaque.

The mural was titled *Christ's Entry into Brussels in 1889*, and it was painted in 1888 by the Belgian artist by name of James Ensor. There was a bit more to the description than that, but my patience was at its end. I reached up and, ever so carefully, ran my fingertips over the clean plastic top of the plaque.

A strip of tape.

That was all. A mere strip of Scotch tape, about three inches long.

I found the guide book in the pocket of my jacket, opened it to its first page. Then I slowly and gently peeled the tape off the top of the plaque, making sure that it didn't curl in upon itself. In the few seconds before I transferred it to the front inside cover of the book, though, I quickly examined it.

Neatly flattened against the tape was another strip of tape, and enclosed within those two strips, like a lab specimen captured within a flexible microscope slide, was a single strand of hair. A human hair, silver-grey, its follicle still attached to one end like a minute dewdrop.

I carefully plastered the tape and its valuable cargo within the cover of my book, then I closed it and walked away to study the other paintings in the room. The French impressionist movement was really ahead of its time; I took the opportunity to relish the other Monets and Cezannes on display, always keeping an eye on the mural. The young couple cruised through the room and stopped for a moment to gaze upon the Ensor, then they eventually moved on. A yuppie came yapping through the gallery, giving the masterpieces around him barely more than a passing glance as he quarreled with his agent on his cell phone about how to get Tom and Nicole to read his screenplay. The security guard made his patrol, coming and going like a ghost. I studied trees and rivers and lonely avenues in southern France, and hoped that Green was observing Black's return to the tram station.

About five minutes later, Curly strolled into the gallery, his hands thrust in the pockets of his jacket. Noticing my presence at the opposite end of the room, he hesitated just inside the door, but I kept my back turned to him and pretended not to pay any attention. He brushed his left elbow against the doorframe, erasing the chalk mark Black had left behind, then he slowly walked over to the mural and spent a minute or so in silent contemplation of the Second Coming.

I left the room and entered the adjacent gallery, feeling his eyes on my back. I waited a few seconds, giving him time to feel comfortable, then I quietly slipped to the edge of the door and peered around the frame. By then he had moved to the wall plaque. When his hands emerged from his jacket pockets, I caught a brief glimpse of a plastic sandwich bag.

190

As I watched, he reached up to the top edge of the plaque, ran his fingers across it. His back was turned to me, so I couldn't relish the look on his face, but he went so far as to actually stand on tip-toe to visually inspect the plaque.

Footsteps from outside the room, coming closer. Curly hastily shoved the sandwich bag back in his pocket and stepped away from the wall, moving a little closer to the Ensor. A moment later, the security guard entered the room. He glided over to the bagman and tapped him on the shoulder, silently admonishing him not to stand so close to the mural. Curly scowled at him, but obediently moved away.

I turned and quickly strode through the room behind me, ignoring the remaining artwork as I followed the signs to the exit. Two quick turns, and I found myself back at the stairway I had taken from the ground floor.

Mickey was impatiently waiting for me just outside the front door, her arms folded across her chest. She started to say something, but I cut her off. "Did you see Black come out?" I asked, and she nodded. "Green, did you get a clear shot of Black?"

"Caught him on the way back to the tram." Ed's voice came clearly through the earpiece. *"Jesus, Blue, what the hell happened to . . . ?"*

"Never mind that now. I've intercepted the drop." Michaela's mouth opened and her eyes widened in surprise as I took her arm and led her away from the museum entrance. "Black's handler is still inside. Where are you positioned right now?"

"Directly above you, on the roof," he replied, and I instinctively looked up. I couldn't see the flycam from where I was standing, but the rooftop was three stories above me. *"What does he look like?"*

"Tall, curly blond . . . never mind. Can you see me?"

"No. Can you get a little farther away from the building?" Mickey followed me as I took a few more steps out onto the promenade. *"Okay. Got you both. Now who am I looking for?"*

"Wait a minute, and I'll introduce you." I looked back at Mickey, favored her with my most annoying grin. "You're still smoking, aren't you?"

She hesitated. The boss had been bugging her to kick the habit ever since she joined Falcon Associates, and she had conned him into believing that she had given up cigarettes. But I could smell tobacco on her breath, which meant that she had sneaked a butt while I was inside. "Of course not. I've . . ."

"Gimme one." I looked over my shoulder to check the door. Black's handler hadn't appeared yet. "Green, get airborne and come down low."

She had just dug her pack of cigarettes—Gitannes, yuck—from her handbag and shook one out for me when Curly pushed open the door. Judging from his gait and the expression on his face, he was mighty upset just now. Good. I was about to piss him off even more.

"Blue, what are you . . . ?"

"Just do it." I snatched the cigarette from Mickey's pack, then turned and walked toward Curly just as he was striding past us.

He was almost about to brush past me until I stepped in front of him, raising the cigarette to my mouth. "Pardon me, *signor* . . . do you have a light?"

I used the only word of Italian I knew beyond a restaurant wine list, but that stopped him. The handler hesitated. "Sorry," he said, and I wasn't surprised to hear an Italian accent, "but I don't smoke."

192

A faint whirring sound from just above us. "Neither do I, to tell the truth," I said, then I suddenly pointed above his head. "Hey, look up there . . . !"

He pivoted on his heels, looked up . . . and there was the flycam, a miniature helicopter with a camera lens protruding from its bulbous fuselage, hovering barely ten feet away. Its propwash stirred his hair as he stared at it in gapemouthed shock.

"Have a nice day," I said, then I put my arm around Mickey's waist and walked her away from the museum.

Curly stared up at me from the miniatures liquid crystal screen of the Panasonic portable DVD player, his face frozen in a timeless expression of astonishment. The flycam had captured him beautifully; I had little doubt that, once the images were analyzed by the boys and girls in Intelligence, they would be able to match his face against their files of known covert operatives. Before I passed the disk to them, though, I wanted to make a hard copy of this shot for myself, just to pin up on my bulletin board.

I heard the flight attendant coming down the aisle, and snapped the player shut before she could ask me to switch it off. The American Airlines 767 was still climbing to cruising altitude; it was highly doubtful that the minuscule electromagnetic field generated by the player would interfere with the cockpit instruments, but I didn't want to get in an argument with the person whom I would depend upon to deliver Bloody Marys all the way home to Washington. She passed through the first-class cabin with a silent look of admonishment in my direction; she knew what I was doing, and I knew that she knew, but neither of us were willing to lock horns over the issue.

Michaela still wasn't speaking to me. She idly flipped

through the copy of *The New Yorker* she had picked up just before we boarded the plane, and continued the cold-shoulder treatment she had been giving me ever since Mr. Coffey picked us up in the Spookmobile outside the Getty. I sat up front with Ed; we chatted about the assignment until we reached LAX, where he dropped us at the main passenger terminal before driving the minivan over to the air cargo center for shipment back to Dulles International. Mickey and I were taking a separate flight to Reagan National. All the time Mickey quietly fumed in the back seat; I had to ask her twice to burn me a second copy of the flycam footage, and even then she did so grudgingly. I decided to let her stew for a little while longer; we had a four-hour flight in front of us, so we certainly had time to hash things out when Mr. Coffey wasn't around.

So I savored my Bloody Mary—a little on the bland side; next time I'd have to ask the flight attendant if she had any Tabasco sauce—as I gazed down at the arid, overdeveloped landscape falling away beneath the plane. The late afternoon sun illuminated the suburban sprawl west of Cucamonga, catching the thick plume of smoke rising from the latest forest fire in the San Bernadinos and tinting it a lovely shade of red.

The overhead console made its *dink* sound, signaling that the pilot had switched off the seatbelt sign and that we were now free to move around the cabin or play with our little electronic toys. I opened the DVD player again and took another moment to relish the look on Curly's face one more time, then I switched it off and unbuckled my seat belt. The business traveler sitting in front of me cranked back his seat a few inches, and the close-up view of the airphone nestled in his seatback reminded me that I had some unfinished business of my own.

I started to reach into my jacket for my wallet when Mickey shifted her legs, folding her left knee over her right. The sole of her high-heeled boot lightly kicked my ankle, and she muttered something that almost sounded like an apology. That was enough of an icebreaker for me.

"S'okay. No problem." I made a little show of trying to get at my wallet, even though it was easily within reach. "Hey, do you have the company phone card? I can't get to mine."

"Hmm? Yeah, sure." Mickey unclipped her seat belt, turned the magazine face-down in her lap, then reached forward to pull her shoulder bag from beneath the seat in front of her. "Calling in?"

"Uh-huh. I want to let them know what to do about the package." That being the small plastic bottle in my jacket which contained the strand of hair I had found in the Getty. Ed had volunteered to take it with him to Washington, since his flight was scheduled to arrive shortly before ours, but I was reluctant to let it out of my sight. I pulled the phone out of its recessed cradle and swiped Mickey's card through the slot, then dialed the company's secure switchboard number.

"Falcon Associates," the operator said.

"Blue Priority One," I said. "Cardinals over Orioles in the eighth inning."

This was the password which not only verified my identity, but also informed them that I was speaking on an unsecured phone. "Thank you. How can I direct your call?"

"Shipping department." That was the code word for Forensic Science. A brief pause, then the phone buzzed a few times. I checked my watch; it was 4:45 Pacific Standard, which meant that it was a quarter to eight in D.C. I hoped someone on the third floor would be working late.

I was about to give up when the phone was picked up on the seventh ring. "Forensic . . . I mean, Shipping Department," a distracted male voice said.

I immediately recognized its owner: Jim Kessler, one of the sharper pencils in our desk drawer. The boss had recruited him only last year from the FBI, where he had been working overtime for slave wages at its National Crime Lab. Jim wasn't earning much more at Falcon, to tell the truth, but at least he didn't have G-men breathing down his neck all the time. We were drinking buddies when we were off the clock.

"It's Blue. What's happening, dude?"

"Nothing much. Just chillin' in the loading dock." Which meant that the boss had him stay late at the lab to wait for my call. "I hear you've got something interesting for us."

"Oh, yeah. You're going to like this one." I resisted the temptation to go into details. "Look, we're probably not going to get into D.C. until well after midnight your time, so you might as well go home."

"Thanks, pal. I appreciate it." I could hear him smiling over the phone. The last thing he wanted to do was spend the night at the office, waiting for two field operatives to come traipsing in from California.

"No problem, but look . . . can you get access to an electron microscope? The sooner the better. Like, first thing tomorrow morning?"

A sigh. He wasn't off the hook yet. "Yeah, sure," Jim said after a moment. "I know some people I can call."

"Give 'em a buzz tonight, willya? I'm sure the boss is going to want us to hop on this as soon as possible."

"I'll set it up before I leave. You're going to owe me one for this, you know."

I knew what he meant: steak dinner at our favorite Georgetown watering hole, with yours truly picking up the bill. It wasn't a hardship; after knoshing on light-weight California cuisine for the last four days, I was ready for some East Coast red meat and potatoes. "No problemo. You the man."

"Yeah, yeah . . . see you tomorrow."

"Nighty-night," I replied, but he had already hung up. I let the phone cord retract the receiver back into its socket, then I turned to Mickey. "Done. I'll bring it to the office in the morning."

"Uh-huh." She had picked up *The New Yorker* again and was skimming the film reviews. She was putting on a pretense about not being much interested in my conversation, but I knew that she had been hanging on every word. "So what's this about an electron microscope?"

"Nothing. Just operational details." Two can play this game; I touched the armrest button, let my seat fall back a few inches. The video screen was descending from the ceiling two rows in front of us; I reached into the seat pocket and pulled out the plastic bag containing the headphones. "Any idea what the movie is?"

"The new *Star Wars*, I think." Mickey reluctantly put aside her reading material to pull out the in-flight magazine; she aimlessly riffled its pages back and forth before surrendering to the inevitable with an exasperated sound. "Okay, I'll bite. Why do you need an electronic microscope?"

I ripped into the bag, pulled out the headphones. "Let's talk about you first. You're upset about being left outside, aren't you?"

Mickey hesitated, still playing with the magazine. "You could put it that way, yes," she finally replied, dropping her voice a little. Not that she really needed to; across the aisle,

197

an elderly man was loudly blowing his nose into a wad of tissue while his wife tucked an airplane blanket around her shoulders and snuggled into her seat for a nap. "I was supposed to tail Black into the museum while you stayed outside. At the last minute, you changed the plan. I'd like to know why."

She did know how to cut straight to the chase, didn't she? "Because I saw Black's contact and you didn't, and there wasn't enough time to warn you." I thought about it a moment, then decided that straight truth was better than a polite lie. "Also, I couldn't trust you to be as discrete as I needed you to be."

"Uh-huh." She nodded and shoved the in-flight mag back in the seat pocket. "And that has something to do with the way I'm dressed."

"That's part of it, yes. It's hard to keep a close tail when you're dressed like a fashion model. I was afraid that either Black or Curly would spot you, so I cut in." She opened her mouth to object, but I raised a hand to cut her off. "But that's only half of it. I saw something that indicated to me that this wasn't going to be a simple letter drop."

"The magazine? Oh, c'mon . . . I noticed that, too."

The flight attendant picked that moment to stop by and inform us of tonight's dinner choices. I opted for the steak tips and Mickey requested the linguine, and I asked for another Bloody Mary. Two more cocktails on a full stomach, and I'd snooze through the rest of the trip home. When she was gone, I picked up the thread of the conversation. "I'm sure you noticed the magazine. It was an obvious giveaway . . . why would anyone carry reading material into an art museum? But I bet you were thinking that he would drop it somewhere, and someone else would pick it up later. Right?"

Mickey didn't say anything, but the look in her eyes told me that this had been her thought at the time. "But that wouldn't work," I continued, "because major museums are positively fanatic about their appearance. If Black had casually dropped it on a bench, you can bet that it wouldn't have remained there two minutes before a security guard would have picked it up and tossed it in a waste can."

"Uh-huh." She raised an incredulous eyebrow. "And you figured that out immediately."

"No . . . or at least not immediately. It just seemed like an amateurish way of going about a letter drop, and we were clearly dealing with pros. And I ruled out a brush contact because there weren't enough people around. If you want to hand off something to someone, you do it in a crowded place, like an airport terminal, where there's so many people around that if anyone's watching . . ."

"I know what a brush contact is, thank you."

I had no doubt that she did; I had read her Mossad dossier shortly after she had been hired by Falcon Associates. Mickey was good. She had to be good, because the boss didn't bother with second-raters and wash-outs. But she was used to dealing with crazy Palestinian bomb-throwers, not the cooler variety of American industrial spy. "Sorry," I said. "Didn't mean to sound patronizing. I just don't think you would have tumbled onto Black's game if you had been looking for the obvious." I allowed myself a chuckle. "He's a sly kinda guy, our Mr. Black. If I had been one step behind him, he might have gotten away with it."

Mickey opened her mouth to ask the obvious next question, but again we were interrupted by the stewardess. She gave me a fresh Bloody Mary and handed Mickey her ginger ale, then quietly asked that I lower my window shade. Unnoticed by either of us, the in-flight movie had started;

199

special-effects starships and Jedi masters were leaping across the narrow screen. I was almost tempted to curtail our chat and put on the headphones.

"The hair you found?" Mickey's manner had thawed a little; she was no longer irate so much as she was curious. "You didn't explain what . . ."

"Oh, right. The hair." I sipped my drink—still a bit too bland, and not enough vodka in it either—and put it aside. "Black's a biochemist who works at a major biotech firm, right? That means he has access to all sort of advanced technology, not the least of which is the stuff they use for genetic research."

"I understand that. But what does that have to do with . . . ?"

"He needed to smuggle a lot of company information out of his lab, but he couldn't do so through ordinary means, right? So he borrowed a trick some researchers at Mt. Sinai University devised a few years ago as an experiment. He took the records he needed, coded them as a long DNA sequence, and transferred them to an organic medium . . . in this case, a strand of his own hair."

Her mouth dropped open as her eyes widened. "You can do this?"

"If you know what you're doing, sure. DNA is made up of a series of nucleotides, and geneticists code them by assigning them letters from the alphabet. Rearrange those nucleotides by their letter-codes, and you've got a form of microscopic cryptography. All you have to do then is impress them on a medium . . . the Mt. Sinai scientists used the back of a postage stamp for their experiment . . . and you've got something like microdot. Only better, because it not only holds more information, but also because you have to know the genetic code they used in order to decipher the message. Sort of like shared-key computer encryption."

I found a new level of respect in Michaela's face as she stared at me. "How did you know about this?"

"I read about it in the *New York Times*." Which was only a half-truth. It was published in the *Times*, yes, and also in *Nature*, but I first heard about it in a classified memo which was circulated around the CIA shortly before I bailed out. "It's actually easy to do, if you know how. A seventeen-year-old girl from Long Island duplicated the same feat only a year later. Earned her a prize in a high school science contest."

Mickey was impressed. "Smart kid."

"Finding the message is only half the battle, of course. Once Jim locates it with an electron microscope, he'll still need to determine the exact nucleotide sequence which was used to encode the message. Once we've got Black under our thumb, though, he'll probably be willing to sing."

"If he doesn't give us the slip." Mickey frowned. "Your stunt with the flycam . . ."

"It tipped off his handler, sure. He may have already called Black and told him that they've been blown." I picked up her magazine from her lap and flipped through it. "It's more likely that Curly's probably going to let him twist in the wind while he catches the next flight to Italy. Black's tied down, though . . . wife, kids, a nice house, a career while it's still there. It's going to be harder for him to run, and that much easier for us to cut a deal once we catch up with him."

"I've seen it happen." She gave a little shrug as she sipped at her ginger ale. "My team once had to pursue a car-bomber all the way to Peru before we were able to make a collar."

She didn't say whether her people had made any sort of

201

deal, but I rather suspected otherwise. I handed the magazine back to her. "This isn't the same thing. You're talking about state-sponsored terrorism. I'm talking about companies who hire professionals who, in turn, get poor slobs like Black to take the shitty end of the stick. It's a whole different ball game."

"I see. So you're implying that I'm not ready for his sort of thing." Mickey shoved the magazine into her seat pocket, then pulled out the packet containing her own headphones. "How very enlightening."

One step forward, two steps back. "I didn't say that. I was just trying to . . ."

"Thank you. I'll take your advice under consideration." Mickey withdrew the headphones from the bag, slipped them over her head, and inserted the plug into the audio socket beneath her armrest. Then she pushed back her seat and let herself be lured into a fantasy world where good and evil were clearly delineated, where justice was meted out with light sabers and laser guns.

After awhile, I joined her there. It wasn't a bad movie, if you wanted to escape from reality for awhile.

A Walk Across Mars

It's an image which has remained with us for over twenty-five years, one which appears in every history textbook, has been printed on posters and digitalized on countless web sites. It's familiar even to those who hadn't been born yet and thus don't remember when it was on the front page of every newspaper in the world. It's more famous than the picture of Neil Armstrong descending the ladder of *Ares 2* or the one of Alexei Leonov standing on the Martian surface between the raised flags of the United States and the Union of Soviet Socialist Republics. It looks like this . . .

Two men in Mars suits caked with red dust, struggling across the stony tundra of Utopia Planitia. The figure on the right is barely able to walk: his right leg is limp and twisted, his boot dragging against the ground. His left arm is clumsily draped across the shoulders of the figure on the left, who somehow manages to stand erect; his right arm is wrapped around his comrade's waist, his left hand raised toward the camera. The astronaut on the right is looking down, but the man on the left stares straight at us; his helmet's sun visor is raised, and we can see his face: haggard, exhausted, grimly determined to stay alive.

You've seen this photo countless times. I shouldn't have to remind you what it's about. Lt. Commander Jeffery Carroll and Major David Park, two American members of the International Mars Expedition, returning to Utopia Base after being lost on Mars for eighteen hours. During what should have been a routine sortie, their rover rolled down a dry river channel nearly twenty miles from camp. The rover lost pressure and its high-gain antenna was snapped off, and Park's leg was broken, yet both men managed to survive the crash. With long-distance radio contact with *Ares 1* lost and only four tanks of air between the two of them, they set out across the unmapped wilderness, Carroll half-carrying Park as they fought their way through the cold Martian night until, midway through the following morning, they came within sight of Utopia Base.

The picture was taken by Sergei Roskov, the first man to reach Carroll and Park, and it came to symbolize the International Mars Expedition. There may never be another Mars mission; nearly three decades later, public opinion is still divided over how worthwhile it may have been to spend nearly $100 billion on a project which resulted in few tangible benefits. Yet only the most cynical can deny that the Carroll and Park's ordeal was the great story of 1976 . . . and twenty-five years later, everyone still wants to know how these two men remained alive against all odds.

I know. And God help me, I wish I didn't.

I'm a word doctor.

When someone asks me what I do for a living, I tell them I'm a writer, and when they ask me what I write, I say that I'm a biographer, yet both descriptions are inadequate and somewhat elusive. Oh, I've written a couple of novels, but I've seldom met anyone who has ever read them; my third book was a biography of John F. Kennedy, but since few people today remember the Massachusetts senator who lost to Nixon in the 1960 presidential election, there's not much point in mentioning it. Yet the JFK book received a few favorable reviews—*Publisher's Weekly* called it "one of the best political biographies of the past few years"—and a couple of editors took notice.

Not long after the Kennedy book was published, someone I knew at Random House phoned to ask whether I was interested in doing a little rewrite work on an autobiography of . . . well, since my contract forbids me from identifying her, let's put it this way: she's a legendary film actress, she's not very bright, and she once slept with Jack. Random House paid her a large advance for her memoirs, but she seemed to be having trouble with it—two years later, all she had produced were ten pages—and her editor felt that the time had come for someone else to come in and give her a little advice and assistance.

Advice and assistance. The next time you see a bestseller allegedly written by an actor, a sports figure, a rock star, or a major politician—that is, a celebrity who shouldn't have enough time, talent, or intelligence to write a book—flip to the acknowledgements page. Somewhere in there, usually near the bottom, will be something like this: ". . . and many thanks to so-and-so, for all his advice and assistance in writing these memoirs."

Chances are, this is the person who really wrote the book. The celeb may have gone so far as to actually write the first draft, but more often than not a ghostwriter cobbled together the book from a handful of notes and several hours of tape-recorded interviews. The real author receives a flat fee for his or her work, but it's the celeb who does the book tours and makes late-night guest appearances with David, Conan and Jay. It's not a book so much as it is another consumer item featuring their likeness, no different than a cereal box or a wall calendar.

The actress's memoirs sold a couple of million copies, and word got around that I was a reliable wordsmith. Over the course of the next several years, I rendered advice and assistance to a rapper who could barely spell his real name, an actor whom I interviewed in his trailer between takes of his next Oscar-nominated film, a Colorado congressman with presidential aspirations (my least-successful project; his autobiography was published the week after he finished last in the New Hampshire primary) and a radio talk-show host who spent most of his time lying about the size of his . . . um, microphone. I receive my usual mid-five figure fee for these book-products, which resemble literature in much the same way that cheese-product tastes like cheese, and when I feel creative I bang out mystery stories. Yes, I'm a hack, but I'm a damn good hack. It pays the rent, and it beats working for living.

In the autumn of 2000, I got a call from a certain editor with whom I had worked before, wondering if I was presently available. I wanted to work on a novel, my first in quite some time, but Christmas was just a few months away and I needed the money. So I asked who the author was, and my friend in New York told me it was Jeffery Carroll.

I'm not a space buff, but I was aware that he was one of the men in that famous photo. The editor informed me that, twelve months earlier, Jeff Carroll had quietly signed a contract for his memoirs. The deal had been in the seven-figure range, yet his publisher considered it a good investment. After all, Jeff Carroll was not only the pilot who had managed to guide *Ares 2* to a safe landing despite unexpected difficulties, but he was also the man who had carried Dave Park back to Utopia Base. Even more than Alexei Leonov or Neil Armstrong, the co-leaders of the International Mars Expedition, he was considered the hero of the *Ares* mission. Leonov had produced his memoir, *Journey to a Red Planet*, almost twenty years ago—a bestseller then, now out-of-print and largely forgotten—and Armstrong had remained reticent about his role in history, preferring an anonymous life in Ohio. A heart attack had killed Park six years ago, so no one would ever get his side of the story. This left Carroll as the *Ares* alumnus most likely to produce a *New York Times* bestseller.

Yet nearly a year had gone by, and Carroll hadn't delivered so much as an outline. When the editor phoned Carroll's literary agent to inquire about the delay, he was told that Jeff Carroll had recently been diagnosed with liver cancer. Although chemotherapy had knocked it into remission, no one was sure how much longer he would live. Carroll still wanted to publish his memoirs—in fact, now faced with his own mortality, the former astronaut was determined to tell his story—yet it was no longer possible for him to write the book himself.

Was I interested in taking the job? Of course I was, and not just because the money was good. For some time now, I had wanted to write about someone whose fame had come from something less ephemeral than pop culture. Jeffery Carroll wasn't the product of starmaking machinery; he had once walked on Mars, and this was a more significant achievement than making movies or cutting rap albums.

So I told the editor to fax me a contract, and that's how I became Jeff Carroll's confessor.

Jeffery Carroll lived in western Massachusetts, his home an 18th century cedar-shingle farmhouse on a hilltop outside Northampton. A country road no one can find without specific directions, a mailbox with only a number on it, and a view of the Holyoke mountain range: if you wanted to get away from everyone, you couldn't do much better.

His live-in nurse answered the door: a broad-shouldered woman in her mid-fifties, no-nonsense yet polite and soft-spoken in a Yankee sort of way. Since Jeff Carroll's former wife Louise had passed away several years ago—indeed, they had divorced only a couple of months after he returned from Mars—and they didn't have any children, she was the only person who saw Carroll on a daily basis. After taking my coat and offering me a cup of coffee, Dorothy led me through the living room. I caught a brief glimpse of various mementoes—a group photo of the *Ares* crew, a wood model of the Ares 2 lander, his Congressional Medal of Honor framed above the fieldstone hearth—before we reached the glass door leading to a screened-in back porch.

She quietly opened it, peered outside. "You awake?" she asked quietly. A pause. "The writer's here." Another pause, then she stepped aside. "He's expecting you. Go on. I'll bring you your coffee."

In all the pictures I'd seen of Jeffery Carroll during my preliminary research, he had been a robust, dark-haired man with stylish '70s sideburns, his demeanor usually taciturn although the camera had occasionally caught a wry grin. That wasn't the person who waited for me on his back porch; pale and shrunken, nearly bald save for a few whips of white hair, seated in a steel-frame wheelchair with a blanket around his waist even though it was a warm Indian summer afternoon. He was sixty-nine years old. He could have easily passed for ninety.

The years hadn't been kind to him, and he knew it. Carroll peered at me through heavy-lidded eyes. "Who were you expecting?" he rasped. "Neil Armstrong?"

"No, sir," I said. "Never met him."

It was the best I could manage, but he seemed to think it was funny. He grinned and favored me with a dry laugh. "You and me both, and I went to Mars with him. Either he's the smartest guy I've ever known or . . ."

He stopped, shook his head. "Never mind. Rule one . . .

let the living speak for themselves. And if we slander the dead, they're just going to have to sue." The grin faded and he gave me a sharp look. "Think you can live with that?"

There was a wicker chair across from him. I settled into it, placing my notebook and cassette recorder on the low table between us. "No problem at all, Colonel. Besides, the dead can't sue for libel . . ."

"Nice thing to know. Rule two . . . I'm Jeff. Haven't been a colonel in twenty years . . . twenty-two years . . . whatever." His gaze drifted toward the mowed hay field beyond his porch. The fall foliage was at peak; reddish-gold maple leaves lay across the yellow meadow, the wooded hillside draped with harlequin colors. He savored this beauty through the eyes of a man who knew he wouldn't see another autumn.

"This is supposed to be when we get to know each other," he said. "Small talk about things that don't matter . . . how your flight was, how my day has been, how cold it was here this morning, how it's still warm where you live." He sighed. "But you know, there comes a time when . . . well, you just don't have any time left to waste. No offense, but let's just get on with it, okay?"

He was dying, and he was telling me this was to be his final testament. Without bothering to ask his permission to do so, I reached forward to switch on my recorder. He must have heard the sound, for he glanced in my direction. "You ready?" he asked, and I nodded. "Okay, let's get started."

I opened my notebook, flipped to the first page of the questions I wanted to ask. "So, Colonel . . . Jeff, I mean . . . when were you born?"

He ignored me. Still gazing at the autumn hills, he began to speak. "On Wednesday, July 28, 1979, I tried to kill Dave Park . . ." And then he looked back at me. "Or would you rather that I start at the beginning?"

The relationship between Jeff Carroll and Dave Park went back almost fifteen years, when they were recruited from their respective services—the Navy for Carroll, the Air Force for Park—for the U.S. Space Force astronaut training program. At first they were little more than fighter jocks vying for the same job, yet as they made their way through the program the two men developed a deep friendship. Although there was often cut-throat rivalry among the other candidates, Carroll and Park preferred to work together rather than try to trip up the other guy. They helped each other cram for exams, supported one another during survival training in Arizona and worked together to figure out how to beat the cockpit simulators. The wash-out rate was high; although sixty rookies tried out for the USSF during the summer of 1962, only twenty remained eight weeks later. It came as no surprise to anyone that both Carroll and Park received their astronaut wings and were formally invited to join the USSF.

In retrospect, it's easy to see why the pair got along so well, for they had much in common. Both were originally from the South—Jeff Carroll born and raised in Virginia, Dave Park a Florida native—and both had joined the armed services with the ambition of becoming fliers, although only Carroll had seen active duty as a carrier pilot aboard the U.S.S. *Nimitz* while Park was stationed in West Germany. Both had married their teenage sweethearts; Patty Carroll met her future husband when he had played center on the high school football team, and Louise Park found Dave when they had worked together on the yearbook staff. Both were clean-cut, conservative young men who voted Republican, regularly attended church, and had no trouble with being straight-arrows at a time when many guys their age were letting their hair grow over their collars and smoking reefer.

"Maybe that's hard to swallow, but we liked it that way." Thirty years later, there's a wistful smile on Jeff Carroll's face. "I mean, here was all this stuff breaking out all over . . . anti-war protests, sit-ins at lunch counters . . . and we just didn't want to have anything to do with it. Dave and I had our own agenda."

"You wanted to go into space."

"Right on." He laughs, a little self-conscious for using an expression he probably disdained when it was popular. "So far as we were concerned, there was only one thing worth doing, and that was beating the Russians to the Moon." He gave me a sidewise wink. "And, of course, we wanted to be there when it happened."

Yet history didn't work in their favor. While Jeff became a pilot for the Atlas-class shuttles which regularly lifted off from Merritt Island, ferrying into orbit the components of *Space Station One*, Dave opted instead to train as navigator for the lunar reconnaissance mission scheduled to be a precursor to *Eagle One*. Each man thought their career choices would put them on the short-list for the first lunar expedition; indeed, Dave was aboard the *Columbus* when it flew around the Moon on Christmas Eve, 1968. Yet Jeff continued to be a shuttle jockey long after Eagle One touched down in the Sea of Tranquillity; he and his best friend sat in the TV room of Jeff's house in Cocoa Beach, drinking beer and trying not to feel sorry from themselves the night they watched John Harper Wilson set foot on the Moon.

"Why did you get passed up?"

"Politics." Jeff shrugs. "Officially, I was told I was too valuable as an Atlas pilot, and Dave was told that he got the cut because he'd been to the Moon once already. But the fact of the matter was that the Space Force was already on the way out, and I guess we were seen as being part of the old guard."

Dorothy returns to make sure he is comfortable. She asks if I want another cup of coffee; I tell her I do, and take the opportunity to flip the cassette. Jeff waits until I'm ready, then continues.

"The night Johnny Wilson walked on the Moon, Dave and I got drunk. I mean, really loaded. Whiskey, beer . . . we were gonzo. My place was on the beach, so we left the girls behind and went for a long walk on the sand. Just hanging onto each other, not knowing whether we wanted to laugh or cry, doing a little of both. And somewhere along the way, I fell down on my knees and . . . I dunno, maybe it was just the booze, but I made a solemn vow.

" 'Screw the Moon,' I said, 'we're going to Mars. You and me, man, we're going to Mars.' And Dave said, 'I'm with you. Hell or high water, we're going to Mars.' "

It may have been a drunken vow, yet they both remembered it. Robert F. Kennedy was the new President, and he favored the creation of a new civilian space agency which would pursue non-military objectives. On September 6, 1969, Congress passed the Space Act, which established the National Aeronautics and Space Administration. NASA needed a major objective to justify its existence, and the Russians had become interested in establishing *detente* with the Americans, so ten months later the U.S. and the U.S.S.R. signed the International Space Treaty which, among other things, called for a joint American-Russian expedition to Mars.

With the USSF being phased out, many Space Force astronauts tendered their resignations. Carroll and Park stayed on, however, and when NASA and Glavkosmos began putting together the twelve-man team for the International Mars Expedition, they found themselves near the top of the list. On September 2, 1971, the prime crew for Project Ares was publicly announced during a Washington press conference. Colonel Neil Armstrong and Colonel Alexei Leonov were presented as the mission's co-leaders, and standing next to them were Lieutenant Commander Jeffery Carroll, the pilot of *Ares 2*, and Major Dave Park, the navigator of *Ares 1*.

"That was the proudest moment of my life, being introduced as the man who'd land a ship on Mars," Jeff says. "There was a reception for us that evening at the White House, and after it was over, Dave and I went back to the Hilton. We got out of our monkey suits and had a nightcap in the bar. A quiet little celebration, just the two of us. We were on our way to Mars. Nothing could stop us now."

Yet there's no warmth in his eyes, no trace of nostalgia in his voice. "I didn't know it then, but that was the last night we'd meet as friends."

Shortly after Christmas, 1971, the six American members of the *Ares* flight crew relocated to Houston, where they would undergo mission training at the Von Braun Manned Space Center for the next four years. No one liked moving to Texas. Their families had established roots in Florida; the nearest beach was hundreds of miles away, and instead of Route A1A and Disneyworld, all Houston had to offer were miles of strip malls and the NFL's worst football team. Not only that, but every two or three months the astronauts had to fly to the U.S.S.R., where they would spend several weeks training with their Russian teammates at the Star City complex.

"It may have been tough for us, but it was even worse for our families." Jeff shakes his head. "Patty never saw me except on the rare weekend or holiday . . . sometimes not even then. Dave was in Houston a little more frequently than I was, but I don't think he saw much of Louise either. By then they had a little boy, Scott, but . . . well, I don't think Dave got much chance to see his boy grow up.

"After the first few months, I started to notice a change in Patty. She became distant. We'd always been close, never keeping anything from each other. Even when we argued . . . and, y'know, old married couples often quarrel, because that's the way they hash out their problems . . . we always ended up the same way. Usually in bed." A reticent smile, quickly gone. "But now there wasn't even that. We'd have a disagreement over something, and she'd simply surrender. 'Whatever you want, Jeff,' even when I knew she didn't like it. But we didn't . . . I mean, she wouldn't . . ."

"A problem with sex?"

His face darkens. He glances away. This isn't something he's comfortable talking about. "When we . . . when we did it, it wasn't because she wanted to. Before we moved to Houston, there had never been . . . y'know, that sort of problem. Now I was spending twelve, sometimes sixteen hours a day at the space center, and then I'd be gone for a few weeks, either off to Russia or up to the Wheel, and then I'd come home and . . . well, she simply didn't want to be with me."

All of a sudden, he became impatient. Tossing aside his blanket, Jeff raised himself from his wheelchair, let his felt slippers touch the floor for the first time. "It's too cold out here," he muttered, reaching for the gnarled walking stick resting against the wall. "Dorothy! Coming in!"

The porch door opened, banged shut. His nurse gently

helped Jeff hobble across the porch, scolding him for walking without permission. I looked away as she guided him into the house; for the first time, I noticed the aluminum bedpan tucked beneath his wheelchair. Dorothy returned a minute later; she gave me an apologetic smile as she picked up the bedpan. "Give us a moment," she said quietly, then she whisked through the porch door into the living room.

I made a few notes, put in a fresh tape. Early afternoon; the day was warm but a northern breeze had come in, rustling the fallen leaves beneath the porch. Looking out over the mountains, I noticed a daytime moon hovering in the bright blue sky. Jeff Carroll never went there, but Dave Park was one of the first men to see its far side. I found myself wondering what it must be like to see another world, not as a distant and abstract object but as a real thing . . .

But when you're so far from Earth, what is it that you leave behind?

"You can come in now." Framed within the porch door, Dorothy waited for me. "He's a little tired, but we wants to go on." And, softly: "Please . . . be gentle. This is taking a lot out of him."

I picked up my recorder and notebook. The interview would continue, but I doubted it would be gentle. There were too many secrets, and my subject was unburdening himself of them, one at a time.

Ares 2, the larger of the two ships which went to Mars, was a monster. With a wingspan of 450 feet and weighing more than 1,800 tons, it was the largest vehicle ever assembled in space. Twenty-one Atlas flights were needed to carry its components up from the Cape, and sixteen more to bring up the pieces of *Ares 1*, the passenger vessel which would remain in orbit above Mars and eventually bring the crew back to Earth.

During winter of '74 and '75, Jeff Carroll was a regular visitor to Space Station One. His training in Houston and Russia now largely complete, one of his major tasks was overseeing construction of *Ares 2*. It wasn't easy. Several racks of electrical cable were laid in backward, two of the enormous fuel spheres belonging to the booster stage had hairline fractures which weren't discovered until after the spheres were test-pressurized, and one of the astronauts building the vehicle was killed while the return rocket was being mated to the wing fuselage. Jeff found himself sleeping in a narrow berth aboard the Wheel more often than in his own bed back home, and sometimes it would be weeks before he'd see his front lawn again.

"And all this time, Dave was in Houston." As he speaks, Jeff gazes at the polished wooden model of *Ares 2* upon the coffee table. "Most of his training was now being done in the simulator at Von Braun, so he wasn't going to Russia quite so often, and once *Ares 1* was finished he came up to the Wheel only a couple of times. I'd see him now and then, usually during mission briefings, and we'd say hello, sometimes grab lunch. I'd ask how Louise was doing, and he'd ask how Patty was doing, but . . . well, since we weren't seeing much of either of them, it was just polite conversation."

He's looking at the framed photo of his late wife, placed on the rough oak mantle above the fireplace. Dorothy quietly enters the living room, the floor creaking beneath her rubber-soled shoes. "Then one night in late May, just after the Memorial Day weekend, I returned early from a trip to the Wheel. Wasn't supposed to be back for another day or so, but at the last minute I managed to snag a ride back to the Cape aboard a cargo shuttle, then grabbed a commercial flight out of Orlando to Houston. Patty's birthday was coming up, and I wanted some time to go shopping for her."

He picks up a glass of water, takes a sip. "It was raining that night, really coming down hard. Didn't get home till around midnight. I was about to pull into the driveway when I saw there was already a car parked in front of the garage. I recognized it at once . . . it was Dave's Camaro."

He glances at me. "Guess you can already see where this is leading, right?" I say nothing, and he goes on. "Anyway, I drove down the street, then circled back and parked across from the house under a tree. Turned off the engine and waited. About a half-hour went by, then the front door opened. Someone came out . . . he was wearing a raincoat with the hood pulled up over his head . . . and he stopped on the porch. I saw Patty for a moment . . . she was standing just inside the door, wearing her robe . . . and then the guy in the raincoat turned around and kissed her."

A pause. "He kissed her. That's what I saw. Then he dashed out to his car and got in. The car started up, backed out of the driveway, and went down the street. Patty shut the door, and a couple of minutes later I saw the upstairs lights go out."

Jeff looks away. "I sat out there for a good, long time . . . another hour at least . . . not knowing what to do, not even what to think. Or maybe I was thinking lots of things. After a while I started up the car, pulled into my driveway, got out and walked into my house just like I always did. Had a glass of milk in the kitchen, then went upstairs. Patty was asleep, so I put on my pajamas and crawled into bed, trying not to wake her. The next morning I told her I had come home late, but I didn't tell her what I'd seen."

"You didn't . . . ?"

He shakes his head. "No . . . not then, or later. And I didn't take it up with Dave, either. Not that I wasn't tempted. When I saw him the next day, I was ready to punch him through the wall. Instead I left the room, went to the bathroom and threw some cold water on my face. After that, I tried to have as little to do with him as possible . . . but I never touched him, never made any threats, never said a word about what I had seen."

His eyes meet mine. "And you know why? Because I wanted to go to Mars."

Regardless of how angry or hurt he was, Jeff Carroll knew that, if he confronted Dave Park or separated from his wife, it would mean the end of his involvement with *Ares*. Just like the Space Force, NASA management was preoccupied with projecting a squeaky-clean public image; astronauts had been grounded for as little reason as being spotted drinking in a bar. Dave was all too aware that, if anyone discovered that one American member of the Ares team was having an affair with the wife of another member, they both would be dismissed from the mission and replaced by members of the back-up crew. Therefore, Jeff couldn't tell anyone what he had seen that night—not Patty, and not even Dave.

"I just . . ." He sighs, shakes his head. "I just let it go. Chalked it up as a one-night stand, maybe a bad mistake. Whatever the reason, I fell out of love with Patty that night, and Dave was no longer my friend. I tried to pretend like nothing happened. I never saw Dave's car at my house again, but Patty didn't seem to mind when I started sleeping in the guest room. I tried to make love to her a couple of times, but . . . well, it wasn't the same. She just went through the motions, and after the second time I gave up."

"And what about Dave?"

"Dave was . . ." Jeff considers the question, looks away. "Dave was my navigator. I needed him to get to Mars. And that's all there was to it."

On November 2, 1975, *Ares 1* and *Ares 2* simultaneously fired their main engines, and the two giant spacecraft began the long voyage to Mars.

Spending eight months in close quarters with a man who's been sleeping with your wife may seem intolerable, yet *Ares 1*'s crew sphere had three decks, and when that wasn't room enough there were many occasions to taxi over to *Ares 2*. Although it soon became obvious to everyone aboard that Carroll and Park weren't getting along, neither was there any outright animosity. Dave stayed away from Jeff, and Jeff . . .

"I blocked it out." Nestling a mug of hot chocolate against his stomach, Carroll leans back in his chair. With late afternoon setting in, Dorothy brings in some split wood and stokes a fire in the hearth, then retreats to an armchair on the other side of the living room. "Just put it out of my mind as best I could. I played chess with the Russians, wrote in my journal, rehearsed landing procedures with Neil. That sort of thing. When Dave and I had to interact with each other, we did so as professionally as possible." He shrugs. "And that's how we went to Mars. Not as enemies, but not as friends either."

The months went past, each day grinding against the next, as Mars gradually swelled in size, growing from a red-tinted star to a distinct sphere. During this time, the crew regularly received messages from home. Because of the ever-increasing time delay, these communiqués were usually transmitted as text messages, printed out on the com station's CRT screen. Although the Russians and most of the Americans received frequent letters from friends and family back home, Jeff seldom heard from Patty, and even then it was only the most terse greetings. On the other hand, Jeff observed that Dave received frequent letters from Louise. The fact that Louise Park was blissfully unaware that her husband recently had an affair with his best friend's wife rubbed salt in the wound, yet Jeff chose to bite his lip and look the other way. He turned his attention upon Mars, focused upon completing the mission.

It was good that he did so, for landing on Mars was more difficult than anyone expected. When the expedition reached its destination and *Ares 1* commenced its orbital survey, it was then that they found that the landing site was much rougher than expected. Instead of a vast plain of rolling dunes, Utopia Planitia was strewn with boulders, some large enough to damage the landing skids. Leonov was in favor of finding an alternate landing site, but Armstrong held out for Utopia Planitia; the terrain wasn't much better anywhere else they looked, and at least it was flat enough for the high-speed horizontal landing *Ares 2* was designed to make. Never once did anyone aboard seriously consider turning back, although many at NASA were in favor of aborting the mission.

On July 20, the ten members of the landing party boarded *Ares 2*, leaving two men aboard *Ares 1*. With Jeff Carroll in the left seat and Neil Armstrong in the right, the pilot fired the booster rockets for the final time, then jettisoned the stage and commenced the long, swift glide toward Mars.

Back on Earth, hundreds of millions of people were glued to their TVs, watching as Walter Cronkite and CBS science correspondent Arthur C. Clarke delivered a play-by-play commentary on the craft's perilous descent. In Houston, NASA flight controllers listened anxiously to the distant voices within their headsets, all too aware that, if something were to go catastrophically wrong, it would be fifteen minutes before they knew about it.

Yet within *Ares 2*, there was an almost eerie sense of calm. "No one really said anything on the way down," Jeff says, remembering the descent. "I just sat there, right hand on the stick, listening to Neil as he called out the numbers. I kept waiting for something to blow up, but it never did. In fact, it was easier than flying the simulator."

"Weren't you nervous?"

He smiles, shakes his head. "Not really. I knew that if we crashed, we'd be dead before we knew it. So long as we didn't crash, everything would be fine." He chuckles. "Besides, I was too busy handling that beast to have time to be scared."

False modesty or not, it was an extraordinary feat of flying. During the last few hundred feet of descent, Carroll spotted a stretch of ground which seemed a little less rocky; at the last possible moment, he turned the massive ship in that direction. Had he not done otherwise, *Ares 2* would have touched down in the middle of a boulder field, possibly snapping one of the skids and causing the ship to crash. As it turned out, he brought *Ares 2* to a safe landing, albeit one which rattled their teeth.

"Once Neil informed Mission Control that we were on the ground and I raised the return rocket to take-off position, I just lay back and stared up through the canopy. Below me, I could hear the rest of the guys yelling at each other, yelling at me . . . they were going nuts." Carroll shrugs, picks up his water glass. "The only thing on my mind was how weird it was to see a pink sky."

* * * * *

The expedition had been on Mars for little more than a week when Jeff Carroll tried to kill Dave Park.

By then they had unloaded their equipment from the lander and had set up camp: three hemispherical inflated tents and a small, semi-rigid greenhouse, powered by a solar-cell array with a small nuclear generator as back-up. The tents were cold at first, so much that the crew was reluctant to remove their suits after they cycled through the airlock, but after a couple of days the interior temperature rose to seventy-two degrees and they were able to walk around in shirt sleeves. Five men bunked in each of two tents—Carroll made sure that he didn't have to share quarters with Park—and the third tent served as laboratory, mess hall and rec room. A narrow well was plunged through the floor of Tent Three, where it tapped into the permafrost layer deep beneath the Martian regolith. Six days after landing, they had enough water to drink, with even a little left over for the occasional sponge bath.

Once the explorers made themselves at home, the rover was lowered from the lander's cargo bay and assembled on the surface. Designed and built by General Motors, it had oversized wire-mesh tires, four-wheel drive, and was powered by photovoltaic cells. Its maximum distance was fifty miles, which meant that it could travel twenty-five miles in any direction before it had to turn around and come back. The ride was bumpy and its pressurized two-seat cab wasn't much larger than a Volkswagen Beetle, but everyone wanted to take it for a cruise. The first soil tests hadn't revealed the presence of microbiological life, and the water melted from the permafrost was sterile, but everyone was convinced that, if they drove just ten or fifteen miles thataway, they'd find an oasis hiding beyond the horizon.

"One night over dinner, Alexei drew up a list of survey teams," Jeff says. "He and Neil were on the first one, of course, and then everyone else got their turn. I intended to team up with Yuri Antonov, but before I could say so Dave said he wanted to go out with me."

"I thought you two weren't getting along."

"We weren't. That's why it surprised me." Jeff shakes his head. "I think Alexei was surprised, too, because he gave Dave and me a certain look. Like, 'you sure you want to do this?' But Dave seemed insistent and I couldn't think of a good reason to object, so Alexei wrote down our names. We were the third team."

On the morning of July 28, Carroll and Park climbed aboard the rover and set out to the northeast. Their primary objective was a dry channel about twenty miles from Utopia Base; there they were to obtain core samples from beneath the soil of the ancient river bed. Carroll took the wheel, and Park was in the passenger seat. Although the rover was pressurized, Jeff kept his helmet on, only opening its visor. Dave removed his helmet, though, and placed it in his lap.

"We went for a couple of hours or so without saying much of anything," Jeff recalls. "I think we could have gone all day without speaking. Or at least I could have. But we were about eighteen miles from the base when Dave reached over and switched off the radio. Then he looked at me and said, 'Y'know, I think we need to talk.'

" 'About what?' I said. 'I don't think we've got anything to talk about.' And that was the truth, so far as I was concerned. I had done my best to forget it, and the last thing I wanted was to discuss something that had happened thirteen months ago and fifty million miles away.

"But Dave wasn't going to let it drop. 'You know what I

mean,' he said. 'That night you came home early, saw my car in your driveway.'

" 'I think you ought to shut up,' I said. 'I really don't want to discuss it.' He didn't say anything for a while. We were very close to the channel and I was skirting along the edge, trying to find a good place where we could go down and collect our samples. That's when he opened his mouth again. 'Has it ever occurred to you,' he said, 'that you didn't see what you thought you saw?'

"Well, that got me mad. 'Oh, c'mon, you think I'm stupid? What are you going to tell me, you had dropped by to borrow a cup of sugar?'

"I didn't meant to yell, but I was angry. I mean, really furious. 'No, that's not what I'm saying,' he says. 'I'm just trying to tell you that you're not the only one who got hurt that night.' "

Jeff hesitates, stares into the fireplace. I've seen people clam up when they get close to something they've kept secret for many years. Sometimes they fall back, tell you to stop the tape and forget everything you've just heard. But after a moment he takes a deep breath, forces himself to go on.

" 'That was my car you saw, all right,' he said, 'but I wasn't the one driving it. Fact was, I was flying back from Russia that night. If you'd asked me, I would have told you . . . even showed you the ticket stub to prove it.'

"By now I was so furious I wasn't even looking where I was driving. 'If that wasn't you,' I said, 'then who was the guy I saw kiss Patty goodnight at my front door?'

" 'That wasn't me,' he said. 'That was Louise.' "

A long silence. Jeff lets out his breath, picks up his drink. The glass is empty, yet when he turns to call for Dorothy she reappears from the kitchen, bringing him another glass of water. As she bends down to give it to him, she whispers something in his ear. He shakes his head and she nods reluctantly, then turns to leave the room again.

"Patty and Louise . . . I never suspected." The glass trembles in his hand as he takes a sip. "Neither did Dave, for that matter. He didn't figure it out for a couple of months after I spotted his wife leaving my house, and then only after Louise came right out and told him."

"Why did she . . . ?"

"Want to hear something funny?" He grins. "He thought *I* was having an affair with *her* . . . but he didn't say or do anything about it for the same reason I didn't! He didn't want to get booted off the mission!"

The grin vanishes. "So here we were, two stupid bastards, each thinking the other guy's fooling around with his wife when the fact of the matter was that they're fooling around with each other. Two All-American boys off playing astronaut, never suspecting that their All-American girls could . . ."

He shrugs, shakes his head. "Anyway, when he learned the truth, he decided not to tell me. He knew how much it would hurt, and that was the last thing he wanted to do. So he kept mum and hoped things would work out on their own. And when he couldn't stay quiet any longer . . . well, I was hurt all right. In fact, I went berserk."

"You said you tried to kill him."

He looks back at me. "When he told me it was Louise I'd seen leaving my house, I simply couldn't believe it. It was like . . . I don't know, like a red curtain came down in front of my eyes. I forgot where I was, what I was doing, just threw myself at him."

Jeff closes his eyes. "I had my hands around Dave's

throat and he was trying to fight me off when everything turned upside down. All of the sudden, we were rolling end over end down the side of the channel."

The rover crashed at the bottom of the dry channel. Although Dave was knocked out, Jeff remained conscious. The fact that he hadn't removed his helmet is what saved them both, because the rover began to leak air as soon as it came to rest. Jeff found Dave's helmet, put it over his head, and managed to repressurize his suit before he suffered a fatal embolism. He then managed to pry open the door and drag Dave from the wreckage. Dave was alive, but his right leg was broken just below the knee.

Even worse, the rover's high-gain antenna had been demolished, as was the satellite dish which would have enabled them to contact *Ares 1*. However, there were two replacement oxygen tanks in the rover; neither had been ruptured, and since their suit tanks were fully charged, they had enough air for another twenty hours. So the two men had two choices: either remain where they were and pray for rescue, or walk back to Utopia Base.

They decided to walk.

"We worked out a lot of things that night, Dave and I. Perhaps we should have been saving our air, but when you're facing death, it's easier to talk than not to."

The fire is dying out. Jeff reaches over to pick up a cane resting against the hearth, then carefully eases himself out of his chair. It's the first time I've seen him stand unassisted; I almost get up to help him, then remember this was someone who once carried another man on his shoulder across nineteen miles of the most lonesome desert known to humankind. I stay in my seat and watch as he hobbles to the fireplace.

"I won't go into what we talked about," he says as he opens the screen and prods the cinders with an iron poker. "Perhaps some things should be left private. Suffice to say, by the time we made it back to camp, we were friends again. Sergei saw us coming, and just before he reached us he raised his camera and took that shot everyone's seen."

"I've always wondered about that. You've got your hand raised toward the camera. What were you trying to do?"

"A lot of people have asked me that. Everyone thinks I was pleading for help." He shuts the screen, puts the poker back in its rack. "Truth is, I was trying to stop Sergei from taking that shot. I thought we looked like idiots, and I didn't want anyone to see us crawling back into camp with dirt all over our suits."

He moves slowly across the living room. "Dave and I spent the rest of our time on Mars as friends, and we stayed friends long after we returned to Earth. Patty and I divorced not long afterward . . . fact is, we separated even before I came back, but kept it a secret until we were no longer in the public eye. Dave had been trying to patch things up with Louise . . . that's what all those messages were about . . . but she was already in a relationship with another woman . . . not Patty, thank God . . . and she had moved out by the time we got home. She made one brief appearance with him, when we received our Congressional Medals of Honor, but that was the last time I saw her. Patty was there also, under the same pretense, but . . . well, she had her own life, and it didn't include me."

He stops in front of an antique rolltop desk, opens a drawer. "Anyway, that's pretty much it. That's all I have to tell you. You got it, right?"

"Well, yes, but . . ." I glance at my recorder. It holds a two-hour cassette, the second one I've used during our interview, and there's at least twenty minutes of tape left. "There's more, isn't there? I mean, that's just part of the story."

"Uh-huh. The hard part . . . the part I couldn't bring myself to write." As he turns away from the desk, he holds three spiral-bound notebooks. "I hope you don't have trouble with my handwriting, and I apologize for my grammar . . . anyway, it's all there."

I stare at the manuscript as he places it in my hands. He lurches back to his chair, collapses into it with visible relief. "Sorry, but I had to do it this way," he says. "My words weren't . . . well, maybe you can do better."

I open the top notebook, skim a couple of pages. His handscript is neat, his prose effortless to read. Perhaps it could use a little line-editing, but on the whole it doesn't appear to need much revision. "So what do you want me to . . . I mean, what you've just told me?"

Jeff says nothing for a few moments. His gaze returns to the fireplace; he's very tired, and somehow no longer seems interested. "Do with it as you will. It's your book now."

I took Jeffery Carroll's manuscript home and worked on it for the next eight weeks. It was the easiest rewrite job I've ever done: a little chapter restructuring here, some scene embellishment there. His spelling and punctuation were awful, but nothing a good copy-editor couldn't have handled. Easiest money I ever made . . .

Except when it came to writing the chapter where he spoke the truth about what happened on Mars. Even after I transcribed our interview and wrote it as straight first-person text, I went through several drafts, trying to find just the right tone. Yet never could I imagine the way he must have felt, all those lonely hours hiking through the Martian night, coming to grips with the fact that Dave Park, a friend whom he thought had betrayed him, had instead tried to protect him.

So much pain. So much courage.

I was almost through with the book and my editor was breathing down my neck when, two weeks before Christmas, Dorothy called to tell me that Jeff had passed away. He had gone upstairs to take a mid-afternoon nap, and when she went up to wake him for dinner, she discovered he had died in his sleep.

I attended the funeral. Colonel Jeffery Carroll was buried with full military honors at Arlington National Cemetery; the President delivered a brief eulogy, then a Marine Corps honor guard fired a twenty-one gun salute as Navy jets roared across the slate sky in the missing-man formation. I stood in the back of a crowd of nearly five hundred people, none of whom I knew except for Dorothy. I saw her but she didn't see me, and I didn't try to approach her. When it was over, I caught the next flight home.

I finished the book and sent it to the publisher. My editor loved it, and even paid me a bonus. *A Walk Across Mars* was published the following summer and became a major bestseller. If you haven't read it, you should, because it's good and it's true, and most of the words were his own. Except for the parts I decided to leave out.

So far as I'm concerned, that's no one's business. We need heroes. And sometimes, a lie is better than the truth.

Tom Swift and

His Humongous Mechanical Dude

(With apologies to Victor Appleton II)

1. Danger!

"Watch out, Tom!" Junior Bud exclaimed. "You're burning a hole in your crotch!"

Tom looked down to see the smouldering ash which had fallen from the bowl of his bong. Just as his best friend warned him, it had come to rest in the lap of his baggy shorts. "Aw, man!" he said heatedly as he swatted the ember away. "I just bought these yesterday!"

The ash fell to the living room floor, where it left a brown scorch mark in the plush ermine carpet. Tom ignored it as he carefully inspected the four-foot Pyrex tube nestled between his knees. Junior Bud exhaled the lungful of smoke he had managed to hold throughout the emergency. "Bummer, dude," his chum said. "Did you lose any water?"

"Naw. Water's cool. Just gotta reload, that's all." Tom Swift III reached down to the glass coffee table, where a small heap of seedless sensimilla lay on top of the current issue of *Scientific American*. Tom hated having ruined another pair of shorts, but he hated even more wasting good herb. But he had taken too big of a toke from that last bowl, and it had caused him to cough into the bong. Next time, he would have to be more careful. "Wanna see what else is on the tube?"

"Uh . . . sure. Hold on." Junior Bud glanced around the spacious living room for a few moments, searching the coffee table and mahogany end tables, until he found the remote lying on the armrest of his chair next to his elbow. He picked it up and pointed it at the 72-inch flat-screen TV hanging from the wall. It was showing a PBS documentary about Mars. "Boring," he said, and started channel-surfing. "So where's your ol' man, dude?"

"Somewhere in Egypt," Tom said distantly as he stuffed a pinch of dope into the bong's small wooden bowl. "Doing archeology stuff, I dunno." This was an untruth, for Tom knew that his father, the famed inventor Tom Swift, Jr., had flown the Flying Lab out to Redmon, Washington, to play golf with Bill Gates. But that was major uncool. "Where's your ol' man?"

"With your ol' man, I guess." Junior Bud was the son of Bud Barclay, and their fathers had been best friends since their teenage years back in the 1950s. That was long before rock was invented; Tom imagined they must have gone to piano recitals when they weren't building rocket ships or jet-propelled subs. "Think he'll ask you if you got a job yet when he gets home?"

"I'm working on it." Tom located the lighter, flicked it to life. "Went to the mall, filled out some aps. I might get a call from Radio Shack. The manager recognized my name."

"If he calls back, are you going to take the job?" Junior Bud was still playing with the remote, clicking from one channel to another in two-second intervals. Oprah. Boring. Sally Jesse. Boring. African apes. Boring. Some congressman on C-Span. Boring. "Star Trek: The Next Generation." Boring. War in Eastern Europe. Boring . . .

Tom took another hit, a little more carefully this time, and considered the question as he held the smoke in his lungs. Then he exhaled, and after the initial rush subsided, he reached over to the phone and switched on the answering machine. The thought of working bummed him out. "Want some?" he asked, offering the bong to Junior Bud.

"Sure." Junior Bud barely diverted his attention from the TV as he extended his left hand across his right arm. Just as Tom placed the bong in his palm, his friend sat bolt upright in his chair. "Whoa, check it out! My favorite show!"

Tom gazed at the screen. Bud had found some Japanese anime'. Enormous robots vaguely resembling shogun warriors were locked in combat, hacking at one another with giant plasma swords. Every now and then, the action was intercut with guys and chicks wearing skin-tight outfits, their eyes wide as saucers, their mouths tiny ovals moving out of synch with their overdubbed English dialogue.

"Aw, dude, this sucks." Tom shook his head. "Find something else."

"Naw, this is great!" Junior Bud hunched forward, propping the bong between his legs as he stared at the TV. "It's called . . . it's called . . . well, I don't remember what it's called, but it's great." He reached for the lighter, then pointed to a blond-haired girl wearing what looked like a school uniform. One of the robots had just picked her up in his fist, and she was screaming in a shrill, high-pitched voice. "Watch, man. I bet she gets her clothes ripped off."

Tom watched, and sure enough, a few seconds later the robot tore away the girl's blouse and kerchief. She had a nice pair, he had to admit, but watching anime' wasn't exactly his idea of getting off. If anything, it only made him more frustrated. The last time he had a regular girlfriend was while he was still in college, but she dumped him after he dropped out in his freshman year, and ever since then the only time he got laid was when he picked up some high school skank at some rave club on Long Island. Junior Bud couldn't be doing much better if he was getting aroused by cartoons.

"That robot's a wimp," Tom said, trying to change the subject. "My dad's got a bigger one than that."

"No way." Junior Bud finally lit the bong. He sucked in a long hit, then raised his mouth from the smoking tube and regarded his lifelong friend with unfocused eyes. "That mofo's fifty feet tall," he croaked. "It can't be bigger than that. It's scientifically impossible."

"Way, dude. It's . . ." Tom stopped to think about it for a moment, but found he couldn't remember just how tall his father's robot was. "Well, it's bigger than that."

"Sure. As if."

"Truth, dude," Tom swore as he reached for the bong. "It's down at my dad's plant, in the warehouse. He even let me work it once."

"No way." Junior Bud exhaled as he put his Nikes up on the coffee table. "Your ol' man never lets you near his stuff."

Junior Bud was correct. The elder Swift was reluctant to allow his son to use any of the miraculous inventions he and Bud's father had devised during their youth. At least not since the time when Tom had borrowed his ultrasonic cycloplane and attempted to fly it to New Jersey for the Monsters of Rock show at the Meadowlands. Fortunately, Tom ejected from the craft before it crashed in the Long Island Sound, but that escapade had caused him to be grounded for a month.

"Yeah, well, he's out of town." On sudden impulse, Tom stood up. "I know where he keeps the keys. C'mon, I'll show it to you."

"Aw, man . . ." Junior Bud stared at the TV. " 'The Simpsons' are coming on in a minute."

"You've seen it before." Tom picked up his cap, put it on backward. "Let's go."

2. An Amazing Errand

Tom and Junior Bud climbed into Tom's roadster, a bright red Jeep Wrangler with pneumatic jacks and monster speakers, and tore down the driveway of the Swift family estate where Tom lived in the guest house. They headed for Swift Enterprises, but first they stopped at the mall in the nearby town of Shopton because Junior Bud remembered that the new Fugazi CD was due out today. They spent a few minutes in the record store, looking for boarder music while trying to ignore the assistant manager following them through the aisles. Tom had been caught shoplifting in the store twice already, but each time the manager had been persuaded not to press charges after Mr. Swift made a few phone calls. Tom picked up four CDs and put them on his American Express card, then they left the mall and continued to his father's plant.

Swift Enterprises was a sprawling complex of laboratories, machine shops and aircraft hangars spread across four square miles. The original facilities had been built by Tom's grandfather, and Mr. Swift had expanded the plant by developing some useless wetlands adjacent to the runways. As they roared up to the gatehouse in front of the main entrance, an elderly security guard stepped out of the shack to greet them.

"Turn that down!" he shouted, cupping his ears against the music blasting from Tom's car stereo.

"What'd you say?" Tom asked indeterminably.

"I said . . . turn . . . that . . . *down!*" the guard bellowed, angrily pointing to the CD deck beneath the dashboard.

Tom turned to give Junior Bud a querulous look. "I think he wants you to turn it down, dude," Bud said. He had his hands clasped together in his lap to conceal the pipe they had been smoking since leaving the mall.

"Oh, yeah. Right." Tom pushed the Pause button. "Hi, Mr. Ames. How are you today?"

"What are you doing here?" Harlan Ames demanded. The former head of security for Swift Enterprises, he was one of Tom Swift, Jr.'s oldest friends, and Mr. Swift had found meaningful employment for him at the plant after the company had been forced to downsize. "I thought your father was out of town."

"Yes, sir, he is," Tom said. "He's . . . uh, in Egypt right now."

"He told me he was going to Washington state." Mr. Ames' eyes narrowed suspiciously. "What are you doing here?" he asked again.

"Umm . . . I left my sunglasses in his office," Tom said. "I just came by to pick them up."

Mr. Ames said nothing for a moment. "If you left your sunglasses in your father's office," he said at last, "then what's that you're wearing?"

Too late, Tom suddenly realized his error. "Oh, these are my other sunglasses," he lied opaquely, pointing to his retro-style Ray-Bans. "I left my good ones here. I'd really like to get them, 'cause I'm going surf . . . I mean, to a job interview tomorrow, and the sun really hurts my eyes,

235

y'know, and so I'd like to go hit my dad's office, y'know, see if they're there, which I'm sure they are, and . . ."

"Yeah, yeah, sure." Mr. Ames turned toward the shack, then he stopped to look back at the younger Swift. "You say you've got a job interview tomorrow?"

"Yes, sir," Tom said. "At a major high-tech company."

"Uh-huh. I bet." Mr. Ames shook his head in disgust as he marched into the gatehouse. A few seconds later he emerged with a temporary vehicle pass, which he stuck behind the windshield of Tom's Jeep. "It expires at closing time," he said. "Go get your sunglasses."

"Thanks, Mr. Ames." Tom rubbed the bridge of his nose with the middle finger of his right hand. "Nice to see you again."

Mr. Ames glared at him, then shuffled back in the gatehouse, grumbling as he pressed the button which opened the electric gates. "If I didn't know better," he muttered, "I'd swear you were adopted."

"Senile ol' coot," Tom crowed as he floored the gas pedal.

A few seconds later, he pulled up in front of the main office building. Parking the Jeep in the slot marked *Reserved—Swift*, Tom climbed out and, followed by Junior Bud, sauntered through the glass doors of the entrance. The receptionist gave him a sullen glare but remained quiet as he marched past the front desk, and Bud paused to help himself to some chocolate mints she kept in a bowl on the counter before he trailed his chum down the ground-floor hallway to the executive suite.

His father's secretary, who had been there since, like, forever, spotted Tom as he strode into the suite. "I deposited your trust-fund check yesterday," Miss Trent said quickly, swiveling around behind her desk as she feigned a broad smile. "Your dad said that if you needed more, I could fax him and . . ."

"Naw, naw. That's cool." Tom waved her off as he headed straight for the closed door of his father's office. "I just stopped by to pick up my sun . . . uhh, I think I left my jacket in his office, last time I was here."

"Oh . . ." She seemed confused. "Well, I haven't found any jackets that look like yours," she added helpfully, "but if your father did, he might have hung it in his closet . . ."

"He probably did." Tom opened the door, reached inside to turn on the ceiling light. "Thanks, I'll find it myself."

"Man, she's really nice," Junior Bud said as Tom shut the door behind them. "What's her name? I can't ever remember."

"I dunno." Tom shrugged. "Miss Something."

The office had once belonged to his grandfather, but Mr. Swift had moved in shortly after the founder of Swift Enterprises passed away. The walls were lined with framed photos of the elder Swift, many taken in exotic places like the Amazon rainforest or Antarctica, and the shelves were filled with scale models of exotic-looking aircraft, submersibles and spaceships, a few of which were chipped or missing pieces after Tom had played with them on the floor as a kid. Half-hidden behind a battered model of the jetmarine was a photo of the three Swifts, taken during Tom's high school graduation. Tom was still wearing his hair long then, and he was flashing a two-fingered love sign at the camera. His father was smiling, his left arm around his son's shoulder, but somehow his expression seemed embarrassed. His grandfather scowled from his magnetic levitational wheelchair.

"Hey, dude," Junior Bud murmured as Tom walked

237

around behind the desk, "where does your ol' man keep the booze?"

"Forget it. He doesn't drink." Tom opened the top drawer, peered inside. Everything was neat and tidy: sharpened pencils, rubber bands, thumb tacks, blank notepads, an ancient slide rule. Only his father would still use a slide rule.

"Bummer." Bud prowled along the shelves, checking out the models and pictures, until his eye fell upon an ungainly contraption: four oversized dragonfly-like wings mounted upon a slender fuselage, with a propeller behind its rear stabilizer and a broad plastic fan attached to its nose. "Yo, what's this thing?" he asked, picking it up. "Some kinda airplane?"

Tom looked up from the desk. "Whoa, dude! Be careful with that! It's mine!"

"Huh? What'dya mean, it's . . . ?"

Junior Bud's thumb accidentally found the switch on the object's underside. The wings fluttered, then blurred into a flurry of motion as the aft propeller buzzed to life. Suddenly the miniature aircraft lifted off from Bud's hands and rose toward the ceiling.

"Aw, man . . . !" Tom dove beneath his father's desk. "Don't move, whatever you do!"

"Huh?" Bud watched in amazement as the miniature aircraft began to circle the room. He lifted his hand to point at it. "Is this something your ol' man . . . ?"

All of a sudden, the drone turned around and hurled itself straight toward Junior Bud. "Hey!" he shouted. "Jeez, it's . . . !"

Then the plastic fan smacked him in the face. "Oww!" Bud yelped, then he backhanded the contraption across the room. It hit the wall behind the desk. One of its wings

238

snapped and the device fell to the floor, its propeller still buzzing. "What the . . . ?"

"The ornithoptic insect annihilator." Tom crept out from beneath the desk and carefully picked up the broken automaton. He located the power switch and turned it off; the contraption gradually stopped purring, and it died in his hands. "The flying flyswatter," Tom murmured, regarding it with forlorn nostalgia. "My greatest invention."

Tom had designed the ornithoptic insect annihilator a few years ago in an attempt to impress his father. It was meant to be a robotic drone which would automatically patrol a room, seeking out house flies and mosquitoes with its onboard motion detectors and getting rid of them without human intervention. His father had authorized a small production run based upon Tom's prototype, but the flying flyswatter hadn't worked as intended; although it did an admirable job of killing flies, it also had an unfortunate tendency to home in upon anything else that moved. Although Mr. Swift canceled plans to distribute Tom's invention on the American market, Swift Enterprises made a small profit by selling its overstock to the Ukrainian National Army.

"Aw, man," Junior Bud said. "Sorry I busted it."

"Never mind, man. It sucked anyway." Tom carefully placed the flying flyswatter back on the shelf, then returned to the desk. He found the key ring for which he had been searching in the top left drawer. "Got it," he said, shoving the keys into a pocket of his shorts. "C'mon, let's go see the robot."

Outside the office, they found Miss Trent still sitting at her desk. "Did you find your jacket, Tom?" she asked.

"Uhh . . . oh, no, ma'am." Tom kept his hands in his pockets to keep the key ring from jingling. "Guess I must have left it at home. Sorry to bother you."

"Well . . . all right, then." She gave Tom an uncertain look. "I have to call your father in Washington in a few minutes. Do you want me to tell him anything for you?"

"No, no, that's okay," Tom said reaffirmingly as he walked toward the door. "I'll see him when he gets home. Catch you later."

"I thought you said your dad's in Egypt," Junior Bud said as they passed the reception desk again. He grabbed some more mints from the bowl and gave the receptionist another smile, which she pointedly ignored.

"Egypt, Washington . . ." Tom gave a world-weary shrug. "What's the difference?"

3. Fabulous Inventions

Tom drove his Jeep across the plant grounds to an enormous warehouse on the other side of the runway and parked in another reserved slot with his last name painted on it. The buzz he had collected before leaving home was beginning to wear off, so after looking around to make sure no one was in sight, he and Junior Bud stoked up the pipe and took a few hits. Then he stashed the pipe beneath the glove compartment and they climbed out of the Jeep.

Mr. Swift's master ring contained nearly thirty different keys, along with a miniature remote which Tom remembered to use to deactivate the security system. It took several minutes for Tom to locate the proper key, but finally he managed to unlock the front door. The warehouse was pitch-black inside, and the two chums spent several more minutes wandering about in the darkness before they located the light switch next to the door.

"Whoa, wicked!" Junior Bud exclaimed as the ceiling

240

fluorescents flickered to life. "What's all this shit?"

Across the vast interior of the warehouse, all the way to the far wall, were parked machines and vehicles of all shapes and size, some larger than others. Each was covered with spotted plastic sheets or dusty canvas tarpaulins; crates of spare parts were stacked nearby, and electrical cables snaked across the concrete floor.

"Stuff my dad invented." Tom led his friend down the center aisle. "That's his electronic retroscope, and over there's the triphibian atomicar . . ."

"What's that thing?" Junior Bud pointed to the largest object in the warehouse, a massive machine which vaguely resembled a enormous gyroscope. "A thermonuclear subatomic can-opener?"

"Naw, man, it's . . . uh, it's the . . ." Tom shook his head. "I forgot. He flew it to the Moon once, though."

"Cool."

They made their way to the back of the warehouse, and poked around crates containing the disassembled remains of the space solartron, the atomic earth blaster and the spectromarine selector, until behind a wooden cradle containing the hull of the jetmarine they found a man-shaped object hidden beneath a tarp. A paper sign taped to its front read *Ator*.

"Here it is," Tom said, as he reached up to pull off the sheet. "My ol' man's robot."

Junior Bud gaped at it. "Aw, dude," he exclaimed, "you're such a liar! It's only seven feet tall!"

"Uhh . . . I thought it was bigger," Tom admitted in a small voice.

He also remembered it being a bit more impressive. The robot was plated with silver-grey Tomasite plastic save for the chain-mail covering the rotary joints of its arms and

241

legs, with old-fashioned dials, knobs and buttons arrayed across its chest. It had three-fingered claws for hands, and a pair of tube-shaped eyes protruded from its bucket-shaped head, from the top of which rose a slender wire aerial. For some weird reason, his father had chosen to give the robot a hinged jaw.

"Man, this thing's a piece of crap." Junior Bud stepped closer, rapped his knuckles against the robot's chest. "Doesn't it have any . . . I dunno, laser beams or anything?"

"Chill," Tom said frostily. "This was one of my dad's first inventions, okay?" He searched his memory. "I think he built it for use in nuclear power plants, but something screwed up." Or maybe it didn't screw up. His father was pretty sharp, but sometimes his inventions were only used once. Like the levitating roadway he had designed to help logging companies drive trucks into the Amazon rain forest. Greenpeace loved that one . . . "So it ain't C-3PO. It's still pretty radical."

"Yeah, right. More like C-3PO's grandfather." Junior Bud walked around behind the robot. "Hey, check it out. It's still plugged in."

Tom stepped around behind Ator. Sure enough, a fat yellow power cable led from a socket on the robot's back to an electrical outlet on the warehouse wall. "Cool," he murmured. "They must have kept it plugged in to keep the batteries from dying."

"Maybe it still works." Bud grinned at him. "Think you can make it?"

Tom shrugged. "Sure. Why not?"

4. The Return of Ator

Tom and Bud rummaged around the warehouse until they located the crate containing the robot's control unit, a wooden box with toggle switches, analog meters and black plastic knobs on its Bakelite shell. "The world's first remote," Tom muttered as he opened it up to look inside. "Look . . . it's got vacuum tubes and everything."

Bud peered into the box. "I've got an old Fender amp I could use them in."

"No way, dude," Tom said decisively. "My dad'll get pissed if he finds this thing missing."

The control unit needed new batteries, but Tom found some D-cells in an equipment locker and inserted them within the unit. When he flipped the power switch, the box hummed to life and the dials glowed orange-red. Tom remembered that the knobs controlled the robot's movements, but when he turned one of them, Ator remained still. The two chums puzzled over this for a few minutes until Tom snapped his fingers. "Aw, man!" he exclaimed. "I forgot to turn the robot on!"

"I'll get it." Junior Bud sauntered over to the robot and inspected its chest panel until he found a button marked Power. He pressed it, but still nothing happened. "Maybe we gotta unplug it first," he said, then he went around behind the robot and jerked the power cable from its back.

There was a low electrical throb from deep within Ator's chest, and then its eye-tubes emitted a bright yellow glow. "Yeah, that did it," Tom said. "Get out of the way and lemme see if I can make this thing go."

Tom turned the right knob to the right, and Ator's right arm swung upward in a swift, flat-handed arc. "Hey, look at that!" Bud yelled. "It's doing the Hitler thing!" Tom

243

pushed it to the left, and the other arm raised to same position. "Cool," Bud said. "Now it's doing Frankenstein."

"Shut up," Tom snapped. "I'm trying to get it to walk." He studied the control unit, struggling to make sense of its various dials and toggles. It had been many years since the time the senior Swift had showed him how to operate Ator, and even then it had been only for a few minutes. If the right knob controlled Ator's arms, then what moved its legs? He turned the left knob to the right. Ator took a step forward, its right leg making a metallic grinding noise as its foot settled on the cement floor with a solid clunk. Tom turned the knob to the left and the robot's left leg followed suit.

"Real impressive," Bud said. "But you said it was sixty feet tall."

"Don't start with me," Tom began.

The two friends played with the robot for a while, getting it to walk forward, then backward, then to swing its arms back and forth. At first Ator moved slowly, the chain mail covering its joints rasping with each movement it made, its eyes flickering a bit until Tom discovered how to increase the voltage. After that the robot was easy to control; Tom marched it down the warehouse aisle, then stopped it in the middle of the warehouse floor.

Tom had just succeeded in getting Ator to do the hokey-pokey when they heard a car drive up outside the warehouse. He ran to a nearby window, peered out just in time to see Harlan Ames getting out of a white Land Rover with rack lights mounted on its roof.

"We gotta blow," Tom hissed. "It's that old guy again."

When he looked back around, though, Junior Bud was nowhere to be seen. And the control unit was missing!

No time to worry about that now. The elderly security

guard had already checked out Tom's jeep, and now was walking toward the warehouse door. Tom dashed past Ator, still standing on one leg, and headed for the front door. He got there in time to meet Mr. Ames just as he opened the door. The old watchman stepped back in alarm, his right hand falling upon the taped handle of his night stick, before he recognized the young heir to the Swift fortune.

"What the heck are you doing in here?" he demanded.

"Just looking around," Tom said, searching for an explanation. "I think I left my jacket in here."

Mr. Ames gave him a skeptical eye. "You told me you were looking for your sunglasses."

"Uhh . . . whatever." Tom reached over to switch off the lights, then stepped through the door and slammed it shut behind him. "Thanks for letting me look. I think I left them at home or something."

He started to walk past Ames, but the guard raised a hand to stop him. "Hold it right there, son. Where's your buddy?"

At that instant, Tom spotted Junior Bud creeping around the side of the warehouse. He held the control unit beneath his right arm, and while Mr. Ames had his back turned to him he moved quickly and quietly to Tom's jeep. "Who?" Tom said innocently, trying to stall the guard.

"Don't play dumb with me. I know he's still in there." Pulling his key ring from his belt, Mr. Ames stepped past Tom to the warehouse door.

"Hey, Tom!" Junior Bud yelled. "C'mon, let's go! We're late for choir practice!"

Startled, Mr. Ames turned to see the other youth sitting in the passenger seat of the Jeep. The control unit was nowhere in sight. "Oh, that guy!" Tom said foolishly. "I'm sorry, Mr. Ames. I thought you meant someone else."

Ames glared first at Tom, then at Bud. "Hey, Mr. Ames," Bud called, "why isn't there a bathroom in there? I had to go around back and find a tree."

The guard took a step toward the Jeep, and for a moment Tom was certain that he would find the control unit under the back seat. "I'll tell my dad we saw you today," he said observantly. "I'm sure he'll want to know you've been doing your job."

Mr. Ames stopped, and Tom detected the uncertain look in his eyes. After all, Tom's father was the owner of Swift Enterprises; there was no reason why his son shouldn't be allowed to visit one of the company warehouses, was there? And Mr. Ames was well past retirement age; he couldn't afford to lose his job just because he had harassed the boss's kid.

"Go on, get out of here." Mr. Ames cocked his head toward the Jeep. "Beat it before I go looking for dope."

"Thanks, Mr. Ames. Have a nice day." Tom strolled past him to the Jeep and climbed in behind the wheel. Junior Bud grinned at Mr. Ames and gave him a little wave as they backed away from the warehouse. Ames glowered at them, then turned to make sure that the door was locked.

"Oh, man, you scared the piss out of me," Tom expelled. He glanced in the back of the Jeep as he drove toward the front gate. The control unit was on the floor below the seat. "And why the hell did you take that?"

"I dunno." Junior Bud turned around to pick up the box. "I just thought it looked cool."

"Dude . . ." Tom shook his head. "My dad's gonna be wicked pissed when he finds out it's missing."

"Are you kidding? He probably hasn't seen it in years." Junior Bud put the unit in his lap and absently fiddled with the knobs. "C'mon, lighten up. Let's go back to the mall."

5. A Strange Encounter

Twilight had fallen upon Shopton by the time Tom and Junior Bud returned to the mall. They smoked another bowl out in the parking lot. Bud played with the control unit, then they left the box in the Jeep while they went into the mall.

The two pals were hungry now, so they visited the food court and got some pizza, which they heartily consumed at a nearby table while eyeing the girl working behind the counter at Arby's. Junior Bud went over to ask her if she wanted to go party after she got off work, but she ignored him until her manager came out front and told Bud to leave. Bud did so, but not before he pocketed a handful of ketchup packets; he got his revenge by mashing them on the floor beneath their table. "Anarchy rules!" he shouted as they left the food court. The Arby's manager stared back at them in confusion.

They wandered in and out of stores until they found their way to the ten-screen cineplex at the other end of the mall. They had already seen most of the movies playing there, and the ones they hadn't seen were lame, but since there was nothing else to do they decided to see again a Robert DeNiro gangster movie which hadn't sucked too much the first time they had seen it. Tom was out of cash and the nearest ATM machine was all the way back in the food court, so he whipped out his trusty AmEx card and put the tickets on the plastic. Bud paid him back by buying popcorn and a box of Skittles.

They managed to sit through the first half of the film before they remembered how it ended. Bud expressed his critical displeasure by throwing the rest of the popcorn on the floor, then they got up and left.

"Life sucks," Tom said vacuously as they walked out of the theater.

"Yeah, dude." Junior Bud shoved his hands in his pockets and glared at the children waiting in line with their parents for the latest Disney movie. "Let's go back to your place and smoke some dope."

"Yeah, cool. Maybe we can catch 'The Real World' on . . ."

It was at that moment that they came upon the Radio Shack where Tom had applied for a job yesterday. The middle-aged store manager who had given him an employment application was standing just inside the door, demonstrating an answering machine to an elderly woman. Tom ducked his head and tried to quickly shuffle past, but the manager turned just in time to spot him.

"Hey, Tom! Hold on!" He excused himself from his customer, then stepped out into the mall. "Come back to see about that job?"

"Umm . . . yeah, sure." Tom glanced at the name tag pinned to his red vest: *Rick Brant*. "I just happened to passing through, and I was wondering . . ."

"Of course you were." Mr. Brant regarded him curiously. "Say, have you visited an eye doctor lately? Your pupils are blood-shot."

"Uhh . . ." Damn! Wrong time to leave his Ray-Bans in the car. Junior Bud had drifted away to study the lingerie on display at Victoria's Secret next door. "Just came from the movie. I think I was sitting too close to the screen."

"Sure." Mr. Brant seemed unconvinced. "Anyway, about that job. I looked at your application, Tom, and . . ."

"I won't be able to start next week," Tom said quickly. "I've got something else going on, and . . ."

"Perhaps that's just as well," Mr. Brant said, "because I wasn't going to offer you the job anyway." As Tom gazed at him in astonishment, the store manager went on. "I think I need someone a little more . . . well, mature . . . to work here."

"Mature?" Tom exclaimed childishly. "I'm twenty years old, man! How mature do you gotta be to run a friggin' cash register?"

He hadn't meant to shout, but the old lady standing nearby glanced over her shoulder to glare at him. Mr. Brant gazed at him stoically as he folded his arms across his chest. "When your father was only seventeen . . ."

"Hell with my father!" Tom said infernally. "I'm sick of hearing about him!"

"I don't doubt you are. I would be, too, if I were you. But I was the same age as he was way back when, and all I wanted to do was the same things he was doing. I was an inventor once myself. I . . ." Mr. Brant sighed and shook his head. "Never mind. It's a long story. But I didn't have the opportunities you have now. If I did, do you think I'd be here?"

Tom started to retort, yet the wisecrack he wanted to make somehow couldn't find its way past his lips. There was a certain sadness in Mr. Brant's face, and Tom suddenly realized that he was gazing upon his own future. Spending his waning years in a New Jersey shopping mall, price-marking toy RC cars and trying to show some old biddy how to operate an answering machine . . .

"Rick!" The grey-haired woman turned to bark at Mr.

Brant. "How do you get your voice to come out of this thing?"

"I'll be right with you, Mrs. Drew." Mr. Brant rubbed his eyes. "I swear," he whispered beneath his breath, "she doesn't have a clue." Then he looked at Tom again. "Son, it's been a long time since I was twenty, but I think I know what guys your age would say. Dude . . . get a life."

Before Tom could reply, Mr. Brant turned and walked back into the store. "All right, let me show you how this works . . ."

Junior Bud noticed the wounded expression on Tom's face as his friend slowly walked away from the Radio Shack. "Hey, man, what was that all about?"

"I dunno," Tom said cryptically. "Let's just get out of here."

6. Robot Amok!

Life sucks. On the other hand, why did his world feel so empty?

Tom contemplated this notion as he and Junior Bud moseyed their way toward the entrance. Maybe getting stoned and hanging out in the mall wasn't all that life was about. It might not be holding down a job at Radio Shack, but seeing all those things his father had invented a long time ago had made him wonder if there was more to living than just getting by. All his other friends were either in college or had steady jobs; they had ambitions that went beyond finding a good party next weekend. What was he doing tonight? Going back to his parent's house to do bong hits with Junior Bud.

I'm mature, he thought. I'm twenty years old. How responsible do you have to be to get some respect?

When they reached the front entrance, they were startled to see people rushing through the glass doors. A fat lady in a Hawaiian-print muumuu nearly collided with Tom as she ran screaming past them. A yup was yelling into his cell phone; a couple of teenagers stared through the windows at something outside. From the far distance they could hear the *whoop-whoop* of an approaching police cruiser.

"Whoa," Bud murmured as they sauntered past everyone. "What'dya think this is all about?"

"Dunno," Tom said vacantly. "Let's check it out."

A crowd had gathered on the sidewalk outside the mall, their attention focused upon the parking lot. The blue lights of the police car strobed against the yellow sodium lights at the far edge of the lot, but it was gridlocked behind traffic attempting to leave and wasn't getting any closer. More people came toward them, and they joined the throng outside the mall even as Tom and Bud pushed through the mob.

Tom stopped at the edge of the sidewalk. Now he could see the cause of the commotion.

Ator was striding through the parking lot, its claws raised menacingly, its eyes flickering in the dark Long Island night with each step it took. An empty shopping cart stood in its path; instead of stepping around it, though, Ator picked it up and hurled it through the windshield of a nearby Toyota. Bystanders dashed for cover as the giant robot marched past them, a mindless juggernaut which paid no attention to any obstacles in its way.

"Aw, shit," said Tom with great feeling.

Ator picked up the front end of a double-parked Volkswagen and shoved it against the Datsun minivan next to it. It couldn't be mere coincidence that Ator happened to be here. After all, the robot had still been activated when they left Swift Enterprises. Somehow or another, Bud must have done something with the control unit which caused the robot to follow its radio signal from the warehouse to the mall.

"Umm . . ." Junior Bud stepped back. "Maybe we oughta check out the arcade."

Tom's first impulse was to follow his friend's advice. If they made themselves scarce, maybe they wouldn't catch the heat for any of this. But the robot would still be here, and people could get hurt.

"Naw, man," he said negatively. "This is our fault. We gotta do something about it."

He didn't hear an answer. When he looked around, Junior Bud was no longer standing next to him. Through the crowd, he caught a glimpse of his friend as he dashed across the parking lot, heading for where they had parked the Jeep.

"Hey!" Tom yelled. "Hold up, dude! You gotta help me here!"

Yet Junior Bud was way ahead of him. He got to the Jeep first, and snatched the control unit from behind the back seat. "I'm getting rid of the evidence!" Bud yelled back as Tom ran after him. "I'll call you tomorrow or whatever!" Then he turned and ran down the row of parked cars, clutching the box against his chest.

"Wuss!" Tom shouted boldly. "That's the last time I . . . I . . . " He couldn't think of a decent threat, and besides, Junior Bud was already halfway across the parking lot. "See if I invite you to my next party!"

He heard a crash from behind him, and turned just in time to see the robot pick up an abandoned baby stroller and pitch it against a lamp post. Ator was still tracking the signal from the control unit; Tom had little doubt that the robot would follow Junior Bud clear across Long Island, in the meantime leaving behind a trail of destruction.

Now the robot was headed his way. Behind him, Tom could hear more police cruisers approaching the mall. Yet he knew that the Shopton cops were ill-equipped to take down a seven-foot robot. Like it or not, he was the only person around who knew how to stop Ator before it harmed someone.

"Oh, hell," Tom muttered warmly. "Maybe I can still get into the Army when this is all over."

The robot was marching down the row when Tom stepped directly in front of it. "Hey!" he shouted, waving his hands over his head. "Yo, Ator! Mechanical dude! Stop! Pull over! Chill!"

Yet the robot didn't pause for an instant. Too late, Tom remembered that voice-recognition software hadn't been invented when his father had cobbled this big mother together. He was still wondering why Dad hadn't been a little more cutting-edge when Ator swung its right arm at him.

Its claw nearly took off the top of his head before Tom hurled himself to the ground. He yelled in pain as the asphalt skinned his knees and the palms of his hands, and he rolled out of the way just in time to avoid being trampled by the robot.

Tom picked himself off the ground, watched as Ator stomped past him. All right, so calling a time-out obviously wasn't going to work. But maybe he could reach the power switch on its chest panel. Tom hesitated, then he lunged after the automaton.

Ator didn't detect his presence until Tom leaped onto its back. He wrapped his arms around its head and blindly scrabbled for the chest panel farther down the robot's thorax. For a few moments Tom was sure that he could reach the power button; from somewhere in the distance he could hear people shouting, urging him to hang on. But now Ator was aware that something was hindering its movements. It swung around, its left claw reached back to grab Tom's shirt.

Tom yelped as the claw ripped against his skin, then the robot tore him off its back and tossed him aside. His shirt ripped as he skidded across the pavement; fireflies danced across his vision when the back of his head connected with the ground.

For a few seconds, Tom lay prone on the ground, the breath knocked out of him, blood running from his scraped back. He hadn't hurt this bad since he had played goalie for the Shopton High soccer team. Of course, he had been bounced from the team after the coach had discovered a joint in his locker, but that wasn't the point. Not only was he in considerable pain, but he was also good and pissed.

"Dude," Tom murmured hotly as he staggered to his feet, "you are serious toast."

He dug his hands into the pockets of his shorts as he lurched toward his Jeep, and found his keys just as a Shopton police cruiser pulled into the row. A cop jumped out and yelled at him to stop, but Tom ignored him as he crawled behind the wheel and jammed the key into the ignition. The engine rumbled to life, and Tom slammed the stick into first gear and left rubber behind as he punched out of the parking space.

Ator was dead in front of him as Tom's Jeep tore down the parking lot. He shifted to second and put the pedal to the floor, and braced his hands against the wheel as the headlights caught the sleek surface of the robot's back.

"Eat me!" Tom spat, and an instant later the Jeep's front end slammed against the robot.

254

Ator's chest snapped forward and its arms flung outward as the robot wrapped itself around the hood. The left headlight shattered; friction sparks whisked past the windshield and metal shrieked against metal as Ator was dragged beneath the vehicle. Tom felt a hard multiple bump against the tires as he ran over the robot, yet when he hit the brakes and looked back over his shoulder, the robot was still intact. Although there was a large dent in its back and one of its eyes was broken, nonetheless Ator was clambering to its knees.

Damn, but the old man built 'em to last, didn't he?

Tom grabbed the stick and jammed it into reverse, then planted his foot on the gas pedal. The Jeep's tires screeched as it hurtled backward toward the robot. Ator was almost on its feet again when the Jeep's rear bumper caught it square in the middle of the chest.

Its right arm connected with the roll-bar just behind Tom's head. Tom ducked, but kept his foot against the gas pedal. He heard voices shouting at him, and at the last second he glanced at the side mirror and saw police officers running away from their cruiser, then his Jeep slammed straight into the cop car.

Jagged pieces of Tomasite were strewn across the parking lot as the robot was crushed between the two vehicles. Something made a loud implosive sound from deep within the robot, then Ator's remaining eye went dark. Its jaw sagged open as its limbs suddenly went limp, and then the robot sagged forward and sprawled across the back of the Jeep.

Tom climbed out of the Jeep. "It's okay, officers!" he shouted with authority, raising his hands. "Everything's under control! Just call my dad, he'll take care of everything!"

"I'm sure he will." One of the cops was already pulling out his handcuffs. "You have the right to remain silent . . ."

7. A Hero's Reward

Tom opened his eyes when he heard the door to the cell block open. He yawned and sat up as a police officer approached the door of the holding cell. "Okay, you're free to go," the officer said as he unlocked the door and pushed it open. "Your bail's been paid. There's someone waiting for you out front."

A dapper young gentleman carrying a briefcase stood at the front desk of the Shopton police station. He introduced himself as Mr. Hardy, a senior partner with the law firm of Hardy, Hardy & Sons and he waited patiently while Tom relaced the sneakers of his basketball shoes before he escorted the young man out to where his car was parked.

"The charges include damage to private property, reckless driving, possession of a controlled substance, and operation of dangerous equipment within city limits," Mr. Hardy said as he drove Tom toward his home. "We may be able to plea-bargain them down to lesser charges, once the judge has been informed that you were acting to prevent the robot from causing any further damage . . ."

"Solid." Tom hungrily eyed the Pizza Hut they had just driven past. "Hey, can we stop somewhere? I'm starving."

Mr. Hardy ignored him. "We can be sure that there will be civil suits as well," he continued. "Swift Enterprises has already received a call from the mall, and we'll probably be hearing from the insurance companies representing the owners of the various cars the robot damaged."

"Has my dad phoned yet?" Tom asked. He imagined

that the elder Swift would be righteously pissed about all this. Indeed, Tom was prepared to be grounded for at least a month.

"I spoke with your father about an hour ago. He's flying home as soon as he's concluded his business with Mr. Gates." The attorney allowed himself a judicious smile. "Among other things, we discussed the possibility of you completing your education."

"Go back to college?" Tom shrugged. "Yeah, well, I guess that'd be cool. Maybe some place up in New Hampshire." He'd heard about some wicked party schools in New England. Besides, he had always wanted to try snowboarding.

"Actually, we were thinking of sending you a little farther away." Mr. Hardy's smile became a broad grin. "New Zealand, maybe . . . or perhaps Guam."

Tom stared out at the passing street lights as he contemplated a prolonged visit to some far-away land. Little did he know that the *Hydroponic Marijuana Cultivator* lay in his future, and the exciting adventures that this invention would bring.

"You don't think we could stop for a taco, do you?" he asked saucily.

About the Author

Allen Steele was born in Nashville, Tennessee, and received his B.A. in Communications from New England College and a Masters Degree in Journalism from the University of Missouri. Before turning to science fiction, he worked as a staff writer for newspapers in Tennessee, Missouri, and Massachusetts, as well as Washington, D.C. A two-time winner of the Hugo Award in the novella category, he lives with his wife, Linda, in Whately, Massachusetts.